Trey bent low ove̶̶̶̶̶̶̶̶̶̶
her from their g̶̶̶̶̶̶̶̶̶̶

"Laugh," he said, his face perilously close to hers.

"What?" Her eyes were wide with alarm.

"Laugh." He whispered the harsh command. "Like the sort of woman who should be out alone with a man at this time of night."

Still she did not comprehend. Speechless, she just stared at him, her pupils dark with surprise and, if he was any judge, with sudden want.

So Trey did what he must. What some part of him had burned to do since he'd first laid eyes on her. He pulled her hard against him and seared her with his kiss.

* * *

An Improper Aristocrat
Harlequin® Historical #924—December 2008

Author Note

I came to romance as a reader long before I even conceived of being a writer. Broken marriages were common in my experience as I was growing up. Looking back now, I realize how lucky I was to discover romance as a teenager, and to find so many wonderful examples of strong women and the men who value them. Every time I picked up a romance novel I learned a lesson about characters struggling with difficulties in life and fighting their own personal demons. I struggled and fought along with them, and rejoiced as they truly earned their Happily Ever Afters. I think I picked up a few valuable lessons along the way.

An Improper Aristocrat is my second novel for Harlequin Historical. I hope you enjoy riding along with Trey and Chione on their journey to a happy ending.

DEB MARLOWE

An Improper Aristocrat

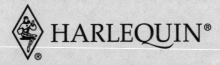

HARLEQUIN®

TORONTO • NEW YORK • LONDON
AMSTERDAM • PARIS • SYDNEY • HAMBURG
STOCKHOLM • ATHENS • TOKYO • MILAN • MADRID
PRAGUE • WARSAW • BUDAPEST • AUCKLAND

Recycling programs
for this product may
not exist in your area.

ISBN-13: 978-0-373-29524-1
ISBN-10: 0-373-29524-3

AN IMPROPER ARISTOCRAT

Copyright © 2008 by Deb Marlowe

First North American publication 2008

www.eHarlequin.com

Printed in U.S.A.

Available from Harlequin® Historical and
DEB MARLOWE

Scandalous Lord, Rebellious Miss #885
An Improper Aristocrat #924

DON'T MISS THESE OTHER
NOVELS AVAILABLE NOW:

#923 HER MONTANA MAN—Cheryl St.John

Protecting people runs through Jonas Black's blood,
and Eliza Jane Sutherland is one woman who needs his strong
arms about her. Despite blackmail and dangerous threats on their
lives, the attraction between Jonas and Eliza is undeniable—
but Eliza bears secrets that could change everything....
Every woman needs a man who will fight for her!

#925 THE MISTLETOE WAGER—Christine Merrill

Harry Pennyngton, Earl of Anneslea, is surprised when his
estranged wife, Elise, arrives home for Christmas—especially
as she is still intent on divorce! But when Harry and Elise find
they are stuck with each other under the mistletoe, the magic of
Christmas is just what they need to reignite their love!
*Mistletoe works its magic as passion is rekindled in this festive
Regency story....*

#926 VIKING WARRIOR, UNWILLING WIFE—
Michelle Styles

War drums echoing in her ears, Sela stood with trepidation on
the shoreline. The dragon ships full of warriors had arrived—
but it wasn't the threat of conquest that shook Sela to the core.
It was her heart's response to the proud face of Vikar Hrutson,
leader of the invading force—and her ex-husband!
Now the warrior must conquer his woman's heart!

To Irene. Her lessons were innumerable and invaluable. She introduced me to the romance genre and she showed me every day in a hundred ways the sort of person I would like to be. She was a true-life heroine in every sense of the word.

Prologue

The Valley of the Kings, Egypt
1820

From the shadowed walls of the desert wadi, the French-woman watched. Truly it was him—and from her hidden vantage point he lived up to every whispered tale making its way along the Nile. Her heart quickened.

He sat alone in his tent, scratching out notes by the weak light of his lamp. Narrowing her gaze, she studied him. Ah, yes. The light might be dim, but it illuminated a feast for the discerning female eye: a strong, chiselled profile, impossibly broad shoulders, rugged muscles straining the fine linen of his shirt.

He set down his pen and indulged himself in a lengthy, catlike stretch. Even in so unwary a pose she could sense his power, feel the pull of unwavering confidence and absolute masculinity. Inwardly, she smiled. This assignment, which she had objected to with such vehemence, was going to be no hardship at all.

She crept closer, moving carefully in the mix of rock and sand that littered the valley floor, mentally reviewing all that she knew of this renegade. The Englishman was a legend. He had discovered valuable antiquities in India, Persia and throughout the Orient. In the short time since his arrival in Egypt, he had already made some remarkable finds.

A great man, yes. But here, alone in the cool, dark hours of the desert night, just a man. And one who looked simply weary, and oddly content. Her lips curled wryly. Soon she would fix that.

Her quarry closed his ledger and rose. Stepping lightly, she approached the open tent flap. In one lithe movement she released the catch and stepped inside. Both the canvas and her cloak swirled satisfactorily at her feet.

The Earl of Treyford paused, caught in the act of peeling off his shirt. Fixing his unexpected visitor with an impassive stare, he reached for a name to go with the lovely face. 'Madame Fornier, is it not?' he asked, shrugging back into his shirt.

Her smile appeared to be one of genuine pleasure. 'Indeed. How flattering it is that you remember me, my lord.'

'I make it a point to know my rivals, *madame*.' Deliberately he did not return the smile.

'Rivals?' She pursed her lips. 'An ugly word, and one I'm not at all sure applies to our present situation.'

Trey didn't reply. The less he said, long experience told him, the quicker she would get to the crux of this late-night visit.

'My husband—you met him as well at *le docteur* Valsomaki's?'

At his nod, she continued. 'Fornier, he would be happy with your choice of words. Nothing more would he like than to be considered your rival. He tells himself and anyone who will listen that he is Monsieur Drovetti's foremost agent. But your accomplishments?' She raised a brow. 'He belittles them and says you have only been lucky in Egypt.'

She gave a sad shake of her head and reached up to loosen the fastenings of her cloak. 'Jealousy steals the sting of his words. He has done nothing to equal your feats. I myself saw those figures of Sekhmet you shipped back to England. Very impressive, my lord.'

He inclined his head and watched as the last tie came undone. One lift of her shoulders and the cloak fell away. She stood proudly, her magnificent body skimmed by a shimmering, transparent shift. The effect was infinitely more arousing than even her bare skin would have been.

Trey merely nodded again. 'Thank you,' he said.

She advanced until she stood pressed up against him. 'There are other reasons that my husband envies you.' Her voice dropped to a husky tone that set his pulse to jumping. 'All of Egypt talks of your many lovers. They whisper of your ability to take a woman beyond herself and into a world of passion that few ever know.'

Against his chest he could feel the softness of her incredible gown and all the abundance it showed to advantage. Their gazes locked, then with a coy smile she snaked a hand inside his shirt, running her palm up and over the muscles of his chest. Moving slowly, she stepped all the way around him, trailing soft fingers across his arm and the breadth of his back as she went.

'Surely you were made for these harsh Eastern deserts,' she whispered. 'When first I came here I thought it foolish and arrogant that the men keep so many wives.' Her orbit complete, she pressed into the front of him once again. Trey knew she could be in no doubt about his interest. She cast a sultry look down at the throbbing evidence of it. 'But you…' she sighed '…you are the first, the only man to make me believe. You alone could do it, pleasure so many women, keep them satisfied and happy.'

She smiled up at him. 'Perhaps, in addition to your other talents, you will be the first Englishman to practise poly…poly…' She paused. 'What is the word I want? For marriage to too many wives?'

'Monogamy?' He returned her smile.

She laughed, a dark, throaty sound. 'It is a certainty that no woman would wish to share you. Already I hate all of those on whom you have practised your wiles. I want to tear their hair and scratch out their eyes.'

Her eyes met his boldly. With an unspoken challenge she pushed him gently back until his knees struck the cot. Searching and warm, her hands crept up, sliding slowly along his ribs, his neck, the line of his jaw, before pressing firmly down on his shoulders.

Trey allowed it, sitting on the cot and finding himself at eye level with her lovely bosom. He reached up and pushed aside the fabric, baring first one breast, then the other. 'So, we have established that your husband envies me.' Slowly he traced a finger around one dusky areola. 'And that you envy all the ladies who have come before you.' He teased the other now, circling both erect nipples in an ever-narrowing path.

He watched her shift restlessly, leaning into his caress. 'But what I wish to know, *madame*, is what Drovetti thinks.'

Her breath was coming fast, her pupils dilated with desire, and yet she smiled in appreciation of his tactics. 'The consul-general thinks only of winning the ancient riches of Egypt for France.'

She pressed his hands against her and again he obliged her, cradling the fullness of her breasts and running his thumbs over her peaks.

'And?' he prompted.

'And he thinks you are a talented Englishman with no love for England.' She sighed with pleasure. 'I am to offer you a partnership.'

He laughed. 'Is that what you are offering?'

'That is what Drovetti offers.' She pushed him away and shed the gown, standing confident before him in all of her naked glory. 'This, I offer of my own free will, for nothing other than the pleasure you can give me.'

The smile still lingered on Trey's face. 'And if I accept the one, must I accept the other?'

Her only answer was a hungry look of intense desire. She leaned forward, straddled him on the cot and kissed him deeply. Burying his hands in her hair, Trey abandoned himself to his own inclinations. As was his habit—nay, his life's chosen philosophy—he seized the pleasures of the moment and left the inevitable trouble for tomorrow.

Unfortunately, trouble couldn't wait.

She knelt above him, her hands on the fall of his trousers, when the scream echoed along the craggy walls of the valley. Their gazes locked. Trey could read only puzzlement and alarm in hers as he grabbed her roughly by the arms. 'What have you done?' he demanded, his voice harsh.

'Nothing!' she cried. 'What is it? I must not be found here.'

Another shout. Cursing, Trey flung her away. He was out of the tent and running before the last chilling echo bounded off the rocky outcroppings. His partner's tent was dark, and, he realised after a quick search, empty. He stood a moment in the middle of camp. From which direction had the screams come? His feet and his gut knew the answer before his head, sending him pelting towards the closest tomb.

'Richard!' he shouted into the dark. 'Where are you?'

No answer. He ran harder, gravel and sand making the canyon floor treacherous, but at last he reached the spot. It was the first of eight tombs that had been discovered four years earlier by the Italian, Giovanni Battista Belzoni. Almost invisible during the day, now it was little more than a blacker maw against a background of darkly shadowed rock.

There, just outside the opening to the tomb, he found his partner sprawled against the rough, rock wall, a knife imbedded in his chest.

Trey gasped. 'No!'

He stumbled to Richard's side, frantically feeling for a pulse.

It was faint, but present. His shirt was soaked in blood. Underneath him a dark stain was fast disappearing into the sand. Trey fumbled at his belt, and cursed himself for not bringing a flint.

'Richard. Who has done this?' He clutched the man with bloodstained fingers. 'Never mind. I'll go for help. Just hold on, damn it! Hold on!'

'No.' Richard's voice was faint, but insistent. 'Treyford, stay.' He lifted a feeble hand to the open neck of his shirt.

'Damn it to hell!' Trey cursed. 'Richard, was it the French? What have you got mixed up in?'

'My pendant,' he breathed. 'Bastards…heard you…ran off.' There was a long pause, punctuated by Richard's slow gasp for air. 'You take it.'

Trey bowed his head. The pendant, ancient and carved with old Egyptian markings, was Richard's most prized possession. His partner's breath rasped, sounding harsh and frightening in the dim light, but his fingers still fought to remove the piece. Trey closed his own hand over Richard's and gently lifted the chain from around his neck.

'Chione,' he choked. 'Give it to Chione.'

'I will.' The pendant was warm, but Richard's hand was cold.

'Promise.' Richard was emphatic. '*Promise* me, Trey.'

'I do promise. I will deliver it to her myself.' It was the least he could do to comfort his partner, who was as close to a friend as Trey was ever likely to get.

Richard's grip, when he grasped Trey's arm, was surprisingly forceful. 'My sister. They will come for her. Trey…help her.'

'Of course I will,' he said soothingly.

Richard's grip tightened. His breath was coming now with a sickening gurgle.

Trey squeezed his opposite hand. 'I give you my word.'

Richard's body relaxed. For a moment, Trey thought…

But, no, Richard's hand was moving again, clasping his with grateful pressure.

'Sorry…take you from your work,' he whispered. Somehow he summoned the strength for a faint smile. 'Know you hate…to go home.' Richard's eyes closed. 'Protect Chione.'

'I…' Trey paused until he could go on with a steady voice. 'I swear to you, I will keep her safe.'

It was then, in the darkest time of the early desert morning, that Richard breathed his last, his hand still clasped tight in Trey's.

Trey stayed, crouched where he was, unaware of the passage of time, unaware of anything save the familiar ache of loss. More than a colleague, Richard had been the one person who understood what this work meant to him. Mutual interests, similar drives, complimentary skills; it had been enough to forge a bond of companionship and camaraderie. And, yes, of friendship.

Eventually their dragoman and some of the workmen arrived. Trey saw more than one of the natives furtively making the sign against the evil eye. Spurred on by the headman, a few hearty souls stepped forward to tenderly bundle Richard's body and prepare to carry him back to camp.

'Where is the woman?' Trey asked harshly when the dragoman approached him.

'She slipped away. I let her go.' Aswan cocked his head. 'Shall I find her?'

Trey shook his head. 'Do any of them know anything?' He jerked his jaw towards the milling men.

'I will discover it if they do,' Aswan said firmly. 'We go back. Latimer *effendi* must be prepared for burial. Do you come?'

Trey stared down at the pendant in his fist, then up into the lightening sky. 'No,' he said. The tide of anger inside him was rising with the sun. Grief and guilt and rage threatened to overwhelm him. He experienced a sudden empathy with the howling dervishes he had seen in Cairo; he wanted nothing more at this moment than to scream, to vent his fury into the deceptively cool morning air. Instead, he turned to the opposite direction than that which the workmen were taking, and headed for the ancient trail leading to the top of the cliffs.

It was little better than a goat path and required all of his focus, especially in the poor light and at the pace he was taking it. He was sweating heavily when he reached the top, and he stood, blowing against the cool morning breeze.

The sun was just topping the eastern cliffs, the sky above coming alive in a riot of colour. Trey ignored the incredible vista, looking away as the light crept across the fields and kissed the waters of the Nile. Stately temple ruins and the humble villages came to life beneath his feet. But Richard was dead.

Trey straightened, aware only of his own overflowing bitterness and the bite of the pendant in his grip. *This* was the reason Richard had been killed. Trey was sure of it. Richard had searched relentlessly for the thing since he had first arrived in Egypt, nearly a year ago. The day he found it, he had told Trey that the object filled him with both hope and dread.

Trey could see nothing to inspire such deep feelings. Shaped like a scarab, it looked almost alive in the rosy light of the burgeoning day. Until one felt the empty indentations—in the shape of the insect's wings—where at some time in antiquity thieves had pried the jewels out. Or until one turned it over to gaze at the underside, scored with the old writing.

Such defects had not lowered the value of the thing in Richard's eyes. He had strung it on a chain and never, as far as Trey knew, removed it since. Until today.

Trey ignored the stab of grief and fought to tighten his thoughts. He dragged his mind's eye back over the past months. Yes, it was true. All the strange little occurrences they had suffered had begun after Richard acquired the scarab. They were only small things at first: a few insignificant items missing, their belongings rifled through. Once an itinerary of antiquities that Richard had purchased for the British Museum had disappeared.

Lately, though, the situation had become more sinister. Their rooms had been ransacked and some of their workmen scared off. Richard had refused to discuss the matter, and had scorned the incidents as that which any foreigner might expect to endure in this harsh land.

Trey had not believed him. He had suspected that something more was going on, but he had trusted Richard to handle it. The boy was young, yes, but half-Egyptian himself. Like many of his countrymen he had appeared old beyond his years. He had handled himself with such dignity and their workmen with such ease; it had been easy to forget he hadn't much beyond a score of years in his dish.

And now Richard was dead. Trey should have pushed him, demanded an explanation. He hadn't. He had been too caught up in his work to spare it much consideration. Damn, he thought, letting the sour taste of guilt wash over him, and damn again.

He focused his rage at the pendant, glaring at the offensive thing, for a long moment sorely tempted to pitch it out into the abyss; to leave it once more to the ravages of time and the elements.

But he had promised. Given his word of honour to deliver the cursed thing to Richard's sister. A gruesome memento, in his view. And he had vowed to protect the girl. But from whom? Drovetti? Why would the French want the thing? Why would anyone?

He sighed. It didn't matter; he had promised. He would do it. He turned away and set his feet back on the path into the Valley.

Back to England.

Chapter One

⸻

Devonshire, England
1821

The ominous drip, drip of water echoed against the rough-hewn walls of the hidden chamber. It was true; the idol was here. It sat enthroned on its pedestal, bathed in a mysterious light that set its ruby eyes to glowing. Nikolas reached for it. Almost he had it, but something gave him pause. The glow of the eyes had become more intense. The idol was staring at him, through him, into him. He shook off the notion that the thing could see every stain ever etched into his soul. He reached again, but...

'Excuse me, lass.' Neither the impatient tones nor the broad Highland accent belonged to brave Nikolas.

With a reluctant sigh, Chione Latimer abandoned her rich inner world and slid back into her only slightly more mundane life. She set down her pen and turned towards the housekeeper. 'Mrs Ferguson, I am quite busy. I thought I had asked to be left undisturbed.' She had to suppress a flash of impatience. She had pages to write. There would be no payment from her publisher until the latest installment of Nikolas's adventures was in his hands.

'That ye did, and so I told the gentleman, but bless me if some of us dinna act as high and mighty as the day is long.'

A strangled sound came from behind her. The squat, solid figure of Hugh Hamlyn, Viscount Renhurst, stood right on Mrs Ferguson's heels.

'Lord Renhurst,' Chione said in surprise. 'Are you back from town so soon?' A quick surge of hope had her instantly on her feet, her heart pounding. 'Have you heard something then? Has there been word of Mervyn?'

'No, no, nothing like that.' He waved an impatient hand. 'My steward wrote me in a panic, some sort of blight got into the corn. I had to purchase all new seed for the upper fields, and since nothing momentous was happening in the Lords, I decided to bring it out myself.' His habitually harsh expression softened a bit. 'I'm afraid your grandfather's whereabouts are still a mystery, Chione. I'm sorry.'

Chione smiled and struggled to hide her disappointment. 'Well, of course, a visit from you is the next best thing, my lord.' She filed her papers away, then stood. 'Will you bring tea, please, Mrs Ferguson?'

The housekeeper nodded and, with a sharp look for the nobleman, departed.

'Now what have I ever done to earn her displeasure?' Lord Renhurst asked in amused exasperation.

Chione waved a hand in dismissal. 'Oh, you know how Mrs Ferguson's moods are, my lord.' She shot him a conspiratorial smile. 'I know the perfect way for you to get back into her good graces, though.' She led her visitor over to a massive desk centered at one end of the room. 'You know how she loves it when people make themselves useful.'

She indicated the large bottom drawer of the desk. It was wedged tightly askew and impossible to open. 'Could you please, my lord?' Only with a long-time family friend like the viscount could she ask such a thing. 'All the sealing wax is in there and I've desperate need of it.'

He rolled his eyes. 'I come bearing news and get set to servants' work!' Yet he gamely folded back his sleeve and bent over the drawer. He pulled. He pounded. He heaved. 'Why haven't you had Eli in to take care of this?'

Eli was the ancient groom, the only manservant she had left, and also the one-legged former captain of the *Fortune-Hunter*, her grandfather's first merchant ship. 'He does not come in the house,' Chione explained. 'He claims his peg will scuff the floor, but I think he is afraid of Mrs Ferguson.'

'Oh, for God's sake,' Renhurst huffed in disgust. His fashionably tight coat was straining at the seams, and a sheen of perspiration shone on his brow. 'We're all afraid of Ferguson,' he grunted. 'And you still have not told me what I did to end up in her bad graces.'

Chione smiled. 'It appears that Mrs Ferguson was, at one time, of the opinion that you were on the verge of marrying again.'

The viscount was startled into losing his grip. 'Good God. Marrying whom?' he asked, applying himself and pulling harder.

'Me.'

With a last mighty heave, the drawer came loose. Chione hid her grin as both the sealing wax and the viscount ended up on the library floor. He gaped up at her, and Chione could not help but laugh.

'Oh, if you could only see your expression, sir! I never thought so, you may rest assured.' He wisely refrained from comment and she helped him rise and motioned him to a chair before she continued. 'Can you imagine the speculation you would be subject to, should you take a bride of three and twenty? And though society's gossip is nothing to me, I could never be comfortable marrying a man I have always regarded as an honorary uncle.'

Chione tilted her head and smiled upon her grandfather's closest friend. 'And yet, although I've said as much to Mrs Ferguson, I'm afraid that, since you have no intention of marrying me, she has no further use for you.'

The viscount still stared. 'I confess, such a solution has never occurred to me! I know I've told you more than once that a marriage might solve your problems, but to be wedded to an old dog like me?' He shuddered. 'What if, against all odds, you are right and Mervyn does come back after being missing all these months? He'd skin me alive!'

Chione smiled. 'Mervyn himself married a younger woman, but he did so out of love. He'd skin us both if we married for any other reason.'

'You are doubtless right.' He sat back. 'Not every man in his dotage has the energy that your grandfather possessed, my dear. There is not another man in a hundred that would contemplate a second family at such an age.' He smiled wryly. 'So sorry to disrupt Mrs Ferguson's plans. I suppose now it will be stale bread on the tea tray instead of fresh bannocks and honey.'

'Perhaps not.' Chione chuckled now. 'But I would not put it past her.'

'Actually, I did have a bit of news for you, but before we settle to it, I must ask—where are the children?'

'Olivia is napping.' She smiled and answered the question she knew he was truly asking. 'Will has gone fishing and taken the dog with him. You are safe enough.'

The viscount visibly relaxed. 'Thank heavens. The pair of them is all it takes to make me feel my own age. Leave it to Mervyn to spawn such a duo and then leave them to someone else to raise!' He smiled to take the sting from his words. 'When you throw that hell-hound into the mix, it is more than my nerves can handle.'

Mrs Ferguson re-entered the library with a clatter. She

placed the tea tray down with a bit more force than necessary. 'Will ye be needing anything else, miss?'

'No, thank you, Mrs Ferguson.'

'Fine, then. I'll be close enough to hear,' she said with emphasis, 'should ye require anything at all.' She left, pointedly leaving the door wide open.

Lord Renhurst was morose. 'I knew it. Tea with bread and butter.'

Chione poured him a dish of tea. 'I do apologise, my lord. It may not be you at all. Honey is more difficult than butter for us to obtain these days.'

He set his dish down abruptly. 'Tell me things are not so bad as that, Chione.'

She gazed calmly back at him. 'Things are not so bad as that.'

'I damned well expect you to tell me if they are not.'

Chione merely passed him the tray of buttered bread.

He glared at her. 'Damn the Latimer men and their recklessness!' He raised a hand as she started to object. 'No, I've been friends with Mervyn for more than twenty years, I've earned the right to throw a curse or two his way.' He shook his head. 'Disappeared to parts unknown. No good explanation to a living soul, just muttering about something vital that needed to be done! Now he's been missing for what—near a year and half again? Then Richard is killed five months ago in some godforsaken desert and here you are left alone. With two children and this mausoleum of a house to look after, and no funds with which to do so.' He lowered his voice a little. 'No one respects your strength and fortitude more than I, my dear, but if it has become too much for you to handle alone, I want you to come to me.'

Chione sighed. The longer Mervyn stayed missing, the worse her situation grew, but still, this was a conversation she never wished to have. It was true, her life was a mess, and her family's circumstances were hopelessly entangled. It was universally known, and tacitly ignored, at least in their insular little village and along the rugged coast of Devonshire. Chione coped as best she could, but she did not discuss it. She was a Latimer.

She winced a little at the untruth of that statement. All the world knew her as a Latimer, in any case, and in her heart she was truly a part of this family. She would prevail, as Latimers always had, no matter how difficult the situation they found themselves in.

She stiffened her spine and cast a false smile at Lord Renhurst. 'We are fine, my lord. We have learned to practise economies. Now come, what news have you?'

'Economies!' he snorted. 'Mervyn built Latimer Shipping with his own two hands. If he ever found out what a mess it's become and how his family has been obliged to live…' He shook his head. 'I've spoken with the banks again, but they refuse to budge. They will not release Mervyn's funds until some definitive word is had of him.'

'Thank you for trying, in any case.' She sighed.

'Least I could do,' he mumbled. 'Wanted to tell you, too, that I went to the Antiquarian Society, as you asked.'

Chione was brought to instant attention. 'Oh, my lord, thank you! Did you speak with the gentleman I mentioned? Did Mr Bartlett know anything of use?'

'He offers you his sincerest condolences, but could only tell me that, yes, Richard did indeed spend a great deal of time in their collection before he left for Egypt.'

'Could he not tell you specifically what Richard was looking for?'

'He could not.'

She closed her eyes in disappointment. Chione knew that Richard had been hiding something; something about her grandfather's disappearance, she suspected. Now his secrets had died along with her brother. Trying to ferret out the one kept her from dwelling on the other. But it was more than that. She needed to find her grandfather, and the sooner the better. She refused to consider what the rest of the world believed: that he was most likely dead as well.

'Bartlett did say that he spent a great deal of time with a Mr Alden. Scholar of some sort. He recommended that you speak with him if you wished to know what was occupying your brother's interest.'

Chione brightened immediately. 'Alden,' she mused. 'The name is familiar. Yes, I believe I have read something of his. I shall look through Mervyn's journals.' She turned to Lord Renhurst and smiled. 'Thank you so much. You are a very great friend, to all of us.'

The viscount blinked, and then sat a moment, silently contemplating her. 'You think this is something to do with the Lost Jewel, don't you?' he asked.

'I fear so,' she answered simply. 'But I hope not.'

'I hope not, as well.' His disapproval was clear. 'You are in a devil of a fix already, my dear, without adding in a lot of nonsense about pharaohs and mysterious lost treasures.'

'We might think it a parcel of nonsense, but you know that Richard believed in it. As does Mervyn.' To put it simply, they had *wanted* to believe. The men in Chione's family were adventurers in heart and deed. They craved travel and excitement as fervently as the débutantes of the *ton* craved young and single heirs to a dukedom, as constantly as the opium eaters of her mother's country craved their drug.

Chione cast her gaze down at her tea. What she craved were far simpler things: food for the table, a warmer coat for Will, the ability to pay her remaining servants' wages. But she would achieve none of those by drinking tea with Lord Renhurst.

'Do try not to worry, my lord. We shall muddle through.' Strategically, she paused and cocked her head. 'Listen, do you hear barking?'

The viscount's manner abruptly changed. He set down his dish of tea. 'Well, then,' he said briskly, 'we will scheme together to bring you about, but another time. I cannot stay longer today.'

Chione had to hide her smile at his sudden eagerness to be gone. 'Of course. Thank you so much for talking with Mr Bartlett for me.'

'Certainly.' He paused and a stern expression settled once more over his features. 'I've let you have your way so far, Chione, but I'm watching you closely. If I need to step in, I will.'

'I appreciate your concern, sir.'

He offered his arm, listening intently. 'Will you walk me out? I must be off.'

Chione resisted the impish urge to drag her feet. They stepped outside and she wrapped her shawl tighter about her shoulders. She breathed deep of the sea scent blowing strong on the wind. It was the kind of wind that brought change, her grandfather had always said. She closed her eyes and hoped it *would* bring change. She hoped it would bring him home again.

'Good day to you, Chione. We will speak again soon.' Lord Renhurst's groom pulled his phaeton up to the house and he hurried towards it. He skidded to a stop, however, when a horse and rider suddenly emerged from the wooded section of the drive.

The sun obscured her view, and Chione caught her breath, believing for an instant that she had indeed wished Mervyn Latimer home. The rider approached, and stopped in front of the house, allowing her to see that it was not the imposing form of her missing grandfather, but that of a younger man instead.

A man, indeed, and a specimen of the species like she had never seen.

Most of the men in the village were fishermen, gnarled from their constant battle against wind and sea. Lord Renhurst and her grandfather were older, and stout with good living. Her brother had always looked exactly what he had been—a rumpled, slightly grubby scholar. But this man… She gave a little sigh. He dismounted and she could not look away. He stood tall, broad and powerful. He looked, in fact, as if he could have ridden straight from the pages of one of her adventure novels.

As if he had heard her thoughts, he strode boldly towards the house. The closer he came, the faster her heart began to trip. He stopped and the skin on Chione's nape prickled, every tiny hair there standing at quivering attention.

'Good day,' he said to the viscount, who still stood in the drive. 'I am looking for Oakwood Court.'

His clothing looked as unusual as he. A coat of dark green, made of fine material, but cut loose, with a multitude of pockets. Snug trousers and scuffed, comfortable-looking boots. His linen was clean and his neckcloth a bit limp, as if he had been tugging at it.

'You've found it, sir,' Lord Renhurst replied. Chione thought he might have conversed further if not for a loud and happy bark that sounded suddenly nearby. 'Sorry, must be off,' he said as he edged towards his phaeton. Gravel crunched as the vehicle began to move, then the viscount twisted around on the seat. He looked back at her visitor and advised loudly, 'Good God, man, take off your hat!'

'Oh, yes. Of course.' The gentleman removed said article and turned to face Chione once more. He raked her with an assessing glance and his face softened a bit. 'Can you tell me where I might find Miss Latimer?'

Chione's mouth went dry. Gracious, but the man could not be real. He did not speak, he *rumbled*, with low tones that she could feel, echoing in the bones behind her ear, vibrating in the pit of her belly. His hair was too long to be fashionable, and dark. Nearly as dark as her own, in fact. Yet his eyes were the same colour as the cerulean sky overhead. It was a striking combination, especially when set off by sun-browned skin.

She swallowed and forced herself to gather her wits. 'Yes, I am Miss Latimer,' she said. But Lord Renhurst's last words finally dawned on her and made her realise how near the dog's barking had come. 'Oh, dear,' she said.

The gentleman was oblivious to the danger. 'Miss Latimer, it is a pleasure to meet you at last. I've come a great distance to find you.' He bowed. 'I am Treyford.'

The barking had grown louder still and had changed in tone. Chione could see the beast now, coming from the stables. She was no longer making noise for the sheer fun of it, now she was broadcasting a frenzy of doggy ecstasy.

'The pleasure is mine,' Chione strode down the steps towards her visitor. 'Pray, do excuse me.' She reached up and snatched the very fine beaver hat from the man's grasp just before the dog reached them. Then she turned and threw the thing away with all her might.

Trey's jaw dropped as his brand new hat sailed out to the middle of the gravelled drive. Good God, was the girl mad? Was this why Richard had been so adamant that Trey protect his sister?

He soon realised his mistake. The largest, ugliest dog he had ever seen came out of nowhere and pounced on the hat with a yelp of joy. The creature shook the thing as if to break it, tossed it in the air, growled ferociously at it, then settled down right there in the drive and began to tear into it with powerful jaws.

'I am sorry,' Miss Latimer said, 'but she would have knocked you flat in order to get it.'

The lady looked at him at last. He saw recognition in her eyes—eyes so dark they appeared nearly black. Slightly slanted, they were rimmed with the most astonishing eyelashes he had ever seen.

'Treyford, did you say?' she asked. 'As in the *Earl* of

Treyford? How nice to meet you at last! I feel we must know you already, so frequently did Richard mention you in his letters.' She cocked her head at him. 'But what a surprise to find you in England, my lord. I had thought you meant to stay and continue your work in Egypt.'

A shout from what he took to be the path to the stables distracted her, and Trey seized the opportunity to study the girl. She looked younger than he had expected. Richard had spoken often of his older sister and it had been obvious that they were close, her support a steady influence that Richard had relied upon. He knew she must be near to five and twenty, but she still looked little more than a girl.

She was also prettier than he had expected—a far cry from the strong-willed spinster he had imagined. Her skin was flawless, with a slight exotically olive tint, but still very pale in contrast to her dark eyes and even darker hair. Her face, finely moulded with high cheekbones, was set in a serious expression, as if she carried heavy burdens.

The shout came again, and Trey recognised her name.

'Chione! Just see what I've got!'

Her face had softened. 'It is young Will,' she said, as if that explained anything. 'Most likely covered in mud, but do not fear. I will not allow him near enough to ruin any more of your wardrobe.'

'Chione!' The boy came into view. He looked perhaps nine or ten years old, and carried a large open basket that bounced against his side as he ran. He was indeed slathered head to foot in mud.

'Beef, Chione!' he called in triumph. 'I was walking past the vicarage with my string of fish and Mrs Thompson called out to me. She vowed she had been longing for her cook's fish stew, and she asked me to trade. An entire joint of beef, can you imagine? I've got it right here!'

'How nice, Will,' Miss Latimer began, but a look of caution

crossed her face as the boy drew near. 'Watch your feet. Careful!'

The warning came too late. The brim of Trey's beaver hat had come completely detached and lay directly in the boy's path. Even as her warning rang out, his feet became tangled and he went down heavily, the basket flying out ahead of him.

The cloth-wrapped bundle within took flight. Trey watched, prophetically sure of its trajectory even before it landed, with a splat, in his arms. He looked down at the stain that now managed to decorate both his coat and his linen, and then he glared at the disastrous duo before him.

Miss Latimer was solicitously helping the boy to his feet. 'My lord, we would be pleased if you would stay to dinner.' She indicated the dripping bundle in his arms. 'As you see, we shall be dining on roast beef.'

Chapter Two

Trey was in the grip of an excessively bad mood. He had travelled halfway round the world, only to end up in Bedlam. He
had given his word, and so he had given up Egypt. And he had
ended up in a madhouse.

It hadn't been his first impression. He'd left the village this
afternoon, taking the coastal path as directed, and he'd thought
this must be one of the most wild and beautiful spots on the
Earth. Oddly enough, he found himself uncomfortable with the
surrounding lushness. After the spare desert beauty of Egypt,
this part of Devon appeared to be blessed with an embarrassment of riches: stunning ocean views of harbour and bay, wood-
lands full of gnarled trees, rocky cliffs, and charming dells
bursting with early springtime displays.

Oakwood Court blended right into the undisciplined vista.
The long, meandering drive left the coastal path and took one
on a leisurely trip through a wooded grove, then abruptly broke
free to cross a sweeping lawn. A traveller found oneself gifted
with a stunning tableau of a many-gabled Elizabethan manor
nestled against a rising, wooded slope. It was a distinctive old
house, full of character.

Trey had never met Mervyn Latimer, Richard's famous

grandfather, who had won a cargo ship in a card game and turned it into one of the biggest shipping companies in England. Yet just by spending a short amount of time in his house, Trey felt as if he knew something of the eccentric old man. His larger-than-life presence fairly permeated the place, along with many fascinating objects that must have been collected throughout his travels.

And although the many curiosities hanging on walls, gracing the tables and filling the shelves of the house were interesting, they were as nothing compared to the arresting collection of human oddities he'd found here.

Directly after Trey's heroic rescue of dinner—the boy's words—his horse had been taken up by the groom. The wizened little man with a peg leg looked as if he belonged in the rigging of a Barbary pirate's ship. Yet he soothed the fidgety horse with a soft voice and gentle hands, and the skittish hack followed after him like a lamb.

Trey, in all his greased and bloodied glory, had been handed over to the housekeeper. A dour Scot if he had ever met one, she wore a constant frown, spoke in gruff tones, and carried heavy buckets of water as if they weighed nothing. Yet she worked with brisk efficiency and made sure he had everything a gentleman could ask for his toilet. Save, perhaps, clothes that fit.

She'd come to fetch him once he was changed into some of Richard's left-behind things, rasping out a crotchety, 'Come along with ye, then, to the drawing room.' He did, stalking after the woman along a long corridor with many framed maps upon the wall, and down a dark stairwell.

One notion struck Trey as they moved through the large house. There was a curious lack of activity. There were no enticing kitchen smells, no butler guarding the door, no footmen to carry water, no maids dusting the collection of bric-a-brac. Trey might be the black sheep of his family and a dark hole on the glittering map of the *ton*, but he had grown up in a substantial house and knew the kind of activity required to run it. The lack was somehow unnerving, and lent the house a stale, unused air. Somehow it felt more like an unkempt museum than a home.

Eventually they arrived on the first floor, and the housekeeper stopped before a richly panelled door. She pushed it open without preamble, stood aside and said, 'In here.' Without even waiting to see him cross the threshold, she shuffled off towards the back of the house.

Trey entered to find yet another room filled with the inanimate detritus of a well-travelled collector. And one animate specimen.

It was a child, of perhaps two or three years. Trey blanched. The only thing more inherently threatening than a respectable female was a child, and this one was both. She was very pretty, with long chestnut curls, but her heart-shaped face was smeared and her grubby little hands were leaving marks on the sofa she stood upon.

'Livvie do it,' she said, pointing down behind the piece of furniture.

Why the devil would a child be left alone in the parlour? Suppressing a sigh, Trey crossed the room to peer into the narrow space she indicated. The wall behind the sofa was smudged with what looked to be honey and a crumbled mess lay on the floor below. 'Yes,' he agreed with the solemn-faced sprite. 'You did do it, didn't you?'

She sighed and abruptly lifted both hands towards him.

Trey grimaced. 'I don't think so,' he said, shaking his head.

She only grunted and lifted her demanding little arms again.

Trey decided to take charge. Children responded to authority, did they not? 'Come down from there,' he said firmly. 'We shall find the irresponsible creature meant to be in charge of you.' He snapped his fingers and pointed to the floor.

The child's lower lip poked out and started to tremble. Great, fat tears welled in her brown eyes. 'Up,' she whimpered.

Hell and high water, were females born knowing how to manipulate? It must be a skill transferred from mother to daughter in the womb. Well, stubbornness was the gift his mother has passed to him, or so he'd been told many times in his own childhood. 'No,' he said more firmly still. 'Now hop down from there at once.'

The tears swelled and ran over, making tracks on her dirty cheeks. *'Uuuuuppp!'* she wailed, and her little body began to shake with the force of her sobs.

Oh, Lord, no. 'Don't do that,' Trey commanded. 'I'm picking you up.' Grimacing in distaste, he plucked her off the sofa, trying to keep her at arm's length. Quicker than a flash, more subtly done than the most precise of military manoeuvres, she foiled his effort and nestled up tightly against him.

Trey was suddenly and fiercely glad of the borrowed coat he wore. Underneath the chit's sweet honey smell lurked a more suspicious odour. 'Let's go, then,' he said, 'and find your keeper.'

The door opened with a bang and a distracted Miss Latimer rushed in. 'Oh, no,' she gasped, rushing forward to take the child.

'Shone!' cried the little girl. 'She-own! Livvie do it.'

'I do beg your pardon, my lord.' Miss Latimer strode back to the doorway and shouted in a most unladylike fashion, 'I've found her!'

The dour housekeeper arrived a moment later. She never glanced at Trey, but took the child and scowled at her young mistress. 'She's taken a plate of bannocks with her,' she said with a roll of her eyes, 'so there's no tellin' where we'll find the mess later.'

Miss Latimer shot an inquiring look at him. Trey had not the smallest desire to witness the fuss created should *that* discovery be made. He shrugged and maintained an air of innocence, and the young lady soon bundled the girl and the older woman out of the door.

Miss Latimer winced. 'I must apologise, my lord. Our household has been greatly diminished since Richard's death and

Olivia *will* wander.' She continued on, but Trey was not listening. He knew he was glowering at her, but he could not help himself.

God's teeth, but he could not get over how beautiful she was. Her heavy, black tresses shone, as black as the moods that plagued him, as dark as any he had seen in his travels to the east. It was the perfect foil for her exotic skin, just exactly the tawny colour of moonlight on the desert sands.

Her eyes, framed by those lush lashes, agitated him. They were too old for her young and beautiful face. It was as if she had experienced too much sorrow, too much of the dark side of life, and it could not be contained. It spilled out of her, tinting her gaze with mystery, with *knowing*.

He realised most men would find her beauty fascinating, but damn it, this was exactly the sort of situation in which a man couldn't afford to give in to attraction. Women like this came with a multitude of strings attached, and Trey hadn't thrown off his own yoke of responsibility so he could take on someone else's.

He could see that his glare was unsettling her. He knew that she was at best unnerved, and at worst unhappy, at his presence. He did not care. He was unnerved and unhappy, damn it, so she might as well be, too.

He had come to England to aid an ageing spinster facing an undefined danger. He had been fully prepared to root out the trouble, deliver the damned scarab, and then quickly return to Egypt. There had been no mention of thick eyelashes and long ebony hair. He was not supposed to be dealing with children, and their flying joints of meat and their artful tears. In fact, the only danger here appeared to be to his wardrobe.

And the girl was still talking. Trey had the sudden, nearly irresistible urge to get up and walk out, to drop the scarab in her lap and to never look back. He suppressed a sigh at the thought, for he knew he could not do it. But damn Richard for getting himself killed and thrusting his responsibilities in his lap! He rubbed his temple and wished the girl would stop talking. He wanted to get this over with and get back to his work as quickly as possible.

Miss Latimer did stop, at last, as the door opened again and young Will, freshly scrubbed, bounded into the room, the dog at his heel. The boy dutifully made his bow and went to kiss her. The dog made a beeline for Trey, collapsed upon his Hessians, and gazed adoringly at him, tongue lolling.

'Oh, dear, I am sorry,' Miss Latimer said yet again. 'She has a hopeless passion for gentlemen.'

'Mrs Ferguson says she likes their accessories—particularly the ones made of hide or leather.' Will grinned.

'Will—take the dog outside.'

'She will howl,' warned Will. He turned to Trey. 'Morty likes you, Lord Treyford. Do you like dogs?' he asked ingenuously.

'For the most part,' Trey said, reaching down to scratch behind the beast's ears and lift her drooling head off of his boots. 'Morty?' he asked.

'Her real name is Mortification,' Will explained. 'Squire named her because he said he was mortified that such an ugly pup came from his prize bitch. I shortened it to Morty so her feelings wouldn't get hurt.'

'Will saved her life,' Miss Latimer explained. 'Squire was going to have her destroyed.'

'I gave my last guinea for her,' said Will. 'She's my best friend.'

Women, babes and puppy love. Good God. No wonder Richard had fled to Egypt.

'I've asked Mrs Ferguson to save a bone for her,' she continued. 'She will have it in the kitchens, so you may be left in peace, Lord Treyford.'

As if summoned by the mention of her name, the housekeeper appeared in the parlour door. Without ceremony she snapped her fingers at the dog. 'Come, you hell-spawned hound. Bone!'

Evidently the dog was familiar with the word. She rose, gave herself a good jaw-flapping shake, then trotted off after the housekeeper, casting a coquettish glance back over her shoulder at Trey.

The damned dog was *flirting* with him.

He looked up. The girl gazed back, expectation clear in those haunting eyes.

Trey faltered at the sudden, strange hitch of his breath. Something sharp moved in his stomach. This was, suddenly, all too much for him. Too much clutter, too many people. Hell, even the dog seemed to want something of him. Trey knew himself for a hard man, surviving in a harsh world. He lived his life unencumbered, with relationships kept to a minimum and always kept clearly defined. Servant and master, buyer and seller, associate or rival. It was simpler that way. Safer. Neither of those attributes, he was sure, could be applied to this family, and that made him uncommonly nervous.

The intense stare that young Will was directing at him only increased his discomfort. Suddenly the boy opened his mouth and a barrage of questions came out of him, like the raking fire of a cannonade.

'How long did it take to sail back to England? How hot is it in Egypt? Did you see any crocodiles? Have you brought back any mummies? Did you climb the pyramids? Were you afraid?' Red-faced, the boy paused to draw breath. 'Will you tell us over dinner? Please?'

Trey's breath began to come faster. He cleared his throat. 'Yes, well,' he said, trying to keep the harshness from his voice, 'actually, I've come to your home with a purpose, not on a social visit.' The boy looked mutinous, and Trey rushed on. 'I need a private moment with your sister, lad. I've a sort of… message, from Richard for her.'

The boy's expression cleared of its clouds. 'My sister?' he scoffed. 'She don't know enough words to have a proper conversation, my lord. Did you mean Chione?' He shot a devilish glance at the young lady, then turned to Trey, eyes sparkling as if sharing a great joke. 'Chione's my niece, not my sister!'

Now Trey was flustered, something that did not happen often. Niece? What sort of tangled mess had Richard dropped him into? He knew with certainty that there was only one answer to that: exactly the sort he had spent a lifetime avoiding.

Will was staring at him now. 'Didn't Richard tell you anything? He wrote us all about you. You see, my papa is Chione's grandpapa, so I get to be her uncle. And Olivia gets to be her aunt! Isn't that funny?'

It wasn't funny. It had been a long time since Trey had felt this awkward. But there was no way he could tell the boy how he had discouraged Richard's tendency to talk of his family, of anything other than their work. Trey didn't like chitchat. He liked focus, and determination, and hard work. He liked travel. Distance. Adventure. There was nothing wrong with that. So why was his stomach churning now?

He breathed deeply. It was too damned late to avoid this fiasco, but he'd be damned if he didn't extricate himself in record time.

Miss Latimer helped him take the first step. 'Will, why don't you run along and help Mrs Ferguson with dinner? Lord Treyford and I will take a stroll in the gardens. If that is acceptable, my lord?'

Trey nodded and watched as the boy started to protest, then hung his head. 'A pleasure to meet you, my lord,' he said, and turned towards the door.

The boy's dejected profile was impossible for Trey to ignore. He let loose a silent string of curses. But he was all too familiar with the heavy weight of childish disappointment. 'Hold, lad,' he said roughly, and the boy turned. 'Egypt is as hot as blazes. Yes, I climbed the pyramids, and, no, it was not the least bit frightening. I've been uncomfortably close to some crocodiles, too. Egypt is full of wondrous things.'

Trey closed his eyes. Just the thought of Egypt calmed him. He hadn't expected it, but the country had beguiled him. Time flowed differently there; he'd had a sense that the secrets of the past were just out of his reach, hidden only by a thin veil of mist.

'And the mummies? Did you bring any back?' The boy's eyes were shining.

'No, although I encountered plenty, both whole and in pieces.' He glanced over at the girl. 'Perhaps I will have time to tell you about it before I must go.'

'Thank you, my lord!'

Miss Latimer wore a frown as she rose to her feet. 'Just allow me to stop in the front hall to fetch my wrap, and we can be on our way,' she said.

Good. Perhaps she was as eager to be done with this as he.

Chione wrapped herself well against the chill and led their guest outside, once again restored to her habitual poise. She should be grateful that he had made it easy for her to slip back into her normal, contained role, she told herself firmly, for she had been acting a fool since her first glimpse of Lord Treyford.

She had scarcely been able to help herself. All of that overt masculinity and absolute self-assurance touched something inside of her, stirred to life a part of her that she would rather be left slumbering.

And then she had heard it in his voice. That all-too-familiar longing when he had spoken of the wonders of Egypt. She knew that tone and exactly what it meant. *He was one of them.*

Like her grandfather, her brother, and even her father. Never happy where they were, always pining for something more exotic, more adventuresome, more dangerous. Or perhaps, just *more*.

That tiny wistful note that had crept into the earl's voice; that was all it took to effectively quench all of the flutterings and tinglings and ridiculously rapid heartbeats that had plagued her every time their eyes met.

An adventurer—just like the others. With that realisation she reached for calm, breathed deep and let the veneer of her assumed identity fall back into place. They stepped down into the formal garden and he grudgingly offered her his arm. She took it, then had to school herself not to gasp as a slow, warm burn started in her fingertips, flowed like honey through her, and settled in a rich puddle in the pit of her belly.

Perhaps she wasn't rid of all of those stirrings. Yet.

'You are very quiet, Miss Latimer.' Though his voice was rough, there was a hint of irony hidden in it. 'Not at all like your brother.'

Chione had to smile at that. 'No, indeed. Richard was many things, but quiet was not a label he was often burdened with.' She swept aside a low hanging branch and held it back invitingly. 'He was too full of life to keep quiet for long.'

He did not answer and they walked in silence for several moments. Despite her disillusionment, Chione could not but acknowledge her heightened awareness of his looming presence. It was more than the sheer size of him, too. The air fairly crackled around him, as if the force of his personality stamped itself on the surrounding atmosphere.

She wondered just what it was that brought him here. Not a happy errand, judging by his nearly constant frown, but really, who could blame the man? Since his arrival he'd had his hat eaten, his clothes bloodied, been entertained in the drawing room by a toddler and quizzed by a little boy. They should count themselves lucky he hadn't run screaming back to the village.

Chione was glad he was made of sterner stuff than that. 'Richard wrote of you so often,' she began. 'I know he held you in very high regard. Forgive me if I am rude, but I was surprised that you did not know of our…unusual family. Did he not speak to you of us?'

She had chosen poorly, perhaps, because his frown deepened. 'He spoke of you,' he said gruffly. 'And of your grandfather.' He paused. 'I should have asked sooner—is he still missing? Have you had no word of him?'

'No, not yet. Soon, I hope.'

'Do you still have no idea what might have happened to him, then?'

'On the contrary, there are many ideas, but no proof of anything.'

'It has been what? Two years? And yet you hold out hope?' He sounded incredulous.

'Not two years, yet, and indeed, I do have hope. I hope every day that this is the one that brings him home. My grandfather has been in a thousand scrapes and survived each one. He told me once that he meant to die a peaceful death in his bed, an old man. I believe he will.'

The earl looked away. 'Richard felt much the same,' he said.

Chione felt a fresh pang of loss at his words. Yes, Richard had understood. She blinked and focused intently on the surrounding wood. The forest was alive around them as the birds and the insects busily pursued all the industries of spring. She sighed. Life did go on, and Richard's responsibilities were hers now.

'I am happy to have the chance to thank you for the letter you sent to us, on my brother's death. It was a comfort to know that he had a friend like you with him when he died.'

For a long moment, Lord Treyford made no reply. The path had begun to climb and he paid careful attention to her footing as well as his. When at last he did speak, he sounded—what was it—cautious? Subdued? 'That is truly what I've come for, what I've travelled all this way to do. To speak to you about Richard's death.'

He fell silent again. Chione waited, willing to give him the time he needed. She harboured a grave feeling that she was not going to like what he had to say.

'Richard's last thoughts were of you,' he finally said. They had come out on a little ridge. A bench had been strategically placed to take advantage of the spectacular view. The earl motioned her to it and gingerly lowered himself beside her.

His gaze wandered over the scene. 'When one hears of Devon, it is always the desolate beauty of Dartmoor.' He paused. 'It seems that nothing here is as I expected.' His gaze was no longer riveted on the view. Instead it roamed over her face, the blue of his eyes more than a match for the sky overhead. After a moment the intensity of his regard began to discomfort her.

She ducked her head and ruthlessly clamped down her own response. She breathed deeply, gathering her strength and reaching for courage. She raised her head and looked him in the eye. 'Tell me about Richard's death.'

It was enough to sweep clear the thickening tension between them. 'Yes,' he said. 'Of course.'

He reached into an inner pocket, drew something out. 'Just before he died, your brother asked me to give this to you.' He took her hand from where it rested in her lap and placed the object in it.

It was sharp-edged, and warm from the heat of his body. For several moments that was the sum of Chione's impressions, for she could not see through her sudden swell of tears. She breathed deeply again, however, and regained control of her emotions. As her vision cleared she got her first good look at the object.

Only to be seized by something uncomfortably close to panic. A wave of nausea engulfed her and she let the thing fall from her suddenly lifeless fingers.

Good God, he had found it.

Chapter Three

~~~~~~~~~~~~~~~~~~~~~~~

Trey watched, shocked, as Miss Latimer dropped the scarab as if it had seared her. She sat lifeless, eyes closed, fists clenched, neither moving nor speaking. He could see the sheen of sweat upon her brow. She really was frightened.

'Miss Latimer?' He grasped her cold hands and began to chafe them. Still she sat, frozen. 'Miss Latimer?' Already unnerved, he began to get impatient. 'Damn it, answer me!'

'Yes.' Her voice was faint.

'What is it?' Her eyes were opened now, but glazed, her focus obviously fixed on some inner torment. 'What ails you?'

There was no response. Trey bent down and retrieved the scarab, still on the chain that Richard had worn around his neck, and tried to press it into her hand.

'No,' she said sharply, shying away.

He closed his hand around it, feeling the bite of the insect's sharp legs. 'Richard's last wish was for you to have this,' he said roughly.

'I don't want it.' The words emerged in almost a sob. She clapped a hand over her mouth, eyes wide as if in horror at her own lack of control. Trey watched as she drew a deep breath and stood. 'Do you hear me, Lord Treyford? *I do not want it!*'

Trey was dumbfounded. Here was yet another twist to this horrifyingly convoluted day. He stared at the girl, wondering where the calm and remote young lady he had walked out with had gone. 'That is unacceptable,' he said flatly. 'I made a pledge to your brother that I would deliver it to you.'

She looked unimpressed.

'I gave my word of honour.' As far as he was concerned, that was the end of the matter.

Apparently it was for the girl, as well. It quickly became obvious that he had pushed her past the point of restraint. She stood poised, indignation in every taut line of her body, those incredible dark eyes glittering with emotion. 'I don't give a tinker's damn for your honour,' she ground out. 'Family honour, a man's pride, I've had my fill of it. It is all just fancy trappings and convenient excuses for doing whatever fool thing engages you, regardless of who you hurt or neglect in the process.' She cast a scornful glance over him. 'You keep it, Lord Treyford, and if by some miracle you do find the Jewel, then you may keep that as well.'

'Jewel?' Trey asked. He was getting damned tired of feeling like the village idiot, not understanding who was who or what was happening around him.

She let out a distinctly unladylike snort and turned away from him.

'Now, you wait just a moment. Keep it?' Hastily Trey got to his feet, trying to tamp down on the flickering rise of his own anger. 'Keep it, you say? If I had wanted to keep the cursed thing I would have stayed in Egypt,' he said, growing more furious with each word. 'I would not have abandoned my plans, given up my work, and tramped halfway around the world to this…' he swept his arm in an encompassing gesture '…this insane asylum.'

He rubbed a hand across his brow, dampened the flames of his temper, searching for patience. 'Months, this has cost me months.' With a sudden fluid movement, he thrust his arm out, dangling the scarab from its chain, forcing her to look at it. 'This thing meant something to your brother. It was so important that he spent his dying breath securing my promise to see it returned to you. And you ask me to keep it?'

For the briefest of moments he saw a stricken expression cross her lovely face, but then her eyes narrowed and her expression hardened. 'I know what it meant to my brother, and, worse, what it means to me.' She looked as if she meant to go on, but could not. Her spine straightened as she grappled with her emotions.

Trey was fighting the same battle, and losing fast. He glared at the girl, feeling helpless in the face of her irrational reaction, and resenting her for it. 'I promised Richard,' he repeated harshly. 'He lay in the sand with the life spilling out of him, and he took my hand and made me promise. To deliver this, and to protect you.'

'Protect me?' The sound that came from her was bitter, ugly. 'From what? The folly of trusting in selfish, egocentric men?' She raked him with a scathing glance. 'That lesson I have—finally!—taken to heart.'

She turned away, shaking with the force of the emotion racking her, and Trey could see the moment when she gained a measure of control. She turned, dashing the tears from her face, her voice once more composed. 'I apologise, sir, for taking my grief and anger out on you. I cannot… I need to spend some time alone just now. I trust you can find your way back on your own?'

She did not wait for an answer to her question. Trey stared in disbelief as she walked off, following the path farther into the wood. He stood watching her for several moments, debating whether to chase her down, before he glanced at the scarab in his hand. Turning, he walked back up the path towards the house.

He passed it by, going straight to the stables to fetch his

horse. The wiry groom silently readied his mount, and Trey set out at a brisk pace, more than eager to put a stop to the most unsettling day he had experienced in years. He wished, suddenly and intensely, that he could send the scarab and a note and be done with the matter, that he could be free to make plans to return to his work.

The thought brought on a sudden longing for the simplicity of his time in Egypt. Long days, hard work, hot sun. It had been vigorous and stimulating. Hell, even the complexities of dealing with the wily Egyptian *kashifs* were as nothing compared to the chaos he'd unwittingly stumbled into.

There were too many things here he just did not understand. He had a promise to keep, it was as simple as that, but he could not quiet the worrisome thought that things were much more complicated here than they appeared on the surface.

Aswan had secured him a room in the village's best inn. The former headman—who had consented to leave Egypt and travel as Trey's manservant—expressed a substantial amount of surprise at his employer returning in a different suit of clothes from the one he had sent him out in. And though he was not usually the sort to chat with a servant, or anybody else for that matter, Trey found himself spilling the whole muddled tale as he stripped for a proper bath.

Now, as he gratefully sunk into the steaming tub, Aswan occupied himself brushing out Richard's coat. 'This vicar's wife, who made the trade with the boy,' he mused, his clever fingers making quick work of the task, 'she sounds most worthy. Should I wish to meet her, would it be frowned upon?'

Trey stared at the man. 'No, but why the hell should you wish to?' He regretted the harshness of his words when the Egyptian man raised a brow at him. 'If you do not mind my asking,' he said.

Aswan bowed. 'You may ask, *effendi*.' He returned to his

work while he spoke. 'It is not often that one hears of a woman so generous and so wise as well. She accomplished her task, pleased the boy, and saved the young lady's face all at once.'

'Saved the young lady's face?' Trey wondered if there was some miscommunication at work here. 'From what?'

'From the discomfort of accepting charity. This is something of which you English do not approve, no?'

Trey sat up in the tub. 'Do you mean to say that that girl has been reduced to taking charity?' He experienced a sudden vision of the dusty, empty halls of Oakwood Court.

'Reduced? That is a good word,' Aswan said. 'Reedooosed.'

'Aswan.' His warning was clear.

'Yes, sir,' the man relented. 'It is common knowledge in the village that they are in trouble. The elder of the family, he is gone—no one knows where—yes?'

'Yes,' Trey said impatiently.

'His business—it goes on. There are the men who look after it.'

'Directors.'

'Directors. But the old man's own money, it is…iced? Froze?'

'Frozen? His assets are frozen?'

'Yes! And the family is left to support themselves until the old one is found. With Latimer *effendi* crossed over, it is difficult for them.'

Trey sank back into the warm depths of the tub. Well. That explained quite a bit. Perhaps it also explained Richard's pleas for him to help Chione? Could her trouble be as simple as a lack of funds?

In any case, it gave him a clear reason to ride back out there first thing tomorrow. If Miss Latimer did not wish to keep the scarab, perhaps she would allow him to sell it on her behalf. After that, other arrangements could be set up to see the family through, at least until there was some word of Mervyn Latimer.

With hope, however slight, that his time in Devonshire might actually be near an end, Trey could at last fully relax. He heaved a sigh and laid his head on the back of the tub.

Poor Nikolas was still trapped in the tomb of the Ruby Idol.

Chione had fled to the library upon returning to the house, shutting herself in and the ugly truth out. Here she had sat at her desk, staring at the empty page before her, aware of how much more crucial that payment from her publisher had become, and yet unable to put a single word to paper.

She told no one the terrible news. Not yet. Mrs Ferguson brought her dinner in on a tray. Will came through seeking his lost atlas. Each time she pretended to be busy scribbling. They would know soon enough. Perhaps her household had accepted the truth long ago, along with the rest of the world, leaving her clinging to fruitless hope alone. Now, as the darkness grew around her and the house slipped into silence, she was forced to let that hope go.

He was dead. Her grandfather was dead. She had known it the moment she had seen that scarab. He had been obsessive about it and had worn it on his person always. In some way that she did not understand, the thing was tied up with the story of the Pharaoh's Lost Jewel. Richard, who had shared his unflagging interest in the ancient mystery, had believed that to be the reason that Mervyn Latimer kept the scarab close, but Chione had always believed it to be a symbol, a remembrance of his beloved son and of all the people he cared for, lost in the course of a long and dangerous life. For him to be parted from it, something catastrophic must have happened. But how had Richard come to have it? Why? A sound escaped from her, a rasping, horrible sound. It didn't matter. They were both gone and she was alone.

The place deep inside of her where her hope had been, her faith in her grandfather's ability to survive anything, was empty.

But not for long. Pain, and, yes, anger and betrayal too, rushed at her, filling the hollow spaces, until she could contain herself no longer. She stood, unable to bear even the light of the single candle on her desk. She fled to the darkest recesses of the library, to Mervyn Latimer's favourite stuffed wing chair, and, flinging herself into it, gave in to her grief.

Long minutes passed as her inner storm raged, battering her with emotion. She cried for her grandfather, her brother, for her parents who had died long ago. She cried for the two children upstairs who were orphans now, just as she had been. She cried for herself. But gradually the howling wind of grief abated, leaving her spent.

Unflinching acceptance, warm approval, boundless love—these were the things her grandfather had given her, what she would never feel from him again. The thought loosed another painful, racking sob. He had taken her from chaos and given her security, happiness, a family.

Chione had been born in Egypt, to the Egyptian wife of Mervyn Latimer's son. But her parents had died when Richard was an infant, and Chione a child of only eight. She had rec-ollections of them, of her mother's soothing hands and Edward Latimer's booming laugh. But she had other memories too, harsh and ugly memories that she had locked away, hidden from the world and even from herself.

She had no wish to bring them to light again. And for a long time there had been no need to, thanks to Mervyn Latimer. He had come to Egypt, carried both Richard and her to England, taken them in, and raised them with love.

Now he was gone and their roles were reversed. It was Chione who was left alone, with two children who had no one else to turn to. Chione was the protector now, and though the weight of yet another role might be heavy, it was one she would embrace. Not just because she already loved those children as if they were her own, but also because it was fitting somehow.

Here was her chance to give back some of what she had herself been given. Acceptance. Family. Love. And if it came with a price, well, then, she was happy to pay it.

The thought had her rising, going back to her desk. She pulled out the well-worn letter from Philadelphia and spread it with gentle fingers. America, a land where people focused forwards instead of back, where new ideas were welcomed instead of shunned. She thought she might have flourished there, been of use, accomplished something truly worthwhile. A tear dropped on to the vellum, blurring the ink. Carefully, she folded it and put it away. Her dreams might need to be smaller now, but they would be no less important.

The untouched dinner tray still sat on the edge of her big desk. Chione saw that Mrs. Ferguson had placed today's post on it as well. Wearily she glanced at the notice from the butcher, a cordially worded reminder, which none the less explained why she had sent Will to fish for their supper today. She put it aside and picked up the next, and then she stilled. It was a letter from Mrs Stockton.

The woman was grandmother to Will and Olivia, though a cold and self-involved one at best. Chione read the note quickly and with distaste. Yet another hint for an invitation to visit. The horrid old woman had shown no inclination to become involved with the children after their mother, her daughter, had passed on. She had even refused to see Olivia, the infant her daughter had died giving birth to. Her renewed interest in them had not come until after Mervyn Latimer had been gone long enough to cause concern—and when the possibility of his fortune passing to her young grandson occurred to her. Well, she would have a long wait before she received what she was hinting for; Chione had enough trouble without inviting it into her home.

Her home, yes. Her children, her responsibility, and not just now, but for ever. Chione straightened her spine and looked to her empty paper with new determination. She doubted the trustees would believe the scarab to be as definitive a sign as she did. Which meant no money coming in and no further hope of rescue, either. It could be years before they decided to release Mervyn's funds. Her writing had made the family a little more comfortable in the past few months. It would have to do more in the future. Dashing the last tear from her eye, she took up her pen and bent to work.

Nikolas had at last scrambled free of the collapsing tomb when she heard the noise. She dropped her pen and lifted her head, straining to hear.

Chione might not be a mother, but she had the instincts of one. She knew all the noises the old house gave forth as it settled during the night. She knew the far-off buzzing that was Mrs. Ferguson's snore. She hunched her shoulders each night against the gritty sound of Will grinding his teeth in his sleep, and she recognised the occasional thump that was Olivia falling out of bed. This sound was none of those.

Her candle had burned low, its pool of light spreading no further than the paper she had been writing on. Heart thudding, she left it and rose to slip into the hall.

The noise had come from upstairs. Chione paused long enough to cross to the wall where a collection of antique knives was hung. She slipped one from its mount, an ancient flint blade with an ivory handle. At the foot of the stairs she removed her sturdy boots, then silently padded up in stocking feet, instinctively avoiding the creaking spots.

Halfway up, she froze.

A muffled sound had come from below, from the direction of the kitchens. Someone was in the house. One person moving about, or two? It did not matter; she had to check the children first.

Chione eased on to the landing and trod as silently as she could into the hall. There was another, smaller noise that still sounded loud in the inky darkness. Her room, she thought gratefully, not Will's and not Olivia's.

But Will's room was nearest and the door was slightly ajar. She put her back against the wall right next to the door and listened. Nothing. Peeking in, she saw only Will, sprawled out fast asleep. But where was Morty? Her customary position at the foot of the bed was empty.

Chione found the dog a little way down the hall, bristling silently directly outside the closed door to her own room. Sending out a silent prayer, she crouched next to the dog and placed one hand on the knob. The ivory knife handle in her other hand had grown warm. She gripped it tightly, breathed deeply, then gave the knob a quick turn and thrust the door open.

Morty was through in an instant, emanating a dangerous rumble as she went. A bark, a crash, a thump. Cautiously, Chione followed the dog in. Her window was open. Bright moonlight spilled through it, illuminating the shambles her room was in, framing the figure crouched in the window frame, and blinking wickedly off the long blade he held over Morty's head.

Chione didn't stop to think. She hefted the well-balanced blade and threw with all her might. The black figure grunted, then turned and went out the window.

'A very nice throw,' a deep voice said right behind her.

Chione gasped, and her heart plummeted to her feet. She spun around and fell back. Two large and capable hands reached out to steady her and she looked up, directly into the brilliant blue eyes of the Earl of Treyford.

Chapter Four

Trey waited until the girl had steadied herself before he released her.

'There are more below,' he said in a low voice. 'Fetch the boy, I'll get the girl. Where is she?'

He had to give credit where it was due. Miss Latimer did not bluster, swoon, or ask idiotic questions as he had half-expected her to do. 'Across the hall,' she whispered, and, taking the dog, turned back towards Will's room.

Trey crossed the hall and stealthily opened the little girl's door. He sent up a silent request to whichever deity might be listening, hoping that the babe would not squall when awakened. He need not have worried. Nerves of steel must pass with the Latimer blood, along with those incredible eyelashes. Hers lay thick against her round, little cheeks, until he hefted her into his arms. Their one brief meeting must have made an impact, for she peered up at him, then tucked her head against his shoulder and promptly went back to sleep. He heaved a sigh of thanks and crossed back to the hall.

Miss Latimer was already there, along with a wide-eyed, young Will.

'We must move quickly and silently,' Trey whispered. He

shook his head when Miss Latimer would have taken the little girl from him. 'No, I'll hold on to her, unless we run into one of them. Then you take her and run for the stables.'

'Mrs Ferguson?' she asked.

'Is already there, with my man and your groom. They should have a vehicle ready when we get there.' Trey nodded and set out for the stairwell. 'Quietly, now.'

She reached out a restraining hand. 'No, Lord Treyford. This way.' She took a step backwards, and gestured farther along the hallway.

He might have argued, but Will grasped his forearm and hissed, 'Listen!'

Everyone froze. From the direction of the stairwell came a soft, ominous creaking sound.

Trey promptly turned about. 'Lead on,' he whispered. 'As fast as you can.'

They did move quickly, passing several more bedchambers before taking a connecting passage to the left. Almost at a run, they reached the end of that hallway in a matter of moments. Trey cursed under his breath. There was nothing here except a shallow, curved alcove holding a pedestal and a marble bust. Not even a window to offer a means of escape.

There was no time for recriminations. Trey's mind was racing. Could these be the same bandits who had murdered Richard? Was it possible they had followed him all the way from Egypt? If it were true, then they were desperate indeed, and he had to keep these innocents out of their hands. 'Back to one of the rooms. Are there any trees close to this end of the house?'

'No, wait a moment.' Miss Latimer was part way into the alcove. It was hard to discern in the near darkness, but he thought she was probing the wainscoting. 'Ah, here we are,' she whispered.

He waited. The dog gave a soft whine. There was a grunting sound from Miss Latimer's direction. 'Give it a push, Will,' she urged. 'No, there. Go on, hurry!'

The boy disappeared into the alcove, followed closely by the dog. Trey moved closer and could only just make out the outline of an opening in the curve of the back wall.

'In you go,' said Miss Latimer calmly. 'I will come behind you and close it.'

'Archimedes, is it not?' Trey said with a nod towards the bust. 'Someone has a fine sense of irony,' he whispered as he squeezed past her in the tight space.

He, in the meantime, had a fine sense of all the most interesting parts of Miss Latimer's anatomy pressing into his side as he passed. No, she was not the dried-up spinster he had expected, but apparently neither was he the jaded bachelor he had believed. One full-length press—in the midst of a crisis, all clothes on—and his baser nature was standing up and taking notice. Ignoring it, he moved past.

He had to stoop to enter the hidden doorway, and found himself on a tiny landing. Ahead he could barely discern a narrow set of stairs. Then the door slid home and the blackness swallowed them.

He reached out a hand. The other wall was mere inches away. If he had stood erect and unbowed, his shoulders might have brushed both sides of the passage. Suddenly she was there, close against him again, her mouth right at his ear. 'Archimedes fought and died. We shall run and live.'

Her words were in earnest. The situation was serious. And still a shiver ran through him as her breath, hot and moist, caressed his skin.

Trey muffled a heartfelt curse. His head was still bent in the low-ceilinged corridor, an awkward position made more so by the child resting against his shoulder. Danger lay behind and the unknown ahead, and he must face it saddled with a woman and two children. This was hardly the first scrape he'd found himself in, but it ranked right up there with the worst of the lot. And despite all this, still his body reacted to the nearness of hers. To the scent of her hair. To the sound of her breathing in the darkness. For some reason he did not fully comprehend, all of this infuriated him.

'Go,' he said in a low, harsh whisper. 'I'll be right behind you.'

She moved on silent feet down the narrow stairs. Trey followed, one arm cradling the child close, the other feeling the way ahead. At the bottom, the passage continued in a bewildering set of sharp turns. Several times Trey's trailing fingers found the empty air of a connecting branch, but Miss Latimer passed them by, moving forward at a good pace and with an air of confidence that he hoped was well founded.

Presumably the upkeep of the secret corridors was not high on the housekeeper's duty list. Cobwebs clung to his hair, stuck to his face, and soon coated his seeking hand. Dust, disturbed by their passage, hung in the air and tickled his nose. Desperate, he turned his face into his shoulder, trying not to sneeze. The occupant of his other shoulder had no such compunction.

How did such an immense noise come from such a small person?

The adults both froze, listening, hardly daring to breathe. Not far away, on the other side of the passage wall, sounded a triumphant shout.

Once more he felt the press of that lithe body, soft against his. 'We're near the upper servants' quarters,' Miss Latimer whispered. 'They will waste time searching them. There is another set of stairs just ahead.'

For just that moment, her scent, light and fresh, engulfed him nearly as completely as the darkness. But as she moved away and they began to descend the second stairwell, the air grew dank and the walls moist. They were moving underground.

'Where?' Trey growled quietly.

'The bake house,' she replied.

It was not far. In a matter of a few minutes they were

climbing out of the clammy darkness, emerging into a small, stone building, still redolent with the rich, yeasty smell of fresh bread. Will stood on a box, just next to one of the high windows.

'There was a man at the kitchen door, but he went into the house a moment ago,' he whispered.

Trey turned on the girl. 'Who are they?'

'You don't know?' Her startled look was authentic, Trey judged. 'I have no idea!'

Perhaps not. He decided to leave the rest of that conversation for later. 'How far to the stables?' he asked, handing the child over.

'Not far,' said Will.

'Past the gardens and the laundry, beyond that grove of trees,' Miss Latimer answered. 'Perhaps a quarter of a mile.'

Trey suppressed a groan. It might as well be a league, with this ragtag group.

'We will stay off of the path,' he ordered in dictatorial fashion, 'and under the trees as much as possible. If you see anyone, drop to the ground as quick as you can, as silently as you can. We'll go now, before the sentry comes back to the kitchen door.'

Moonlight was streaming in the high windows; he could see the worry in Chione Latimer's eyes, though she had displayed no other sign of it. 'I'll go first,' he said. 'To the back of that garden shed.'

He paused, and caught her gaze with intent. 'If something happens, go back into the passages and find another way out. Don't stay there, they will find their way in, eventually.'

Her expression grew grimmer still, but she only nodded.

Trey went to the door and opened it a fraction. He stood watching for a short time, but saw nothing, heard nothing except the usual nighttime chorus. The noise, in and of itself, was reassuring. Taking a deep breath, he plunged out of the door and sprinted to the shelter of the tiny garden shed.

Nothing—no shouts of alarm, no explosion of gunfire, no whistle of a knife hurtling through the air. He looked back at the seemingly empty bake house and motioned for his little group to follow.

They came, silent and swift. When they had reached him and stood, gasping in fright and fatigue against the old wooden wall, he felt something alien surging in his chest. Pride?

He pushed it away. Emotion, never a safe prospect, could be deadly in a situation like this, and besides, his stalwart band still had a long way to go. He took the child back again and nodded towards the nearby grove of trees.

What followed had to be the longest fifteen minutes in the history of recorded time, let alone in Chione's lifetime. Like mice, they scurried from one place of concealment to the next, always stopping to listen, to test for danger. They saw no one. Eventually they reached the stables. In the moonlight Chione could see that the great door stood open a foot or so. Morty, who had been sticking close to Will's side, suddenly surged ahead, tail wagging, and slipped in the building.

Chione sighed and hefted Olivia a little higher on her shoulder. She'd endured a maelstrom of emotions today, and now it seemed they were all coalesced into a heavy weight upon her soul. The scarab, she thought. It had to be that damned scarab.

She had barely set one foot in the door before she found herself enveloped in Mrs Ferguson's arms, the housekeeper's heavy rolling pin poking her in the side. For one, long, blessed moment, she leaned into the embrace. All she wanted was to just collapse, sobbing, into the older woman's arms, and not only because of the handle digging into her ribs.

'What did you mean to do—make the man a pie?' Lord Treyford asked the housekeeper with a nod at her weapon of choice.

'Wouldna be the first heathen I beat the fear of God into

with this,' Mrs Ferguson answered, releasing Chione to brandish her rolling pin high.

'Speaking of heathens, that is my man, Aswan,' Lord Treyford said, waving a hand at the man standing watch near the door.

He bowed, and Chione's skin prickled. She handed the still-sleeping child to the housekeeper. It had been a long time since she had seen an Egyptian face. 'With you be peace and God's blessing,' she said in Arabic.

He bowed low, but did not answer. He looked to the earl. '*Effendi*, we should go now.'

They had everything ready for a quick escape. Will's sturdy Charlemagne had already been hitched to the pony cart. He was the last left; the other horses had been sold to finance Richard's trip to Egypt. Her heart heavy, Chione tried to ignore the empty stables, the stale atmosphere.

Would the house look as forlorn, when those men did not find the treasure they had come for? Would they destroy the place in revenge? Steal away Grandfather's collections as a substitute? Or, God forbid, set the house ablaze in their anger?

She stiffened her spine and raised her chin. Let them. All of her valuables were right here. And tonight, they were under one man's protection. She looked for the earl and found him watching her. Inexplicably, she felt her spirits lift.

'Can you drive the cart?' he asked her. 'Aswan and I will ride.'

She nodded. He put his hands on her waist to lift her up to the seat, and Chione felt her hard-fought-for composure slip. She waited for him to release her, but his large grip lingered. One heartbeat. Two. Three. A swirling flood of warmth and unfamiliar pleasure flowed from his hands. It filled her, weighed her down, slowed her reactions, and very nearly stopped her mental processes altogether.

With difficulty she broke the contact, moving away from his touch, berating herself as she settled on the seat and took up the reins. Could nothing—not grief, danger or exhaustion—temper her inappropriate reactions to the man?

She turned to watch as old Eli helped Will and Mrs. Ferguson into the back of the cart and found that, yes—something could. Shock, in fact, proved most effective. 'Who is that?' she gasped. An injured man lay in the front of the cart, curled on to a makeshift pallet.

'Watchman,' Lord Treyford said tersely. 'His fellow came to alert us when they spotted the intruders lurking about. We found him out cold. Eli has seen to him.'

She stared as he took the lead of the village hack Aswan led forward. 'A watchman? Then you were expecting trouble?' The accusation hung unspoken in the air.

'No, not exactly,' he bit out, swinging up and into the saddle. He spoke again and the timbre of his voice crept even lower than his usual rumble. 'I promised Richard that I would bring you the scarab. When he begged me to, I promised to protect you. But truly, I thought it to be a dying man's fancy. Not for a moment did I believe that any danger connected with the thing wouldn't be left behind in Egypt. I never imagined the sort of trouble we've seen tonight.'

He made a grand sweep of his arm, indicating the stable, the wounded man, the cart packed full of her dishevelled family. 'I expected to come here and find Richard's spinster sister facing a civilised problem: a neglectful landlord, investments in want of managing, a house in need of shoring up. *Not* a girl barely out of the schoolroom, grubby children, flirtatious dogs and village gossip. *Definitely* not a hysterical tirade, secret passages and a narrow escape from armed intruders in the night!'

His mount, sensing his ire, began a restless dance. Seemingly without effort, he controlled it, bending it to his will even as he continued his tirade. 'The answer to your question is "No". Thanks in part to everyone leaving me in the dark—no,

I was not expecting trouble. In fact, you have only Aswan, who had the foresight to suggest a lookout, to thank for our presence here tonight.' He glared at her from the back of his horse and finished with a grumble. 'Not that we were much use, in any case.'

Chione should have been insulted. She stared at his flashing blue eyes, his big frame emanating pride, anger and chagrin, and she was once more reminded of the exaggerated characters in her novels. The Earl of Treyford was prickly, harsh and bossy. He was also clearly angry with himself for not anticipating tonight's events and honest enough to admit that it was his servant's precaution that had saved the day—or night.

Though he might be the last to admit it, Lord Treyford was a man of honour. And she was not so easily subjugated as a restless mount.

Clearing her throat, she met his defiant gaze squarely. 'Then I extend my most heartfelt thanks to Aswan, my lord,' she said with all sincerity, 'for I am very glad that you are here.'

Her conciliatory tone mollified Trey, but only for a moment. In the next instant, he grew suspicious. In his experience women used that tone when they wanted something. Her wants did not concern him, only his own needs.

Unfortunately, he became less sure just what they were with every passing moment. Guilt and frustration gnawed at him, and he resented the hell out of it. He had years of experience behind him, decades of avoiding people and the tangled messes they made of their lives. And look what one day in the Latimer chit's presence had brought him to.

'Let's move,' he said as Aswan opened the door wide enough to get the cart out. 'Will says the track through the wood will bring us out on to the coast road. From there we'll go straight to the inn.'

Cautiously, they set out. The forest lay in silence; the few noises of their passage were the only discernible sounds. The coastal path was deserted as well, leaving Trey no distraction from the uncomfortable weight of his own thoughts.

There was no escaping the truth. He hadn't taken the situation seriously, had not considered that something like this might happen. The thought of that girl, those children and what might have been was unbearable.

Damn it—he was tired of being kept in the dark! What did everyone but him know about that wretched scarab? What was it about the cursed thing that could possibly have stirred these bandits to follow it halfway around the world? He didn't know, but he was damned sure going to find out.

To that end, and to the hopeful thought that the sooner he dealt with these sneak thieves, the sooner he could shake the Devonshire dust from his boots, Trey left his ragtag group in the care of the disconcerted innkeeper and turned his horse's head back the way they had just come. Fortunately, the first watchman had not been idle. He had a half-dozen men gathered, and though they were armed only with cudgels and pitchforks and one battered French cavalry pistol, they were eager enough. Trey gave them a terse set of instructions and they set out again for Oakwood Court.

But it was to no avail. The intruders were gone, leaving behind only a thoroughly searched house and a flattened juniper bush below the open window of Miss Latimer's chamber.

The taste of frustration was not one Trey was overly familiar with. Now he found it had a sour flavour that he did not care for at all, especially when he'd spent the last four-and-twenty hours having it forced down his gullet. So he was in a foul mood as he took to the saddle for what—his third trip today?— back to the little village of Wembury. Aswan wisely kept his own counsel and without a murmur took possession of the horses as they dismounted once again in the inn's courtyard.

The innkeeper, Mr Drake, had evidently been awaiting their

arrival. Trey eyed the man with a bit of distaste; he found him rather dandified for a proprietor of a backwoods inn.

'Lord Treyford, your…guests have all been accommodated. I must warn you, though, that the boy has been put on a cot in your room.'

'Thank you,' Trey answered. 'Of course, you will apply all of their expenses to my account.'

'Yes, sir. Thank you, sir. I had wondered…'

Trey was sure he had. In fact, he was sure that the whole village would be wondering by morning. But that was the least of his worries. Was he going to have to wait until morning to get some answers? 'Are they all abed, then?' he asked.

'Aye, they are.' The man leaned in close. 'Had you any luck, sir?'

'Only the ill sort.'

'Bad news, that is, my lord.' He shot Trey a wry look. 'Today all the good citizens of Wembury will be a-twitter with the gossip. Tonight they'll be wide-eyed in their beds, sure that they will be the ruffians' next victims.' Sighing, the innkeeper shook his head. 'Every rusty blunderbuss in the county will be hauled out of storage, just like in those hungry, restless months after the war. Back then, old Jeremiah Martin shot his own brother in the arse, thinking he was a run-down Peninsular veteran come to steal his prized hog. We'll be damned lucky if no one is killed.'

Drake heaved another sigh, then slapped a hand down on the counter, startling Trey. 'Well, then, my lord, I've an extremely nice brandy laid out in the private parlour, should you like a nip before you retire.'

Trey hesitated only a moment. It was obvious that Mr Drake was not averse to a little soporific gossip. Suddenly, despite his usual scruples, Trey discovered he might not be averse, either. He needed answers, and he might finally begin to ask the right questions if he had a better understanding of the situation. And tired though he was, somehow retiring to a chamber with Will—and no doubt the dog—held little appeal.

The private parlour was more elegantly done up than one would expect, and the brandy was indeed very fine. Trey leaned back into the comfortably stuffed chair. 'I would like to think that discretion is one of the services my money will buy, Mr Drake.'

'Certainly.' He returned Trey's look with a sober one of his own. 'In this case, however, my discretion is of no use to you. The men who rode with you tonight, they will talk.'

Drake held up the decanter and, at Trey's nod, poured them each a second drink.

'Gossip, superstition, unlikely tales of the supernatural, and the mysterious,' Drake said as he settled back into his chair, 'they are all an integral part of the atmosphere here. The locals thrive on it, repeat it and embellish it.' With a lift of his chin he indicated the floors above. 'Your friends, they are favourites, both in the locals' hearts and in their whispered conversations.'

'But what the hell is a wealthy shipping merchant like Mervyn Latimer doing setting up his family here?' Trey nodded his head towards the ceiling. 'Shouldn't the lot of them be living in Plymouth, close to the shipping offices?'

Drake sighed and took a drink. 'Mervyn is a man who likes his privacy. Not easy to come by when you are famous twice over. In addition…' he leaned closer and lowered his voice '…there are rumours that the young lady has dealt with her share of snobbery.'

Trey raised a brow in question.

'It's her foreign blood, I suppose, although if you ask me it's a damned shame. A lovelier girl you couldn't ask to meet, in every way. But you know how dreadful people can be to an outsider. Here, in a smaller society, it is easier for her.'

'Not to mention that here the people are more needful of her grandfather's money?'

'That too. In any case, we've our own deep-water quay, and

in his sloop Mervyn could be at his main offices quickly enough.'

Trey took a drink and thought a moment. 'It seems to me that the girl is a sight more needful of her grandfather's money than anyone else.'

'And so she is,' sighed Drake. 'But without proof of Mervyn's death—no body or any known catastrophe such as a shipwreck—the company remains in the hands of its board. Without his influence that group squabbles more than the local Ladies' Aid Society. So much so that the courts have ordered Mervyn's shares frozen pending investigation into the matter.'

'And who knows how long such an investigation will take?'

'Who knows when they will even begin, is the question.'

'So,' Trey mused, 'the girl is accepted here, but left near to destitution and still gossiped about?'

Drake flashed Trey a rueful smile. 'But who among us could resist—especially when you throw in such a topic as the Pharaoh's Lost Jewel?'

The jolt of excitement Trey felt had him sitting up a little straighter. Miss Latimer had mentioned a jewel, had she not, when he tried to give her the scarab?

'I don't know the legend,' he said, striving for a casual tone. 'What can you tell me of it?'

'Perhaps I would be better suited to answer that,' a sharp feminine voice said from the doorway.

It should have been impossible for a man of his age and experience, but Trey found himself blushing like a schoolgirl caught gossiping under the covers. Drake, however, seemed unperturbed, rising to greet the Latimer girl with his usual smoothness.

'Miss Latimer, I had thought you abed. Ah, it is not surprising that you should have difficulty sleeping after such a dreadful experience. Shall I warm you some milk, to help you drift off?'

Arms crossed, she leaned against the doorjamb, all injured dignity and unrelenting disapproval. 'No, thank you, Mr Drake.'

'Well, then, since you are awake…' he glanced at Trey with sympathy. 'A message was left here for you earlier. I shall just fetch it.'

He eased his way past her, but her disdain appeared to be focused firmly on Trey. He pasted on his most obnoxious look of unconcern and waved her into the room. 'Good, I am glad you are up. We have much to discuss.'

'Yes, so much that you decided not to wait for me, I see.'

Trey shrugged. 'Drake said you were abed. I merely meant to begin sorting out this mess.'

She glared, but held her peace as Drake returned, a sealed missive in hand. He handed it to her and shot Trey a mute look of apology.

Trey ignored him. A belated sense of uneasiness had him watching the girl instead. Who would be sending the chit a message here? A curious look passed over her face as she broke the seal and began to read.

'Something is not right,' he said. 'Who, besides the people in this room, or asleep upstairs, would know you are here?'

She did not answer. Trey glanced over at her. Even in the candlelight she looked bloodless. Her face was blank, her gaze fixed to the sheet she still held with trembling fingers. Trey had to suppress a sigh of exasperation. Lord, not again.

'What is it?' he asked. 'Miss Latimer?'

Mutely, she handed him the paper.

It was too much; too many emotions for a person to process in a single day. Chione found that her trembling legs would not support her. She sank into Mr Drake's abandoned chair and watched Lord Treyford read the note.

Le grand homme de la vague déferlante, he lives. He is in need of help. Find the coffer.

Alive. For a moment she was convinced that it was an illusion, a hallucination concocted out of her own grief and fear. But the proof was right there in Lord Treyford's hand. Hungrily, she stared at it. Thank God, she had been wrong. Mervyn was alive.

'What is this? A man from the…surf? What nonsense is this, Miss Latimer?'

'*Great* man of the surf. Or something close to that. I think perhaps that part of it was originally in an island dialect.'

'*What* was in—?' His voice, growing loud again with impatience, suddenly broke off, and the look he gave her softened into a sort of exasperated pity. 'Miss Latimer, as much as it pains me, perhaps we should postpone this discussion. I fear the excitements of the day have been too much for you. Let Mr Drake show you back to your chamber.'

'No, I am fine. Do not fear, Lord Treyford. I have not come unhinged.' Chione's weary brain had finally processed the rest of the message. Mervyn was alive, but he needed help. How could she help him? She hadn't a clue as to where he was. And what was the coffer? All at once the fatigue that had swept over her was gone, lifted by her incredible relief, replaced by her anxiety, her need to be doing something, anything, to get to the bottom of all of this. She stood, then began to pace, from the fire to the window, and back again.

'Miss Latimer,' Lord Treyford began with a commanding rumble, 'sit down. I am a man of very little patience, and you have already consumed what small amount I possess.'

Chione swore she could feel his words resonating in the pit of her belly, and for some reason the sensation sent her restlessness spiralling even higher. He wore a tremendous frown and his knuckles were white where he clutched the note she had given him.

Her fingers shook as she went to extricate it. For a moment she was close enough to feel the heat and the aura of masculinity that emanated from him. 'I do apologise, but do you understand what this means? It means I was wrong. Mervyn is alive.'

He ran a hand along his jaw and up to his temple. When he spoke it was with the exaggerated patience one uses with a wayward child.

'I think, Miss Latimer, that it is time for you to sit yourself down and start giving me some direct answers.'

She opened her mouth to respond, but he held up a halting hand. 'No, don't talk. I am going to do the talking, you are going to answer only the questions I put to you. But before we begin, I am going to need another drink. Or two.'

He crossed over to a tray already set with a decanter and glasses. Chione sat in a chair in front of the empty fireplace and watched him toss one drink back immediately and pour himself another. When he returned, he held two glasses. He offered her one.

'Oh, no. I don't think…'

He held up his hand again. 'No. No talking and no thinking. Either is bound to get me in trouble. Take the drink, and just answer.'

He took the chair across from her and sat, staring at her with that broody frown that set her insides to simmering. Chione had had enough. 'Before I answer your questions, I have one of my own. Do you still have the scarab?'

He was startled enough to answer. 'Of course.'

She sat back in her chair in relief. 'I'm afraid I must apologise for my earlier outburst and tell you that I do indeed wish to have it.'

'Tonight would illustrate that you are not alone in that desire.'

She started to speak, but he cut her off. 'No, I do not want to hear protestations that it could have been something else that those thieves were after. We both know the truth. They wanted the damned scarab, and it's only dumb luck that they don't have it right now.'

Chione froze. Had his intentions shifted upon the discovery of the scarab's value?

It seemed he read her mind. 'I travelled here to bring the curst thing to you,' he growled, 'and so I shall. After you have given me what *I* need.'

Chione took a sip from her glass for courage. She managed—only just—not to cough and splutter as it went down. 'And what is it that you need, my lord?' Her saucy delivery might have had an impact if not for the brandy-induced wheeze at the end.

'Information,' he clipped. 'I want you to tell me just what the hell that scarab really is. Why Richard was killed for it, why you damn near swooned at the sight of it, why someone followed me all the way from Egypt, damn it, to try to steal it from you tonight.' The rumbling volume of his voice had raised a notch with each question.

Chione sat silent, considering. He might be curt, temperamental, cranky, even, but Richard had trusted this man. And he had proven himself worthy, keeping his word, abandoning his work, clearly against his own inclination. And tonight he had saved them all.

Chione was many things, but not a fool. She needed to find Mervyn and knew she would not get it done on her own. She needed help. And as much as it galled her to put her faith in yet another adventurer, she wanted his.

'Tell me about the scarab,' he said gruffly.

She took another drink of the brandy. 'For as long as I can recall, it has belonged to Mervyn. He wore it always—in a pocket, or on a chain. When I saw it today in your hands, I believed that it meant that he was dead.'

'Believed. Past tense.' He glanced toward the note she still held in her hand.

'Yes.' She raised her chin in defiance. ' I know you will think that I am foolish, but there is good reason to trust in that note.'

He didn't challenge her statement, or pursue her reasoning. 'Did you know that Richard was searching for the scarab?'

'Not really. He seemed genuinely thrilled to be going back to Egypt at last, and excited about his position with the Museum.' She looked away. 'I suspected that he was also searching for information about Mervyn's disappearance, but he did not confide in me.'

'Neither did he confide in me,' Trey said flatly. 'I do not know just where he found the thing. I do not know if the others who sought it in Egypt are the same ones who were here tonight. I still know nothing of importance, in fact. Yesterday you spoke of a jewel, but the jewels have long since been pried from the scarab. Tonight Drake talks of a Pharaoh's jewel. Tell me now, just what is going on here?'

'It is an old tale, an ancient legend.' Her throat tightened until she thought she might choke on the words, but she forced herself to go on. 'No one is sure just what the Jewel is. Some say it is a collar fashioned in the ancient style, made of gold and inlaid with hundreds of precious gems, others say that it is a huge diamond brought from the deepest Africa. I have also heard that it is an entire cache of jewels, stolen from a great king's tomb long ago.'

'Is the scarab part of the treasure, then?'

'No, the scarab is reportedly the key.'

'The key to what—the cache? Or is it a key such as you find on a map?' She could heard the impatience in his voice.

'Perhaps. I think someone once told Mervyn that the Jewel itself was a map, one that would lead to a lost land of many treasures.'

'I see.' The earl's gaze wandered for a moment. She jumped when he snapped suddenly back to attention and barked out a question. 'What did you grandfather believe?'

'I don't know!' Her hands were clenched to the arms of the chair. 'I was never truly interested in the legend, not in the way that the men in my family were. Did you know that my father was killed because of that cursed Jewel?' She paused and swallowed, but now was not the time to reveal the truth of her family relationships. 'He was murdered just because someone believed he knew something of it! When you showed up bearing that scarab, I knew that Richard had met the same fate and likely Mervyn as well. Now this note says that Mervyn is alive! His fate may hang in the balance and I just do not know!'

Panic reached down her throat and stole her breath away. What if it was true? She had despised the legend, hated the light in her grandfather's eyes when he spoke of it, the excitement in her brother's tone when he talked of leaving, of chasing after a myth. She had resented the way the story grew, interfering with their lives. When talk turned to the legend, she had turned away. And she had been right. Her father had been murdered because of it; most likely her brother had been killed seeking it. But what if her ignorance also doomed Mervyn?

'Calm yourself,' Trey ordered. He refilled her glass. 'We shall sort it all out. Tell me what you do know.'

She breathed deep. Panic accomplished nothing. If there was one thing she had learned from her troubled early life, it was the value of a clear head in a time of crisis. She drank again and drew courage from the warmth the brandy spread through her chest. 'That is nearly all of it,' she said shakily. 'The legend is old. It came to Europe when Bonapart and his delegation of scholars and artists returned to Egypt at the turn of the century. There was talk then, that the scarab had been found, and brought to France.'

'It wouldn't surprise me to find that true. Many items went home with the French.'

'My father was with the English when they fought Napoleon in Egypt. He became interested in the tale and, of course, told his father. And once Mervyn Latimer shows as interest, the rest of the world takes heed. From then on the Latimer name became entangled with the tale, to the extent that many people whispered that the Jewel had been discovered and moved here to Devonshire.'

'Oh, hell.' It was true sympathy Chione saw in Lord Treyford's eyes. 'I can well imagine the shenanigans that have resulted from that rumor.'

'Yes.' She knew her tone was grim. 'There have been incidents over the years. Stowaways, treasure seekers hiring themselves on as footmen, suitors more interested in interrogating Grandfather than in impressing me, that sort of thing.'

'Good God.' He pulled a face.

Chione shrugged. 'I suppose it is the price for living with someone who is more a force of nature than a mere mortal,' she said. Suddenly there was no fighting the swell of tears in her eyes or the sting of grief in her throat. 'I'd pay it a million times over just to have him back now.'

Treyford looked truly horrified now. Chione struggled mightily to control herself, but she was so tired, and her emotions were close to the surface. A sob escaped her despite her best efforts.

The earl stood. He had not flinched once in the face of danger earlier tonight, but now he looked ready to bolt. 'Well, then. You've given me enough to think on tonight. Why don't you go on back upstairs and get some rest?'

A fog-like haze had crept into the room, clouding the edges of her vision. Chione realized how immensely tired she felt. He was right, she would rest. She stood—but immediately began to sway.

'Oh, for the love of…' he stepped forward and placed a steadying hand at her elbow.

'Thank you.' Chione looked up at the blurred form of the earl and sudden tears blinded her further. How she envied his strength, his unfailing steadiness. Treyford knew ugliness, had been immersed in the murky, fetid underbelly of the world. Evidence of it lived there, in his eyes. He'd experienced things that most of the people in her English life could not imagine—just as she had. So often she felt her experiences had set her apart, for ever alone, some part of her still the troubled, disillusioned little girl. For the first time, though, she recognised a kindred spirit. Even better, his was a hearty soul, one that had survived the darkness, conquered it. He was strong and resilient—just exactly what she wished to be.

'How wonderful you have been,' she began. A terrible feeling of guilt made her feel ill. She wished suddenly that she could tell him the truth about herself and her hodge-podge family. But what if knowing caused him to change his mind?

'Yes, yes.' He was not so brave in the face of her emotion—a look of true horror crossed his face now. 'Let's get you up to your room.'

His hand still at her elbow, he set out for the door. But Chione's feet refused to co-operate. She stumbled, only to be caught up hard against Treyford's muscled frame. Instantly her fatigue fled, replaced with a new, humming awareness. The eager, unruly side of her, the persona that she kept ruthlessly hidden, reared to sudden awareness. Through the fog that had descended over her brain Chione allowed herself, for an instant, to look, to touch, to feel.

Heat. Immense strength. Her face was pressed against his chest, her fingers curled tightly around his arms. Instinctively she clutched him harder, because all of a sudden the earth was sliding away beneath her feet.

His arm slid slowly and surely down her body, pulled her up and steadied her. She screwed her eyes shut and revelled in the warmth, the sheer closeness of his strong, solid form. He cleared his throat and she sighed. The scent of him—sweaty male mixed with something foreign and exotic—faded just a bit as she lifted her head and gazed into his stormy blue eyes.

'Are you all right?' His face was set in grim lines.

She nodded.

'I'll take you up.'

He held her close as they navigated the stairs. How long since she had felt like this—truly safe? It made not a whit of sense, but undeniably she felt so, sheltered in the curve of his arm. At her door he stopped.

'You need to sleep.' He said it gruffly. An order.

She found she didn't mind. 'Yes, there will be the children to deal with in the morning.'

'Goodnight, then,' he said.

'Goodnight, my lord. And thank you.'

His relief as he left was obvious. Trying not to feel hurt, Chione opened the door and took herself in to bed.

Chapter Five

Trey came awake when the afternoon sun slanted into the tent and struck his face. It surprised him. He rarely slept during the afternoon rest that Egypt's fierce climate forced on every working man and beast. He pinched the bridge of his nose and thought the men must be enjoying the unusually long reprieve.

Then his hand fell back and hit the soft pillow he rested on, and he knew. England, not Egypt. He threw his legs over and sat upright, feeling the familiar wave of impatience, the pressing need to be moving—on to the next site, the next adventure, or perhaps just away from the ties of the past. Any of the above would suffice.

He reached for his trousers—and froze as yesterday's tumultuous events rushed him, along with the bitter realisation that his stay in Devonshire was likely far from over. Oh, to be sure, there was still that tingling of excitement, deep in his stomach, that came with the prospect of a mystery. He never could resist a challenge, and the riskier it was, the better he liked it. But it was one thing to pit himself—brain, bone and sinew—against an adversary. It was quite another to pitch headlong into a fight he still did not understand, and another thing again to wade into a fracas involving women and children.

And such a woman. Gorgeous, intelligent, strong. The sort of woman who stole a man's breath away, and then began to systematically strip him of everything else he held dear. A temptation even to Trey, who knew better.

What the hell time was it anyway? Where was Aswan? He rose and finished dressing, his uneasiness growing as he ventured forth from his room. The inn was quiet. Too quiet. Only a day's experience of the Latimer family had him expecting some sort of continual upset. But there was no sound of a dog barking, no children shouting, no angry cries from terrorised kitchen staff, nothing.

And no one. The taproom was deserted, as was the parlour. Finally he found Drake in the kitchen, debating the seasoning of a beef stew with the cook.

'Ah, Lord Treyford! You have awakened just in time. You will be first to test the stew and tell Henri that it needs a dash more thyme.'

It smelled heavenly. Trey's stomach rumbled, but he looked away from the dish that the cook set on the table. 'Not just yet, thank you. Where has Miss Latimer got to? And the children? I cannot believe they did not wake me earlier.'

'The young lady? She took her family back to Oakwood first thing this morning. Your man tried to awaken you. When he could not, he decided to accompany them himself.'

'Back—this morning?' Trey choked. 'Damned lot of fools! What if the thieves come back? What if they are watching the house?' He strode out of the kitchen and headed for the front door, calling for his horse as he went.

'But, my lord—' Drake was hurrying behind him '—they took the watchman you hired, and your Aswan as well. We've heard of no trouble, only received orders for supplies and requests for a carpenter and a housemaid. They are surely unharmed!'

Not for long, Trey thought grimly. He threw the saddle over his mount's back himself. *Not for long.*

* * *

Chione had a nose fashioned from an old stocking. She had two large ears made of sturdy grey bombazine, a heavy passenger who kept striking her with his short sword, and, before her, a terrified Roman child barricaded behind an overturned chaise. She also had an audience, although she was sublimely unaware of it.

'*Hannibal am portas!*' shrieked the little Roman girl, resplendent in her toga.

'That's *Hannibal ad portas*, Olivia,' said Chione-the-elephant. She tried to hide her fatigue behind a crisp tone. 'And it was not only the children who feared such a dangerous enemy. The grown-up Romans were terribly frightened when Hannibal climbed over the Alps. It was a brilliant strategy, but he lost thousands of men on the dangerous journey.' Her passenger's shield struck her in the back of the head once again. Chione abruptly sat up, sending him tumbling to the carpet. 'I'm afraid you are just growing too heavy for this, Will.' Hands at her hips, she stretched her tired and aching back.

'Chione!' he complained. 'Surely Hannibal never fell from *his* elephants.'

'He rarely retreated in battle, either, young man, but look how well that served us yesterday,' said a familiar, deep voice from the doorway.

Chione gasped and tore off her long nose before turning. Lord Treyford stood there, amusement and annoyance warring in his icy blue eyes, Morty pressed lovingly to his knee. A rush of heat flooded her. Belatedly she reached up to snatch the ears from her head.

There were times when Chione mourned the loss of her Egyptian heritage, more when she missed the love and guidance of her mother. But there was one thing she had learned at her Eastern mother's knee and had used to her own advantage as she grew, and that was the value of an inscrutable demeanour. It leant an air of mystery and control that gave her an advantage. Right now she sorely needed one.

So she went with the tried and true. She ignored her mortification, and reached deep to find a semblance of composure, for she thought she would rather die than allow the Earl of Treyford to guess how he affected her.

Certainly Will, at least, appeared oblivious to her embarrassment. He had already laid aside his weaponry and greeted the man. 'I wish I could have faced those men last night head on, like Hannibal,' he grumbled, brash with a ten-year-old's sense of invulnerability.

The earl took up his sword to examine it. 'Hannibal had a force of over six-and-twenty thousand, and was fully prepared for many of them to die,' he said with an experimental slash of the air. 'You were part of a much smaller force, and I don't think even one of them could be regarded as expendable.'

Will grinned. 'You are right, of course, sir.'

Chione had recovered her composure enough to become annoyed. 'I have a suspicion that Lord Treyford might be one of those fortunate few who finds himself always in the right, Will.'

He failed to rise to the bait. 'Very often, I do, in fact.'

'Just like my father,' Will said knowingly. 'He always said that if Archimedes of Syracuse was so smart, he would have got the people out while the Romans were still occupied with their sea assault, instead of waiting for them to besiege the landward side. I guess we proved him right.'

'We did. Certainly Archimedes showed us the way last night.' He handed Will his sword back with a nod of approval and the first approximation of a smile she had yet seen from him.

She sighed and swept back a stray lock with tired fingers. He was most likely relaxed because he was here to bid them all goodbye. His servant, Aswan, had accompanied them today, and had been a tremendous help, but he had also mentioned—more than once—his employer's eagerness to be gone.

It had been a blow to hear it. Chione had left the servant and then spent a good part of the afternoon pounding spilled ashes out of rugs, wondering why all the men in her life suffered the uncontrollable urge to run away. With each strike she had meted out a metaphorical retribution. Her grandfather. *Thwack.* Her brother. *Thwack.* And now Lord Treyford. The resulting flurry had the rugs clean in a trifle.

It had been therapeutic exercise. She was in a better frame of mind now. In fact, she thought she might have siphoned off some of the earl's impatience, for that was precisely how she felt right now. There was much to be done, and she had a pressing eagerness to get on with it all. Much of the house still needed to be restored, guards would soon be arriving to be interviewed, and she must begin making arrangements for the search for Mervyn. But beyond a doubt, her greatest need was to bid adieu to the Earl of Treyford. He fractured her concentration, distracting her at a time when she could scarce afford it. What she wanted was his help, and if she wasn't going to get it, then it would be a relief to take back the scarab and be done with him.

And if she repeated that to herself a dozen more times, she might well come to believe it.

'Will,' she began, 'why don't you take Olivia to the kitchens? When Mrs Westcott arrived today she had a pudding and basket full of biscuits. I'm sure the two of you could coax something out of her.'

It was a sure ploy, for Will was a walking appetite. His eyes lit up and he reached for his sister's hand. 'Come along, Olivia. Biscuits!'

Treyford pried the dog's head from his knee. 'And take the dog, please!'

'Come along, Morty. Bone!'

The three of them trooped out. Chione sighed and turned back to the earl.

Her heart began to pound. All of the emotion, all of that

focused intensity, had immediately resurfaced. It shone with unblinking fervour in his eyes, emanated from him as he stalked towards her across the room.

Chione was no strategist, but even she recognised the advantages of retreat. She stepped behind the overturned chaise. Pride forbade any show of weakness, however, so she strove for nonchalance as she flipped it right side up.

He only raised a brow and kept advancing, until his legs came up against the piece and only the narrow expanse of worn cushion separated them.

'Come along, Miss Latimer, rest!' he said in echo of Will's wheedling tone.

She raised her chin. 'Hardly fitting or amusing, sir, since I am neither a child nor an animal.'

The heat of his gaze was nearly palpable as it raked her dishevelled form from head to toe. Despite herself, Chione felt a flush rise to colour her cheeks as the earl slowly shook his head. 'No, you are neither, although I am in no need of a reminder.'

He paused and she struggled to keep her blush from intensifying. 'In point of fact, you are by far the most managing, frustratingly independent woman I've had the misfortune to encounter. You reject me, my help and the scarab soundly, you dispatch a sneak thief in the night all on your own, show us all the route to safety, and then return here, without waiting for me or anyone else, to start the clean up yourself.'

His tone was one of grudging admiration, but he ruined it when he pointed an imperious finger at the chaise. 'Now sit— before I am emasculated any further or you ruin your sterling reputation by passing out. You are as pale as a ghost and nearly trembling with fatigue.' He seized her hand and pulled her around the chaise.

She fetched up close against him, so close that she could feel the heat of his body. She caught herself inhaling, hoping to catch the spicy scent of him, but he let go and gestured for her to sit. 'Did you sleep at all last night?'

Mute, Chione shook her head and sat.

'I thought as much.' He sighed. 'Your lesson was charming and obviously effective, but could it not have waited?'

'The children were restless,' Chione shrugged. 'They are anxious too, and it is reassuring for them to carry on with normal activities in a time of stress.'

'Perhaps they would have been less stressed had they been still safe at the inn,' the earl suggested.

'We have been safe enough,' Chione bridled. 'Your watchmen assured us that all was clear before we left the inn.'

'You should have cleared it with me,' he growled.

'You would not awaken. There was much to be done.' And nothing left to be said. If he was going to take his leave, she wished he would proceed. Perhaps then her jittering, jumping insides would be still, and *she* could be the one to get on with her life.

'Still, a day in the village, even a day confined to the inn, would have been better for the children than returning here and seeing the ransacked house.'

Sarcasm must be as contagious as impatience. 'Ah, I had forgotten your vast experience with children, my lord. Yes, we should have spent the day frolicking while their fears grew apace.' She grew serious. 'Those two children know what loss is. It is far better for them to face a hard truth, rather than to fret and worry and allow their imaginations to take flight.'

Her explanation only appeared to annoy him more. He was pacing now, but he turned back, exasperation evident in the glint of his eye and the rigidity of his frame. 'Could you not simply relax for one day? Could you not give yourself a few hours to recover and your friends the chance to help you with your burdens? Good God, Miss Latimer, what is it that you are trying to prove?'

That had her out of her seat like a shot. His accusations struck true, but she would never allow him to see it. 'I am trying to prove nothing, my lord, only trying to do what must be done. It is no great insult to be called a managing female. It is who I am, what I do. I manage.' She crossed her arms and sniffed. 'Someone must.'

His expression went from exasperated to merely wary. 'Yes, someone must, and I would say you've done a damned fine job with a lamentable set of circumstances. But—'

'Thank you.' Chione had no intention of letting him say anything more. 'Mrs Ferguson and I *managed* to get much accomplished today, in putting the house to rights, and in arranging a permanent set of guards for the estate.'

He looked uncomfortable. 'Yes, we did not get a chance to discuss that note last night, did we? Perhaps now—'

'No, we did not. Nor did I get the chance to retrieve the scarab from you. You do have it with you, do you not?'

'Yes, I have it—'

'Good.' Chione drew a deep breath and tried to throw off both her fatigue and the knife edge of irritability that this man seemed to draw out of her. 'It seems we are for ever arguing. I do beg your pardon and I thank you most sincerely for all that you have done.' She held out a hand and with effort kept it miraculously steady. 'May I have the scarab now?' She gave a little laugh and tried to mean it. 'The relief you will feel at being done with it must only be exceeded by your desire to be quickly gone.'

He pulled it from a waistcoat pocket and willingly handed it over, but he wore a frown as he did so. Chione ignored it, concentrating instead on the scarab. 'The chain is not familiar to me—might it be yours?'

'No. It is in the same condition it was in when Richard gave it into my keeping.'

Chione turned the thing around and around in her hand. Something was nagging at her.

'I admit I am glad to finally see the thing in your hand,' he said.

She could not look at him. 'Yes, your duty is dispatched. Now you may be on your way.'

'Forgive me if I am mistaken, but that sounded remarkably like a dismissal.'

Chione looked up in time to catch the dangerous glitter growing in his blue gaze. 'No, of course not,' she said brightly. 'It is only that Aswan told us how eager you are to return to Egypt.' She forced herself to smile. 'I do wish you the best of luck in your work, Lord Treyford. Perhaps, if you wouldn't think it too improper, I might write to you some time in the future and share the tale of how this all comes about in the end?'

'Write to me?' He sounded incredulous. 'Hell, no.'

She lowered her gaze. 'I am sorry to presume.'

'I'm sorry you do too!' It was almost a shout, but Chione did not startle this time. She rather thought she was becoming immune to his unpredictable spikes in volume.

'Did you expect I would just drop that in your hand and traipse on my merry way?' he raged. 'Shall I offer you my congratulations on a lucky escape from unknown bandits and hop the next ship to Alexandria?'

That was exactly what she had expected—and exactly what she had spent the day alternately dreading and wishing for.

'Was that not your plan?' she whispered. She pooled the scarab's chain into her fist and held her breath.

'No, damn you, it was not!'

He looked truly affronted now, and Chione realised that while she had been so wrapped up in concealing her own feelings, she had wounded his.

'I am so sorry—' she began, but before she got any further the parlour door swung open. They both turned to face a grimy Mrs Ferguson. 'Viscount Renhust has come to call,' she announced. 'Again.'

* * *

Trey was so furious with the Latimer chit's presumptive dismissal of both him and his character that he actually missed the housekeeper's words. Yesterday he would have wept with joy to hear such a casual dismissal. Yesterday he would have kissed Miss Latimer's little, ink-stained hand and been out of Devonshire before nightfall.

But that was yesterday. Today was different, and he refused to consider the notion that anything more than her precarious situation made it so.

Then the housekeeper noted his presence and addressed him directly.

'Ye're here too, are ye? Good.' An older gentleman swept past her into the room and she pointed a finger at him. 'Keep an eye on that one, will ye? He bears watching.' And then she was gone.

The gentleman looked startled to find another man in Miss Latimer's parlour. He gave Trey an appraising glance and a cool nod before turning to the girl.

'Chione, could you please explain just why the servants are abuzz with talk of thieves and midnight raids? The entire coastline is in an uproar. Rumours have you all kidnapped or dead and the villagers under siege from merciless marauders.'

Trey snorted.

'Events have unfolded swiftly.' The girl stepped forward and took the man's arm.

'It would appear so,' he grumped. 'And I've had an irate letter from Mrs Stockton, too. She asks me to intervene on her behalf. It would appear she's willing to send Will off to school.'

'I've already declined such an offer,' Chione bit out. She shot a glance Trey's way. 'And we've more urgent matters to discuss. If I might present you to Lord Treyford?'

But Trey was feeling angry and ill used and incredulous. 'Introductions?' he snorted. 'I have had my fill of this madhouse.

In less than a day I've been attacked by the dog and your dinner, prodded, shouted at, dismissed, and been caught up in a night-time raid by treasure-seeking bandits. Now you insult my honour, disparage my intentions and expect me to sit down to tea like some London milksop?'

'But I didn't, I thought…' the girl sputtered.

'Come now,' chided the gentleman.

Trey ignored him. 'There are six kinds of trouble afoot here and no time for tea parties! As much as you—or I—might bemoan it, the fact is I made a vow.'

'Treyford, did you say, my dear?' Scorn fairly dripped from the other man. 'That does explain it. I'd heard you had the wardrobe of a scarecrow and the mouth of a fishwife.'

'Lord Renhurst!' scolded Chione.

'Renhurst?' Trey repeated. 'You do have the advantage of me. I've never heard of you.'

'Gentlemen, please,' she pleaded. Into the following moment of silence came a soft whine. They all turned to the doorway. There stood little Olivia, with the trailing end of her toga in her mouth, and Will, kneeling, restraining an eager Morty, who obviously wished to join in the fracas.

Trey immediately pulled in on the reins of his temper, but the sight of the children had an opposite and far more spectacular effect on Chione Latimer. Suddenly the quiet, competent young lady was gone and in her place stood a hot-tempered virago.

'Enough!' she cried with a stamp of her fetching little foot, and Trey felt something ease inside of him. He hadn't realised he'd been waiting for something to shatter that implacable calm. Flashing eyes and fiery indignation suited her far more than that air of dutiful resignation.

He had to hide a smile as she pointed at the trio in the doorway. 'You three—up to the nursery and stay there until I come for you.' Two pairs of eyes widened, a tail tucked, and they were instantly gone.

'And you two—' She rounded on Renhurst and Trey with a molten-eyed stare worthy of an ancient Gorgon. Renhurst merely scowled back at the girl. Trey, however, felt the effect of her gaze, hardening in traditional male fashion. He turned away in an attempt to hide it.

She wasn't having it. She marched right up to him and glared into his face. 'Lord Renhurst is here because I asked him.' She spun on her heel and focused her anger on the viscount. 'Treyford is here because *Richard* asked him.'

'Richard?' That brought the other man to attention.

'Yes.' She glared at them both. 'My brother is gone, but I have a chance to save Mervyn, and I'll not let your petty squabbling get in my way.'

She turned those incredible eyes on Trey and he thought her gaze might have softened a bit. 'I am sorry if I injured your feelings.'

Before he could scoff at such a notion she poked a finger square in the middle of his chest. It startled him, but not as much as the warmth that spread from that small contact. It rippled outward and then quickly moved south to contribute to his growing discomfort.

'I know you hoped to deliver the scarab and be gone, but you also said you'd made a vow to protect me. I hope you meant it, because I'm going after my grandfather.' She paused, drew a deep breath and something dark moved in her gaze. Fear? Guilt?

'In a way,' she said, 'your help was Richard's last gift to me, and, by God, I'm going to accept it.'

Trey noted the determined set of her shoulders, caught the hint of pleading that she tried to hide. He acknowledged the rush of desire that this woman roused in him, and the other, more dangerous currents she stirred in his soul. All of his life he had courted danger, craved risk, lived for excitement, and not once had he experienced such a strong sense of forebod-

Chapter Six

Chione let out the breath she hadn't realised she'd been holding. He was going to stay. She shushed the niggling part of her that still resisted putting herself into the hands of yet another thrill-seeking wanderer. She pushed away again the lingering guilt she felt at not revealing the truth about her family relationships. Without a doubt her chances of finding Mervyn had just dramatically increased; she couldn't take the chance of revealing he was no blood relation at all.

Lord Renhurst's shocked tones pulled her back to reality. 'Did you just say he delivered the scarab?'

Chione breathed deep and turned to face the viscount. 'I did. You see, somehow Richard found Mervyn's scarab. Lord Treyford brought it to me.' She pulled the piece from her pocket and watched the conflicting emotions cross his face.

'But, Mervyn wouldn't… If this has left his possession…'

'I know exactly what you are thinking,' she said, 'but, truly, all is well.'

His mouth set, Lord Renhurst reached for the scarab. Chione held it out to him, but was once again distracted by the chain. No, it was the clasp that bothered her. No simple hasp, it was an unusual, cylindrical shape. She pulled it back for a closer look.

It opened easily enough, but unevenly, so she was left with a small, solid, cuff-like disc in one hand and the long, slender cylinder that it fit into, in the other. She frowned. Why should such a short disc require such a long barrel?

It was then that she saw the tiny etching on the disc.

She gasped, 'Look!'

'What?' Both men were on their feet now.

'That mark—it's mine. My name, I mean.'

Treyford stood behind her, peering over her shoulder. She could feel the heat of him against her back, and lower. It settled around her, upon her, found its way inside to send a flush to her face. 'All I see are three wavy lines.'

'Yes, three parallel lines. It's meant to look like water.'

'Your name is water?' Treyford sounded sceptical, and she stepped away.

'No, her name is Chione—it means "Daughter of the Nile".' Lord Renhurst looked troubled.

'It is the mark I used when we played as children, having adventures, making up stories, sending secret messages.' She glanced at Lord Renhurst and gave a faint smile. 'Richard's was a pickaxe, and Mervyn's was a row-boat.' Excitement built inside of her. 'Don't you see? It's a message from Richard, but what could it mean?'

Chione had a sudden thought, and slipping the scarab from the chain, she put the artifact back in her pocket and examined the cylindrical piece once again. She gave a cry of triumph when she spied a thin seam encircling it, but nothing happened when she probed it with her fingernail.

'Here, let me.' Treyford had pulled a knife from his voluminous coat. She handed over the chain and he pried at the tiny line.

Chione was hovering so close she thought she heard the soft click when a hidden latch gave way. Inside the seemingly solid compartment rolled back and Chione froze when a small, white piece of paper fluttered out and to the floor.

With a look of pure disgruntlement, Treyford knelt and handed the rolled paper to her.

There was one word written on it—*Alden*.

Fighting back tears, Chione met the earl's gaze. 'I was wrong,' she whispered. 'This was Richard's last gift to me. Hope.'

It was a fitting gift from her brother, and one that Chione sorely needed during the hectic planning that followed. It served her well as she persuaded, cajoled, negotiated and threatened, until she had everything arranged to her satisfaction.

First both of her reluctant supporters needed convincing that Mervyn was indeed alive and in need of rescue. Neither of the two was inclined to put any faith in the note that had been left for her at the inn.

'You don't know who sent it,' said Treyford. 'It could have been the thieves, or someone working with them.'

Even Lord Renhurst was obstinate. 'I've known Mervyn Latimer for thirty years, and never heard him called something so ludicrous as Great Man from the Surf.'

'But don't you see,' argued Chione, 'that is exactly what makes this all the more believable. Almost no one knew of that name. He didn't want it mentioned. Ever.'

'Why not?' they both chorused.

Chione flushed. 'He was embarrassed. It was given to him by primitives off the coast of South America. He had stopped at one of the more remote islands to trade, and take on water and supplies. His long boat ran aground on a shoal at the mouth of a cove. Mervyn, impatient as ever, dove in and swam the rest of the way to shore, much to the amazement of the natives. They said they had never seen a man as strong as a mountain, with skin and hair as white as the caps of the sea.'

'I understand the name, then, but why the embarrassment?' asked Treyford.

Chione's colour deepened. 'Because the native chief agreed to trade, but he wished a favour in return.'

'What?' Both men were fascinated now.

'He wanted his first wife to have a child with hair the colour of the surf and eyes the colour of the sky.' Chione did her best to shrug her own discomfort off as immaterial. 'So you can see why he wished the story to be kept quiet,' she said earnestly. 'Only someone intimately acquainted with him would have known that name.'

Fascinated, yes, but they were not convinced. Chione despaired of changing their minds, until inspiration struck. 'Eli was there,' she said. 'Ask him.'

As Eli still would not set foot in the house, they all three trooped to the stable. They found the old groom lovingly brushing Lord Renhurst's big bay gelding.

'Eli,' Treyford called. 'Who is *Le grand homme de la vague déferlante?*'

The old man looked to Chione, and she nodded.

''Tis Master Mervyn,' He grunted. 'But if ye be calling him that when he returns, he'll be running you off the place.'

With that hurdle cleared at last, Chione unexpectedly encountered a more tenacious one: the universal conviction that she should stay at home while someone else travelled to speak to Mr Jack Alden.

'I can travel to London and back far more quickly without you,' said Lord Treyford.

'Alden may be a scholar, but he is the brother of a viscount,' Lord Renhurst informed them. 'He'll be far more likely to speak freely with a proper gentleman.'

'Ye won't be going nowhere without a proper chaperon,' stated Mrs Ferguson flatly. 'And I'll not be standing by while the lot of ye run off, leaving the bairns in danger.'

The housekeeper's was the only argument that Chione heeded.

So it was that, after much debate and countless revisions, a plan was devised and settled upon.

First they would circulate the rumour that Chione was in need of funds and planned on selling the scarab.

'No one will have the least trouble believing that,' sighed Chione.

They put it about that Lord Renhurst was going to travel to London to make the transaction for her. Treyford, in the meantime, told everyone he encountered that he was returning shortly to Egypt and his work.

It was hoped that any trouble would follow Renhurst, who would travel armed to the teeth, with his groom, one watchman disguised as his valet, and another acting as a post-rider. The viscount assured Chione that the four of them could dispatch any attackers. They would travel on full alert, at a leisurely pace, leaving plenty of opportunity for mischief. In fact, he was so confident in his own success, Renhurst wrote ahead to make arrangements for the miscreants to be held in Tavistock, where he would wait for Chione and Treyford to meet him.

Treyford would make a show of his departure, but would double back to Oakwood Court in the night. He and Aswan would stay hidden in the house, just in case the attackers were not fooled and staged another assault on the house. If all appeared clear, then he and Chione—and a chaperon, interjected Mrs Ferguson—would leave Aswan, Eli, extra guards and Mrs Ferguson with the children while they met up with Lord Renhurst and then travelled on to speak with Mr Alden.

Leaving the children troubled Chione desperately, though she knew it must be done.

'Why not ask Mrs Stockton to come for a stay?' asked Renhurst once when she was fretting. 'She's a blood relation, I'm sure she'll be happy to help.'

'Absolutely not,' Chione stated in a hard, flat voice. 'I'll stay home myself, or drag the children along to London, before I ask a single thing from that hateful woman.'

Treyford looked up at her in surprise, but she refused to meet his gaze.

After a moment's reflection, Lord Renhurst nodded. 'I can't say I blame you.' He sighed. 'She's scarcely a model grandmother to those children, and I know that she's shown you her worst side more than once. But her mean streak wouldn't be your biggest problem in any case. Once she'd got herself ensconced here at Oakwood, I'd wager you'd have the devil of a time getting her to leave.'

Chione racked her brain and considered at least a hundred different scenarios, but finally had to concede that the children's staying behind was the best alternative. The realisation did nothing to ease her anxiety, however. So when she found herself briefly alone with Lord Treyford, she didn't hesitate to question him.

She was trying to haul a portmanteau unobtrusively to the carriage house, where Treyford was keeping the preparations for their journey hidden. He stood in the doorway, watching the children tumble on the lawns with Aswan. Shrieks of childish laughter rang out as Aswan played the stalking bear to Will and Olivia's Red Indians. Yet the peace of the scene could not soothe Chione's troubled heart.

'Learn-cloth?' asked Aswan.

'No, *loin*cloth,' said Will.

'*Loin*cloth,' the Egyptian repeated, nodding his head.

'I know you are fond of him.' Chione paused beside the earl, indicating the servant and hoping she would not offend Treyford. Aswan appeared to be a perfectly dutiful servant, but he set her nerves on edge. More than once she had felt the heavy weight of his gaze on her, but when she looked, he was always well occupied. 'I need to know that Will and Olivia will be safe. Are you absolutely certain of Aswan's loyalty?'

Treyford nodded his understanding, but kept his eyes on the laughing trio before them. For once Morty had abandoned him and was darting among them, barking madly. 'I trust Aswan implicitly and without hesitation,' he said. 'He has grown attached to the children. I believe he would lay down his own life to protect them, just as he almost did once for me.'

Chione could not hide her curiosity. 'What happened?'

Treyford shrugged. 'Cairo is a dangerous place. I had a gorgeous—and valuable—tomb statue to sell. Word must have spread.'

Chione could not hide the spasm of pain she felt at the mention of the treacherous Egyptian streets.

'Miss Latimer…?' He paused in his story.

'I'm sorry.' She waved a dismissive hand. 'Please, continue.'

But he hesitated. She looked up and into the dark intensity of his searching gaze.

'Please finish,' she asked. 'Will, especially, has been through so much, and we cannot know for sure it would be safe for them to come.' She closed her eyes a moment and clenched her jaw. 'They need Mervyn back, for so many reasons. I must find him, and as much as I appreciate your help, and Renhurst's, I *know* that I should be the one to talk with Mr Alden.' She opened her eyes. 'You must understand how difficult it is for me to leave them.'

Treyford nodded and looked away, back towards the revellers on the lawn. Even in her distress, Chione felt the loss of his regard, as if someone had placed a screen between her and the scorching heat of a fire. She could only be grateful.

'We were caught unawares in the narrow streets of the *Hasanain*,' he began. 'It is a Turkish neighbourhood, in the northern section of the city, occupied by merchants for the most part, and we were not expecting trouble. I should have known better. Life is held far cheaper than gold in that part of the world.' His low, dispassionate tone sent a shiver down her spine.

He rolled a shoulder, as if she had jogged the memory of an old blow. Chione stared. He had shed his coat again, and, as usual, his neckcloth was askew and his waistcoat partly unbuttoned. As he moved, she could see the rippling movement of muscle beneath the soft linen of his shirt. She began to grow warm again, but this time the heat grew from inside.

'I was occupied fighting the biggest Turk I have ever seen. I swear, the man's thighs were as thick as stumps and he had fists like rocks.' He turned then and locked his blue gaze with hers. 'Most level-headed Egyptians would have run, leaving the infidel to his fate. Not Aswan. He stayed, and when I finally finished off that giant, Aswan was dispatching the last of the others. *Four* others.'

He shook his head. 'I've seen more fighting in my life than I care to recall, but I've never seen anyone move so fast, or strike so hard.' His eyes lost focus for a moment, as if he were looking back through the mists of time, then he turned away. 'Aswan is someone you want on your side, Miss Latimer.'

Chione didn't reply. She just stared at his profile in the lengthening shadows while her mind's eye conjured a dramatic, dusty, violent scene half a world away.

'You're not bad in a fight yourself,' he recalled her with a glance askance. 'I should have complimented you before. That knife throw was impressive. Who taught you? Mervyn?'

'No, it was my mother.' She shot him a sad smile. The thought of her mother, of her own burden of secrets, only emphasised the gulf between them. 'A young girl's life is held cheaper than most, in the East. She taught me well to protect myself.'

'A good thing.' He nodded his approval.

Chione wished his approbation didn't warm her quite so much. The story he had told, however, much occupied her mind. She didn't question him further, but later, in the solitude of her room, she wrote long into the night. Before she snuffed her candle and rolled wearily into bed she had completed the next instalment of her story and Nikolas had found a sais, or groom, to accompany him on his travels.

The next morning she recruited Mr Drake into their scheming. He readily agreed to check on the children, and promised to do his best to keep anyone from realising she was gone.

Old Eli, trying to lighten her spirits, even pledged to sashay about the grounds in one of her gowns. Chione laughed at his antics along with everyone else, but she noticed that the earl's smile never reached his eyes. Neither, she suspected, did her own.

At last the time came, and everything was set in motion according to plan. Renhurst departed. Treyford pretended to depart. He came back deep in the darkest part of the night and sequestered himself and Aswan in the unused butler's suite. Chione was left alone to wait.

What she yearned to do—and would not—was to go down to the servants' quarters, to allow Treyford's blunt confidence to bolster her own. Even an ear-bursting disagreement with the earl might come as a welcome distraction.

'Why don't you visit Trey?' Will asked. He had been down to the servants' quarters regularly, and found it odd that Chione had not.

'It is Lord Treyford to you, young man.' Chione said.

'Lord Treyford, then. You haven't been to see him even once.'

'Will, come here to me.' She pulled the boy close and spoke in a grave tone. 'You are old enough to understand that this is no game. The danger is real.' She raised a brow in question and he nodded solemnly. 'No one must realise that the earl and Aswan are here. I want to find your papa, and so does Lord Treyford. By staying hidden, he is taking his role seriously, and so you and I must do the same. We must go on as if they are not here, and everything is normal.'

Will sighed. 'Yes, Chione. But normal is boring and Trey has hunted tigers and dug up mummies!'

Chione knew by the light in his eye that Will would be back down to talk with Lord Treyford. She also knew, despite the yearning in her breast, that she would not.

Though she might fob Will off with talk of duty and danger, the truth was that she was a coward. The earl both fascinated and frightened her. She was uncomfortable with his effect on her, afraid of the ease with which he awakened the *djinn* that lurked in her heart.

For so long she had struggled to bury the passionate, unruly side of her nature. The un-English part. She'd succeeded mostly, tucking away the demon inside of her, along with the dreadful memories of how she had come to be, and the guilt she felt at living a lie.

Then Treyford showed up, easily the most un-English aristocrat she'd ever heard of. He appeared driven by unknown torments of his own, and showed every sign of being as addicted to adventure as the men in her family. And yet it was his uniqueness that spoke to her, and his solid, unhesitant assurance that puzzled her. How did he achieve the one, in spite of the other?

She didn't know. She only knew that something in him reached right down to the hidden part of her soul and whispered it awake. Except that Chione did not wish it to awake, for what would she do with it once Treyford was gone?

And gone he would be. Once Mervyn was found—as she prayed he would be—her tenuous hold on the earl's loyalty would be lost. He would be free and eager to go back to his own pursuits. As would she, Chione reminded herself. The children would be safe and happy, and she would be released from all the worries of the past year.

So Chione waited, and she threw herself into her writing. It was, after all, much easier to craft a hero from fancy and whim than to mould one out of the stuff of real life.

Chione was not the only one chafing at the delay. Trey thought he might go mad in the over-stuffed butler's rooms. If the long boring hours trapped among a profuse assortment of decorative pillows and delicate knick-knackery didn't turn him into a Bedlamite, then the sheer frustration that came with inaction would finish the job.

For hours he paced, from the sole window looking over the kitchen garden, through the sitting room, into the bedroom and back again. Like the fire in the grate, Trey had always been a creature of restless motion, flickering from one task to the next. It was a lesson he'd learned early, and well. Never stay put long enough to put down roots. They invariably became ensnarled with others', and once they had you it was over. If their creeping tendrils did not strangle you, then they blasted you, with demands or criticism, until nothing was left save a dry and withered husk.

Men often exclaimed over the dangers of the life he had led. What they didn't know—could never understand—was that he welcomed such dangers. They were tangible, and thus conquerable. It was with people, and their hidden passions and inexplicable behaviours, where the truest danger lay.

And Chione Latimer was as dangerous a case as he had ever seen. A fixer. Someone who could not resist involving herself in other people's messes, jumping in where angels feared to tread. As a case in point—just look at the ragtag group that made up her household. Or the children. Based on Renhurst's remarks, they had other family. Surely she could have managed more easily had she sent the children to them.

Trey had fully expected, therefore, that Miss Latimer would take advantage of his forced confinement. There was plenty wrong with him, in most everyone's eyes. He'd thought it highly unlikely that the girl could resist the chance to try to fix him.

He'd been wrong. Perhaps he was not worth the trouble, or perhaps he was too difficult a case for even Miss Latimer's skills, for she never so much as poked her nose in the butler's quarters.

It was a relief not to have to fend her off, Trey told himself. Just as it would be a relief to be done with this trip to London. The girl was grasping at straws. His job was to see her safe until she realised her hands were empty. Then he would settle a generous stipend upon the girl and he would be done with her, and all the entanglements of her messy life.

Done, except for that tiny, niggling doubt, that small part of him that wondered why she hadn't been tempted to fix him, too.

Trey was entertaining that very doubt, contemplating that very question as he stood at the window, watching the fading light. In just hours they were to make their late-night departure. Some small sound alerted him, and he turned to find her silhouetted in the door. His heart stopped, then began to race. He saw the trouble in her dark eyes.

'What is it?' he asked.

'There is a rider coming fast up the drive,' she said. 'I think it is Mr Drake.'

It was Drake. Trey waited as Miss Latimer went to meet him. With the door partially open, he heard Drake enter the main hall and sensed the urgency in his voice. She brought him straight in.

'I have had news that may affect your plans,' the innkeeper said without preamble.

The girl stilled. 'Has something happened to Lord Renhurst?'

'No, no.' Drake's tone was one of reassurance. 'I've had a letter from a friend.' He shrugged. 'It may mean nothing, but I thought you'd better decide.' The innkeeper shifted, and scrubbed a hand through his hair. 'It seems a bit silly, now, but…' He breathed deeply. 'I've a friend who runs the George, at Exeter. We've a friendly rivalry, you understand—we vex each other on purpose and exchange news, and such. He's crowing—bragging about his good fortune. He's let all his rooms for the entire week, right along with all the others thereabouts.'

'How nice for him,' Trey said drily.

'I'm getting there, sir,' Drake said. 'Seems there has been a hue and cry that way among the scholarly set. Historians, antiquarians and the like. A great many of them have gathered to debate the authenticity of a new relic—something to do with old King Alfred.'

'But what does it mean to us, Mr Drake?' Miss Latimer puzzled.

'I just thought—if the scholar you are off to consult is at all interested in that sort of thing, he may not be in London at all—but as close as Exeter.'

The girl's eyes grew round as she absorbed the implication. 'Exeter,' she breathed. She rose and rushed out of the room.

Trey exchanged a sardonic look with Drake, but she was back in an instant, a pile of journals in her hands. 'Yes, Mr Alden has written several articles on justice during the time of Alfred the Great, and one on his translations. Surely he would be at such a gathering!' Eyes shining, she embraced the innkeeper. 'Exeter is only two days' travel. We can be there and back within a week!'

Drake's face was flushed, but he was smiling. 'Thought that might be the case.'

Trey was smiling too. Oh, yes, this was ever so much better. He saw the moment when the rest of it hit her. Her smile faded, and she sat abruptly down. Unerring, her gaze sought his.

'But what of Lord Renhurst? He's gone to Tavistock. He'll be expecting us.' She turned back to Drake. 'We cannot wait. What if Mr Alden should leave Exeter? Who knows where he might go from there.'

Trey shrugged. 'I'm afraid you'll have to reconcile yourself, Miss Latimer. It looks like it will be just you and me.'

Chapter Seven

The world outside the carriage window lay silent. Ahead only the faintest tinge of pale blue flirted with the horizon, hinting at the coming day. Inside the carriage the darkness still lay thick and heavy, a fact for which Chione could only be grateful. All of her resources were fully engaged at the moment, wrestling a demon no longer content with its imprisonment.

It was a reckoning Chione had known was coming. She had marked Lord Treyford as dangerous at first sight, when he had vaulted off his horse at Oakwood and strode towards her, eating the ground with his warrior's stride. And she had been right. Every encounter with the man had disarmed her further.

She'd been careful for so long. Kept the fiery part of her soul leashed so tightly that for long periods of time she forgot it. Not so now. No matter how she resisted, the earl had been busily knocking holes in the fortress hidden inside her. The creature inside that fortress was awake now, and quivering with anticipation, for the object of its interest reclined, sublimely unaware, just inches away.

He wasn't supposed to be in the carriage at all. He was supposed to be up on the box. Lord Treyford had emerged from the servants' corridor dressed as a coachman in coarse homespun and a worn greatcoat. Not a very successful disguise, in Chione's opinion, since the rough clothes clashed with his supremely confident manner and only emphasised his powerful form. But he had pulled on a pair of gloves and announced his intention of shortening the journey by taking his turn at driving. Chione had waited for her breath to come back, then had nodded her vigorous agreement and climbed gratefully into the coach with her new maid.

Jenny Ferguson, niece to Chione's housekeeper, had jumped at the chance to act as Chione's maid and companion on their journey. Unfortunately, Jenny had never travelled past the out-skirts of Wembury, and never at all in a closed carriage. They had barely reached Knighton before the girl turned green. Up she'd gone into the fresh air and the company of the well-favoured and unattached driver, and down had come Lord Treyford, into Chione's worst nightmare.

Her eyes kept straying to him, despite the darkness. But the demon inside her didn't need to see. She sensed him, revelled in his looming presence.

Chione thanked all the powers that be for the darkness, for it took a deal of time for her to conquer her foe, time for her to quell the quivering, hollow excitement in her belly and calm the runaway beat of her heart. Yet she persevered.

This…attraction she felt for the earl, it could only be a mo-mentary distraction. Nothing could come of it—how well she knew that! No, other women might think of attracting such a man, might dream of becoming his countess, but not Chione. The heavy burden of her past forbade such a future. Her life was about other things. She had accepted that fact, embraced it.

Her determination only grew with the dawning day. She waged her silent battle, and by the time the sun had climbed high enough to illuminate the carriage interior, she had tri-umphed. She took out a book to keep herself occupied, and her fingers did not even tremble. Much.

* * *

At first Trey was content with the new arrangement. He and the driver could still trade off, and they would each have a chance to rest out of the elements. But whoever had said there was no rest for the wicked must have had an insight into Trey's thoughts. In the darkness, his awareness of his companion seemed a living thing. Her scent, as fresh as rain in the desert, enveloped him in an almost tangible embrace, and he caught himself straining to hear the soft sound of her breath. As the sun rose he abandoned his plans to sleep and gave himself over to watching Chione Latimer instead.

She looked serene in the soft morning light, her lovely face as timeless as the depictions in the Temple at Karnac. For a time he was content to admire the tawny smoothness of her skin, to trace with his eye the graceful curve of neck and cheek, to watch for the lush flutter of her eyelash as she read.

But after a while he began to feel restless. Fidgety. Like a six-year-old who tugs the curls of the girl he admires, Trey had a sudden yearning to ruffle Miss Latimer's calm.

He leaned over to peer at the leather-bound book she held.

'Preparing a lesson?' he asked. 'I do hope it is not something of Homer's. In my opinion, Olivia is too young for man-eating monsters. Not to mention all those conniving suitors of Penelope's. And the seductions.' He paused. 'On second thought, Miss Latimer, I believe *you* are too young for Homer.' She laughed and he held out a hand. 'Perhaps it would be better if I kept that for you.'

She grinned and sparkled up at him as she closed the book with a snap. 'Sorry to disappoint you, my lord. It's only a diplomat's account of the Ottoman Empire.' She cocked her head to one side. 'Plenty of avarice and intrigue in Constantinople, though, so perhaps you might enjoy it at that.'

Trey gave a theatrical shudder. 'Constantinople? Wretched city. Perhaps you would do better to stick with Homer after all.'

A pink flush stole over the girl's cheeks. 'Oh, it's not for the children.' Trey could tell she was striving for nonchalance. 'It's just a bit of research for my stories.'

Her manner—perversely—awakened his curiosity. 'Stories?'

'Yes.'

He raised a brow. 'Bedtime stories? An article for the local paper? Journal entries? I confess I'm at a loss.'

Her flush had turned to the full-fledged burn of embarrassment. 'I should have thought—that is, I assumed someone would have told you.' She raised her chin a notch, as if daring him to judge her. 'It's no secret. I write adventure stories.'

It was not what he had been expecting her to say. But he was learning to expect the unexpected from this girl. She was beautiful, strong, independent. Unsettling. *Dangerous*, whispered the wary, uncompromising part of him. He ignored it.

'Adventure novels?' he asked. 'As in, the serial stories? Like those Nikolas serials? What are the titles—*The Emerald Temple* and *The Scroll of the Sapphire Slave*?'

'Yes.' She nodded. 'Those.'

He was impressed despite himself. 'That sort of thing is very popular. The Nikolas stories in particular. In my travels back to England I was aboard ship with several enthusiasts. They were reading to pass the time, trading copies and talking incessantly of what might happen in the next installment.'

He paused and realised that the note of finality in her voice had meant something. It took him a moment to figure it out.

'Those? You wrote those? You mean to say *you* are A. Vaganti? You wrote the Nikolas series—about the world-travelling adventurer?'

Her face still rosy, she nodded.

Trey stared at the girl sitting across from him. In her prim spencer and plain travelling dress, her hands folded on her book and her blush intensified by the soft morning light, she was an irresistible mix of exotic siren and innocent maiden. She was a conundrum, was Richard's sister, and he was a fool. He stared a moment longer, then he threw back his head and laughed.

She bristled. 'Laugh if you will, but it's kept us warm and fed this winter.'

He struggled to stop, to attain an attitude of detachment as his gaze lingered on her indignant expression. 'My dear girl,' he snorted, 'pray, don't take offence. I only laugh because half my fellow passengers aboard the ship home were convinced that *I* had penned those novels!' He laughed long again. 'Oh, the whispered rumours! They swirled about me like fog. They had themselves convinced that I was returning to England only to deliver the latest story to my publisher.'

She laughed. 'I sent the next instalment to *my* publisher just yesterday. I thought to use the time to plot out the next.' She cocked her head and grinned at him. 'Although I see how the mistake could be made—you do resemble Nikolas, somewhat.'

'So I've been told.' Trey shook his head. 'When I think how those passengers would react, could I tell them that their beloved A. Vaganti is a mere slip of a girl…'

Her grin faded. 'I dare say they would be disappointed.'

But his rusty sense of humour had got a hold of Trey, and he would not let her mood deflate. 'Only to learn that the author who writes such swashbuckling tales gets her research from books.' He allowed the tiniest hint of mockery to invade his tone. 'I know Richard shared your grandfather's thirst for adventure. Aren't you afflicted with the family trait as well? Aren't you pining to get away—to get a taste of what you describe so well for your readers?'

Once again she surprised him. Instead of zinging him with a witty rejoinder, she visibly withdrew. Her body language tightened and her gaze grew shuttered. 'Yes,' she said sombrely, 'there are a few places I would like to see. Paris, perhaps, or Rome. I would like to experience for myself the raw energy of

America. But for the most part, my passions vary widely from the rest of my family's.'

Trey leaned in close and pitched his voice low, just a notch above a whisper. 'It must be the enforced intimacy of our tête-à-tête, Miss Latimer, but I find myself quite interested in hearing of your passions.'

She didn't respond to his teasing. For a moment she didn't respond at all. The delay gave Trey time to wonder just what he was doing. In his urge to unsettle Chione Latimer, what was he doing to himself?

'Perhaps I will share mine, but only if you will reciprocate.'

Trey shrugged, trying not to show how the notion unsettled him. 'Fine, although I take leave to censor my answers to fit a young lady's ears.' He smiled. 'What is it you wished to know?'

'When did you know that you wished to spend your life adventuring? Your estate is in the north, is it not? What spurred you to leave the familiar behind and explore the mysteries of the world?'

He spent several long moments composing his answer. He'd been joking earlier, but he found that a bit of censoring was indeed in order. Not to protect her, however, but him.

'When I was nine years old, I received a present from my uncle—my mother's brother, a younger son who had joined the East India Company. I'd never met him, and truly, I don't recall if he had ever sent me anything before that, but that year, being an accurate judge of young male sensibilities, he sent me a shrunken head and a gorgeous book on the islands of the Caribbean.'

She laughed. 'I would imagine you were entranced.'

'Completely. I studied everything I could on the region. And what was not to love? Voodoo and pirates and tribal beauties—it was all wonderfully exotic.' And so completely unrelated to the rest of his life. 'We struck up a correspondence that lasted until his death. The next year, he sent me a family of carved elephants and the book was about India.' He quirked his mouth at her. 'And that was how it all began. Now it is your turn. I know your brother burned to make advances in the archaeological world. All of England knows of your grandfather's ambition to explore all the unknown places left on our ever-shrinking world. But I wish to know—what are your dreams, Miss Latimer?'

She, too, took her time in answering, and he wondered if it might be for the same reason. 'I want to make a difference, Lord Treyford.'

He leaned back. 'A difference?'

'Yes. Of all people, you should understand. You've travelled so far, seen so much. Like Jenny, most people cannot see outside of their own small lives.'

Trey had an uncomfortable idea where this was going.

'Misery, hunger, want, hopelessness, they abound in the world,' she continued. 'I want to help. Is that something you can at all understand?'

He thought of the downtrodden beggars in India, doomed by and from their birth; he pictured the miserable slaves he had seen in the East, remembered the dirty children scurrying about the streets in cities from Calcutta to Cairo, to London itself.

'Yes,' he said.

She glanced away, but not before he saw the sadness, the pain she tried to hide behind long lashes and quiet competency. His own good humour fled completely, replaced by something more dangerous as he watched her gaze unseeing out of the window.

'My mother was an Egyptian. Did you know?'

He nodded and she went on.

'When she died, Richard was still a babe, and I was not much older. We were alone, frightened, hungry, tired.' She shot him a quick glance and a wry smile. 'I would suppose an earl would have no idea what it means, to feel so helpless.'

'You would be wrong.' The words were out before he knew it.

He didn't want to see the curiosity in her gaze, or the compassion. Luckily she looked away again, at the uncanny brightness of the morning.

'I hated it,' she said with sudden intensity. 'I was so angry, and I felt so betrayed.'

She sighed and sat silent for several long moments.

'Then Mervyn Latimer came. He saved us, gave us everything important in life: love and peace, family and hope. He brought us out of darkness, into the light.' She looked his way once more. 'I dare say you know what I mean, then?'

Trey couldn't breathe. How had they arrived at this place, from the lighthearted banter they had shared earlier? He had the sudden urge to lash out at her, to make her angry so she would forget what she had asked, what she might learn. But that would be running, something he'd been doing for so long, and look where it had got him, right where he had never wished to be. And he had a strange disinclination to diminish himself so, in her eyes. So he screwed up his courage and he said, 'No. I'm afraid no one ever rode to my rescue.'

This time he was the one who turned away. He didn't want to see her reaction.

He imagined it, though. He imagined the pity in her eyes even as he heard her struggle to keep her tone neutral. It made him want to howl.

'We were lucky.' It came out nearly as a whisper. She paused and her voice grew stronger. 'Mervyn is a great man. Richard and I were not the only ones whose lives he has changed. I mean to be like him. I want to help others as I have been helped.'

Trey blinked. Once again she shocked him with the unexpected. She'd suffered loss, pain, hunger, betrayal and yet she wished to help? He thought that Mervyn Latimer must indeed have been a saint, to have raised such a girl.

'I haven't done it yet,' she continued. 'I haven't accomplished much. But I have plans. Once Mervyn is found, I shall make a difference.'

He turned abruptly. 'Don't belittle what you have done. You've touched many people's lives and made them better. The children, the villagers, even that circus troupe that you call servants.'

Her eyes widened. 'Thank you. That is extremely kind of you to say. Except for the circus part, of course, but I promise I won't tell Mrs Ferguson.'

'It's the truth, damn it.' Her modesty irritated him.

She shrugged. 'I do appreciate the compliment, it's only, when I think of all the good that Mervyn has accomplished…' Her voice trailed off.

'Your grandfather is a wealthy man. Such will always have influence in the world. It's easy for him. While you…' Trey raked an appreciative gaze over her well-armoured form '…are undeniably a woman.'

'In a wealthy man's world?' she asked tartly.

'Exactly. I confess it freely, although it's not the thing to admit—but I've always been grateful that I was not born a woman.'

She gave him exactly the same sort of once-over that he'd just given her. 'As are we all.' She smiled.

Trey felt the weight of that look all the way down to his toes. Lord, why did it have to be this innocent girl who made him feel so hot and addled?

'You are right, though, that being a woman will make my goal that much more difficult to reach. Worse than being a woman, though, is being an outsider, belonging to neither of the worlds I have inhabited.' She sighed. 'Commerce, politics, even society, they are the quickest ways to philanthropy, and they are closed to me.'

Trey raised a brow. 'So your sphere of influence is smaller. It means only that you help in smaller ways, one person at a time, and who is to say which is more valuable?'

Her eyes lit up, her countenance softened. She smiled—and the world was alight. Unconsciously, Trey leaned forward, wanting to bask in her brilliance.

She ducked her head a little, still looking at him through the fan of her dark lashes. She was gorgeous. Fearless. With a start, Trey realised that the carriage had begun to slow, but he did not care. He yearned to touch her, to take in some of the light she shone into the world.

As if possessed of a will of its own, his hand rose, brushed her cheek, traced her ear, and caressed the slender column of her neck. He leaned closer still. Her eyes were wide, startled. His slid slowly closed, even as he captured the fullness of her lower lip between his own.

She made a sound, a squeak of surprise, but she did not pull back. Not relinquishing contact, Trey eased across and into the seat beside her. Instinct, or perhaps something more dangerous, had taken hold of him. He gathered her close and pressed a soft kiss on her jaw and buried his face into her smooth, fragrant nape.

The carriage drew to a halt, but he barely took notice. She trembled underneath his hand.

The door opened. Trey blinked and drew back. Frustration swamped him, but at the same time he was oddly grateful for the rescue.

'We've nearly reached Modbury, my lord,' the driver announced. 'Thought we'd water the horses and give the ladies a chance to stretch their legs.'

Slowly, Trey pulled away. He rose and climbed out of the carriage before turning to look Chione Latimer in the eye. 'Your grandfather would be proud of you.'

She made a sound of protest, but he cut her off.

'Your brother, too. You're a fool if you can't see the good you have wrought. A bigger fool, even, than I.'

Before she could respond, he turned on his heel and strode away. So open, and so naïve. She was indeed a pretty, open-hearted fool. He had to wonder if he had ever in his life been so optimistic.

He suppressed a snort. No, he had been born a cynic, and all the formative events of his life had proved the extreme practicality of it. It was this sort one had to worry about, the trusting ones who inevitably got hurt.

He had to keep his distance, watch his step. It was becoming very clear just how easily he could be the one to do it.

Chapter Eight

Lord Treyford did not return to the coach. He took up the ribbons when they got back underway and allowed the driver to rest. As the sun grew higher and the day grew warmer, Chione was able to open the carriage windows. Jenny, who said she could manage the interior as long as she could feel the wind on her face, joined her.

Chione felt nothing but cowardly relief. Treyford had touched her. She rather thought he had kissed her. She put her fingers to her lips. Could you call that a kiss? The nearest thing to it, in any case, and she had let him. Worse, she had wished for more.

With a sigh she dropped her head in her hands. A great, colossal idiot—that's what she was. She'd put herself into the hands of yet another man who would eventually disappear on her, and then she'd nearly kissed him.

Warning bells should have been pealing when he'd touched her. Instead she had lost herself in the low rasp of his voice. Just being in his presence had become a risk. Something about him inspired her heart to open, even as her mind screamed for her to stop. She'd exposed herself, revealed things that she had never discussed with anyone. And he had understood, accepted and even encouraged her.

Her reaction had been instantaneous. She had drunk it in—like water to her parched soul—and immediately begun to crave another taste.

The trembling that beset her had nothing to do with the jolting carriage and everything to do with the insidious effect that Treyford had on her. So dangerous—for where would it stop? Chione had secrets that must be kept, but even now she could feel herself craving the warmth of his regard, the heat of his touch.

No, it was better to stay away. A relief not to have to deal with his overpowering physical presence. Her attraction to the man was a burden, but one she must bear for only a short while. Once Mervyn was found he would be gone. Until then distance would serve her, where her control had not.

So she watched Jenny hanging out of the window and she willed herself not to relive those unsettling moments. Instead she occupied herself with fretting about the children and wondering how Lord Renhurst was faring. Certainly they had seen no sign of trouble; she couldn't help but worry about what that might mean to the viscount. But an hour or so later she had worried herself out. It seemed a futile exercise while trapped in a carriage. She'd brought along Mervyn's journals and she set herself to whiling away the afternoon hours looking for a clue to what the coffer might be.

To no avail. There was no mention of a coffer, the scarab, or even the Pharaoh's Lost Jewel. If you relied solely on Mervyn's journals, you would not even know that such a thing existed. Chione wondered if she might have more luck with Richard's journals, but all of his effects had not yet arrived from Egypt. She must remember to ask Lord Treyford if he knew what had become of them.

She would ask him at their next stop. But she would ask only that. Distance was key.

She never got the chance. Treyford set a gruelling pace. They travelled late into the night, not stopping until Totness for a few hours' sleep.

The next morning she and Jenny had a hurried breakfast in their room and were hustled right back out to the carriage. This time when the girl objected, it was the coachman who came down to switch places, and Chione knew that the earl had reached the same conclusion as she. He was doing his best to stay far away from her.

He succeeded admirably well. They stopped twice to change horses, but in both instances Chione barely caught a glimpse of Treyford. The pace he set continued, relentless but efficient. They rolled into Exeter just as the second evening of their journey faded into night.

Fortunately their destination was easily found. Exhausted but grateful, Chione climbed down from the carriage, instinctively looking for the earl.

He stood with the horses, giving instructions to the ostlers. As the tired animals were led away, he approached. Chione kept her countenance calm, but could do nothing to stop the frantic beating of her heart.

Avoiding her gaze, he took her arm. 'Bring the girl,' he said, voice low, 'and let us search out this friend of Drake's.'

As it turned out, there was no need. A short man, round as a child's ball, came beaming from the taproom before they had taken a step.

'Welcome, welcome!' he called. Breathing heavily, he hustled right up and shook Treyford's hand with enthusiasm. 'An honour it is to have you at the George, sir, ma'am.' He nodded to Chione. 'I've my best private parlour set aside for you. Come in! Come in!'

'I'm afraid you are mistaken…' Chione cast a helpless look at Treyford as the portly little man took her arm to lead her away.

'Not at all!' he insisted, and keeping up an endless stream

of prattle, he dispatched Jenny upstairs and led Chione and Treyford along to a cheerful room, lit by a welcoming fire.

Then he shut the door and his officious manner fell away.

'My lord Treyford,' he bowed. 'Miss Latimer. Welcome to the George. My heavens, but you have made good time!'

'But, sir—' Chione was perplexed '—how did you know to expect us?'

'Our crafty friend Drake, of course. He sent a rider ahead to warn me, but I must tell you that he beat you by only a matter of hours! I've only had time to rearrange a few rooms—no easy matter with all these historians descended upon us.'

'Thank you for your efforts, Mr Cedric, is it?' Treyford had finally spoken up.

'Just Cedric, please, sir. Just Cedric.'

'Cedric, then. Also, I must thank you for your earlier discretion. I assume Drake has filled you in on the particulars of our mission?'

'Only the essentials. And there is no need to thank me. Do anything for a friend of Drake's, I would. Well, then…' he rubbed his hands together '…it's a Mr Alden you're looking to find, is it not? I've sent my own nephew out to make inquiries. Shouldn't be long before we hear something from him.'

Chione could see that Treyford looked ready to object.

'Very discreet, of course,' Cedric said with a raised hand. 'He's a smart boy—knows when to talk and when to listen.'

Treyford shrugged. 'You've made this very easy on us, Cedric.' He cast a glance askance at Chione. 'Miss Latimer's maid should have her bags unpacked by now. Would you mind showing her to her room?'

Chione bristled. 'Thank you, Cedric, but I've been confined to the carriage for the last two days. I find I'm not quite ready to be confined to my room.' She glared at the earl.

'No, of course not,' Cedric agreed. 'So long a journey—and not a decent bite to eat between here and there, I'll wager. You must be famished. My good sister is the cook here, and she is preparing something special for you both. I'll just go out and see to it.'

'Thank you.' Chione ignored Treyford as the little man left. Chin high, she took a seat near the fire. Distance was one thing, but such a high-handed dismissal was another. He'd been the one to run his hands over her, after all. Now he acted as if she were diseased.

'Miss Latimer—' he still hadn't quite met her eyes '—I feel I must apologise. My actions earlier were inexcusable.'

'Which actions?' She knew she sounded testy, but that was precisely how she felt. 'When you kissed me in the carriage or just now, when you dismissed me from your presence like a child?'

'Both, I must suppose.' He shot her a wry look.

'Oh, very well,' she conceded. 'I must take some of the blame as well. It must have been the long empty hours.' She shot him an apologetic grimace. 'Truly, it is not often that I immerse myself in such maudlin sentimentality. I'm sorry you got dragged in.'

'Dragged in, but not under.' He moved at last away from the door, and Chione could see his expression grow serious. Still he did not take a seat, but remained standing, watching her steadily.

'There is something…intangible between us, Miss Latimer. It does us no good to deny it.'

Chione froze in her chair. Still he stared. Waiting.

Slowly she nodded, feeling the heat rush to her face.

'So let us acknowledge it, and thereby disarm it. We both know it is there, but I think we both understand it would be folly to act upon it. We have a job to do. It will go easier if we can be comfortable with each other.'

He was right. She should be grateful he had addressed the problem. How many men would think to lighten such a burden by offering to share it? She was indeed grateful and relieved as well. But somewhere deep inside of her she was forced to acknowledge an unmistakable wave of disappointment, a curious sense of opportunity lost.

'Are we in agreement, then?'

Once more she nodded. She couldn't have spoken even had she wished to.

'Et voilà!' called Cedric as he backed into the parlour, pulling a laden cart behind him. 'Now you shall see how a good English cook trumps Drake's Henri any day. My sister has created a spread that will put anything served in Devonshire to shame!'

He began to pull the covers off of the dishes. 'Eat up, my friends. You will need your strength tonight. My nephew has returned.'

Chione glanced at Treyford, than back to Cedric, the question unnecessary.

'Your man is here. Across town, at the New Inn.'

Trey and Miss Latimer followed the boy through the dark streets of Exeter without incident. None the less, a foreboding prickle had inched its way along his spine. Now, safe in the small lobby of the New Inn, it hadn't dissipated. Instead it settled—a tense throb of awareness—smack between his shoulder blades.

He could not be sure of what it meant, but long experience assured him it didn't bode well. Trey scrubbed his brow in frustration. Then again, perhaps his instincts were befuddled. He glanced across at the woman who'd accompanied him. She was more than capable of driving a man to distraction. And for the first time he was showing himself susceptible to a woman's wiles.

He cursed and began to pace, restless as a caged cat. The boy, at least, had been settled happily into a warm nook in the kitchen. A good thing, since this was taking so long.

The man they had travelled to see was here, mere feet away. Simple enough to climb a few stairs and knock on the door. But no. This was England, where the obsession with social graces made him want to scream. Instead—because he failed to carry so useless an object as a calling card—he'd had to sweat over a carefully worded request, hand it over to a lackey, and wait for a reply. And wait. And wait.

He crossed over to the window, standing well to the side so he could not be seen. Thankfully there was nobody to see outside at the moment, either. 'What the devil did you mean to do in America?' he asked without looking at his infuriatingly calm companion.

'I beg your pardon?' Still she was unruffled.

'Drake told me that before Mervyn disappeared, you meant to go to America. What did you mean to do there? Travel?'

'Yes.' She didn't elaborate, just gazed at him with some curiosity. 'Have you ever been there?'

'No.'

'I think I would have liked it. Americans are very forgiving, I believe. There your past is not as important as your willingness to work, to better yourself.'

Her words increased his agitation. 'You don't need to better yourself,' he said gruffly. 'You are fine as you are.'

'Thank you,' she said, but raised an ironic brow. 'But I think that you understand the wish to begin again? To start anew with the past wiped clean?'

He didn't answer. He started to pace again.

'Stop fidgeting,' she murmured. 'You'll draw attention to us.'

'It's the middle of the damned night,' Trey snapped. 'Who is there to see?'

'You never know who might come in.' She shrugged. 'And we don't want to leave a lasting impression on the clerk.'

'We're making a morning call at midnight,' he began. 'What sort of impression—?' He stopped. Voices outside, faint, but drawing nearer. Damned if the girl wasn't right.

He crossed quickly over and pulled her into a shadowy

corner just as the door opened. A cool waft of air preceded a riotous group of young men into the room. Trey bent low over the girl, shielding her from their gaze with his body. 'Laugh,' he said, his face perilously close to hers.

'What?' Her eyes were wide with alarm.

'Laugh,' he whispered the harsh command. 'Like the sort of woman who should be out alone with a man at this time of night.'

Still she did not comprehend. Speechless, she just stared at him, her pupils dark with surprise, and, if he was any judge, with sudden want.

So Trey did what he must. What some part of him had burned to do since he'd first laid eyes on her. He pulled her hard against him and seared her with his kiss.

For an endless, nerve-racking moment she froze, rigid in his arms. The men behind him had caught sight of them. Whistles and catcalls rang through the small room. Someone shouted some ribald advice and she must have caught on.

Suddenly she answered his kiss. She curled her small hands over his shoulders and pressed herself fully against him. Underneath his mouth, she began to inexpertly move hers.

The dam holding back Trey's desire burst. A flood of passion overwhelmed him. He asked for more, kissed her harder, demanded her surrender. She yielded, and he urged her lips apart.

The men had moved on, but Trey didn't stop. Couldn't stop. She fit against him, soft curves hugging his hardened frame perfectly. He surged inside her mouth, entwined her tongue with his, taught her to kiss him back with long sinuous strokes.

'Ah-hem.'

With a superhuman effort Trey pulled his mouth from hers. She blinked up at him, her expression a gratifying whirl of disappointment and desire. Reluctant, he stepped away.

She staggered, swaying on her feet. 'I think we just left intangible behind,' she said.

Trey only grimaced and gripped her tighter.

'What do we do now?' The question emerged on a whisper.

'We talk to your scholar,' he growled.

Together, they turned to face the waiting clerk.

They'd awakened the man. Jack Alden answered the door in a dressing robe, trousers, and spectacles. He hadn't bothered to comb his hair.

'Lord Treyford,' he said, opening the door wide. 'Do come in.'

Trey stepped in and Alden spied the woman hanging behind him. 'Oh…' he tightened the belt of his robe '…I wasn't aware you'd brought a friend.'

'I thank you for agreeing to see us, Mr Alden,' Trey said. 'May I present to you Miss Chione Latimer?'

The man raised a brow. 'Indeed you may, my lord.' He shut the door and, with a gentleman's grace, bowed over the girl's hand. 'What a great pleasure, Miss Latimer. I was well acquainted with your brother.' He kept the girl's hand clasped in both his own. 'Allow me to offer you my condolences. We lost a great mind when he passed on. And I lost a good friend.'

'Thank you.' She inclined her head, regal as a queen. And every bit as lovely. Trey saw the open appreciation in the other man's gaze and his fists grew tight. 'I am very glad to meet you,' she said.

'Please, sit down.' There was a chair next to the small fireplace. Alden settled the girl into it and waved Trey to take the wooden chair at the small desk. He perched himself upon the rumpled bed.

'This does explain a bit,' he said to Trey. 'I couldn't imagine what the Earl of Treyford wished with me when the boy brought your note. I had not even heard that you had returned to England, but I would have thought you would be in London, what with all the furor over the exhibition of Belzoni's Tomb.'

'Oh, has he opened it, then?'

'To great acclaim. It sounds more like something you would

be interested in than this King Alfred chicanery. I didn't think that English artifacts were what appealed to you.'

'Not as a rule.' Trey lifted a shoulder.

'Forgive us for approaching you at such an odd hour,' Miss Latimer broke in. 'But it is an odd situation we find ourselves in.'

Alden grinned. 'Not surprising for a member of the intrepid Latimer family.'

Trey saw the slightest frown crease her brow.

'No, unfortunately not.'

The scholar must have seen it too. 'Forgive, me, I meant no disparagement. Richard shared some of your family's colourful history. It must be a challenge, that sort of legacy.'

'Every family has challenges.' She raised her chin in that stubborn way she had. The sweet familiarity of the gesture hit Trey hard and unexpectedly. 'Does not yours, Mr Alden?'

He laughed. '*Touché*, Miss Latimer. Mine does indeed, and my family's peccadilloes are nearly as notorious as your own.'

Trey saw her relax. He wasn't relaxed. He was knee-deep in exactly the sort of trouble he'd spent his life avoiding. He stared at the brave set of her shoulders, the serious expression on her face, and he told himself that all was well. He'd caught himself in time. He would escape unscathed, before either of them got hurt.

'And I'm certain you would do anything to protect your family, notorious or not?' she asked Alden with a raised brow.

'Of course,' he responded at once.

'As would I, sir. Which leads me to exactly why we have come in search of you.'

Trey listened as she spun her tale, and he answered several questions that Alden had regarding his work with Richard Latimer. He watched the other man closely, sure that he would scorn such a convoluted account of artifacts, bandits, coded messages and hidden clues. He was wrong. Mr Alden proved an attentive listener throughout. When the girl had finished, he sat back in his chair, took off his spectacles and wiped them absently. For several moments a dead silence hung thick in the room.

Finally she stood. With one hand on the mantel and her earnest gaze fixed on his abstracted face, she asked, 'Have you any idea what your name on that slip of paper might mean, Mr Alden?'

'Yes…' he put his spectacles back in place '…I believe I might.'

She sank back into her chair. 'Thank heavens,' she said in a near-whisper. 'Please, tell me what you know.'

'I think it is more a matter of what you know.'

Trey glanced sharply at the man, but he was already continuing.

'After Richard received the position with the British Museum, we spent a good deal of time together as he prepared to leave.' He looked to Trey with enthusiasm. 'I don't have your experience, of course, my lord, but I do find Egypt fascinating. I have the complete *Description de l'Egypte*. We pored over it and several other works I have in my collection.'

'Did he ever mention Mervyn's scarab to you?' asked the girl. Eagerly she pulled the thing from her pocket.

'He didn't.' Alden's expression flared with interest. 'May I?'

'Of course.'

He took it and inspected it closely. 'Amazing,' he said. 'But, no, Richard did not speak of it. He was remarkably interested in one thing, though.'

'What?' She sounded breathless. Trey was more than a little interested, too.

'A legend. An ancient tale, he said, about an architect's daughter…'

'And a tomb robber!' she breathed.

'So you know it?' Trey noted a particular intensity in his eyes as the scholar asked the question.

'Oh, yes. Mervyn used to tell us the tale often when we were children.'

'I've never heard of it,' Trey interrupted. 'Will you tell it?

She laughed a little self-consciously. 'Oh, it's just another ill-fated romance. There's no historical importance attached to it.'

'Please, I'd like to hear it again as well,' encouraged Alden.

She nodded. She sat a moment, gaze downcast, and when she looked up there was a faraway look in her eyes.

'It begins with an architect in ancient Egypt, a man who helped design the secret tombs of the pharaohs. He was well favoured and a member of the wealthy bureaucracy. He had a daughter, both learned and beautiful. When she came of age he decided to make her an advantageous marriage.'

Trey watched a flush of colour grow in her countenance. She sneaked a quick glance in his direction. He watched her steadily and nodded for her to go on, inwardly cursing the heated reaction that innocent gaze wrought.

'The girl had her own ideas about marriage, as young people often do. She had met a charming and handsome boy, the nephew of a provincial ruler. He pursued her and she loved him madly. It was a respectable alliance, so the father agreed and the marriage was made.'

She breathed deep. 'They were happy for a time. The architect's daughter was already with child when she made a terrible discovery. Her husband was not who he said he was. It was all a lie. He was actually from a notorious…' she paused and glanced at Alden '…family of tomb robbers. He'd only used her to discover secrets from her father. Secrets about the pharaoh's tombs.'

This time she looked at Trey openly and with a challenge in her eye. 'Mervyn always stressed that she was a very intelligent young lady, and now she was an angry one as well.'

'A dangerous combination,' acknowledged Trey.

'The architect's daughter did not let on that she knew her

husband's secret. All the agony she felt at his betrayal was kept hidden. She waited and she plotted. When he made his move she was ready. She tricked him, and trapped him in the tomb he meant to plunder.'

She blinked. Trey could see her gathering herself, pulling back from where the story had taken her.

'So she locked him in with the treasure he had betrayed her for?' Trey thought it a fitting end for the scoundrel.

'No, she took the treasure. Or part of it. She kept it for her daughter.'

'Yes,' Mr Alden agreed, 'and according to Richard the treasure was passed down for many generations of daughters.' He leaned forward, failing to hide his serious expression behind his spectacles. 'What happened to the architect's daughter, Miss Latimer?'

'The legend does not say.' She cocked her head at him. 'Richard and I used to discuss it, though. He always said she would set herself up as a wealthy widow and remarry.'

'And what did you think?'

'I'm sure I don't know.'

'You must have had a theory,' he pressed.

'It's just a legend.' She gave a sheepish little shrug. 'Oh, very well. I once told Richard that I feared that she would hold on to her anger. That she never let herself love again. I told him I believed *that* would be the true tragedy.'

Her answer appeared to energise Alden. He stood. 'Richard was extremely intent on finding any reference he could about that legend.' He walked to the desk and ran his hands along a stack of books there. 'We discussed it at length.' He turned with one of the books in his hand and fixed Chione with a direct look. 'One night, very late, he begged a favour of me. He said if his sister ever came to me, I was to ask her about the legend and most particularly I was to ask that last question.'

Trey was suddenly alert. 'Did he fear an impostor?'

'I can only guess as to his motives—he didn't explain. But

it must be so.' He knelt before the perplexed looking woman. 'I am very glad you gave the right answer, for now I have something to give you.'

'From Richard?' Tears brightened her eyes.

'Indeed. He asked me to keep it close always. But now I may give it to you.' With great solemnity he placed the book in her lap, then opened it.

It was hollowed inside. Trey heard her gasp even as he rocketed out of his chair.

Tucked away lay a shining golden box, perhaps four inches in diameter. She lifted it and they both exclaimed aloud. Hieroglyphs encircled the top edge and each surface featured brightly coloured pictures done in skilled relief.

'They are from the legend,' Chione cried.

Trey saw that it was true. Each side of the box illustrated a scene from the tale she had only just recounted. Most disturbing was the image on the lid: a woman sobbing, leaning on one side of a massively ornate door. On the other side was depicted only darkness.

'But where did Richard find it? Why didn't he tell me?' Sorrow warred with anguish in her voice.

'He would not tell me where it came from,' Alden said. 'I do not believe it had been in his possession for very long, but I cannot say for sure.' He lowered his voice to a whisper. 'Open it.'

Tears streaming down her face, she did. She gasped again and reached inside, pulling out a large, gleaming emerald.

'It's beautiful,' she breathed, cradling it in her palm. Her eyes met Trey's and she held it out to him.

He took it, noted the weight of the thing and the unusual shape.

'The scarab,' Trey rasped. 'Where is it?'

'Here.' Alden passed it over.

Trey turned it so that the head of the insect faced the girl. Very lightly he settled the emerald into the empty space on the right wing. It fit perfectly.

'What does it mean?' she asked in a whisper.

'I don't know—' he raised his head and looked her directly in the eye '—but it looks as if there's one more to find.'

Chapter Nine

⁓⟋⟍⟋⟍⟋⟍⟋⟍⟋⟍⟋⟍⟋⟍⟋⟍⟋⟍⟋⁓

Chione heard the undertone of excitement in Treyford's voice, saw the gleam in Mr Alden's eye and was abruptly brought back to her senses.

'That's all well and good,' she clipped, 'but hardly relevant to the issue. Mr Alden, please do not think me ungrateful. I thank you for the service you have done both Richard and me—but Treyford and I are not seeking the Pharaoh's Lost Jewel. I've come hoping you could shed some light on my grandfather's disappearance.'

'I wish I were in a position to do so,' he said, obviously chagrined.

'Did Richard mention nothing about Mervyn's disappearance?' Chione could hear the desperation in her own voice. 'Did he never discuss any ideas he might have had? Anything about where Mervyn might be?'

'We spoke of it, of course. I remember he mentioned that your grandfather was last seen on Malta?'

'Yes,' she said, hoping for more.

'That's not a very helpful clue, is it? I remember Richard saying he might have left there and gone anywhere in the Mediterranean.'

Her shoulders slumped, but she refused to give up. 'I've often thought that Richard was hiding something. I wondered at the time if he sought that position with the museum so that he might find a way to look for Mervyn. He wouldn't ever admit it, but he didn't precisely deny it.'

'He never mentioned such a thing specifically to me either,' Mr Alden said, his tone slow and thoughtful. 'But I did notice more than once that he attacked his search with renewed vigour when the topic of his grandfather came up—almost as if it motivated him.'

Chione saw Treyford's quick frown. 'What are you suggesting?' he asked.

'I just wonder if the two aren't related.' The scholar's gaze was distant, but he continued to speak with methodic thoroughness. 'Let us just organise our thoughts for a moment. First we have the scarab—Mervyn's prized possession, you say?'

Chione nodded.

'And it is widely associated with the mystery of the Pharaoh's Lost Jewel. Then we have this lovely little box…' he ran a caressing finger along the edge of it '…relating an ancient tale unknown to most, but familiar to Mervyn and your family. And the jewel inside is undoubtedly linked to the scarab.' He nodded towards the artifact, sitting with the emerald still nestled in place. 'So it follows that perhaps the tale is linked to the mystery of the Lost Jewel.'

'You think the emerald is the Pharaoh's Lost Jewel?' Treyford sounded as sceptical as Chione felt.

'No. I'm beginning to believe, though, that the treasure in the legend, the one the architect's daughter passed on to her daughter, might be.'

'It makes sense,' agreed Treyford. 'But still that leaves us with more questions than answers.'

'And none of them gets me any closer to finding the coffer, or Mervyn,' complained Chione.

'I disagree,' Alden said smoothly. 'Look closely. Mervyn is the central figure in both cases. He is the one who binds it all together.'

'What are you saying?' she whispered.

'If we want to find Mervyn Latimer, we're going to have to solve the mystery of the Pharaoh's Lost Jewel?' Treyford asked. In his tone she could hear an odd mixture of anticipation and resignation.

Mr Alden nodded. 'It may be so.'

Everything in Chione wanted to reject the idea. She'd spent her life ignoring the mystery, resenting the toll it had taken on her family. Both her father and her brother had died while pursuing the Lost Jewel. The thought of taking up the chase repulsed her. But what if it were the only way to save Mervyn?

'Even if you are correct, Mr Alden, I have nowhere to go from here. No clue to lead us closer to a solution. Unless there is something else you can tell us?'

'I'm afraid not,' he answered. He knelt before her again and took her cold hand in his.

It didn't help. She felt empty, dejected. She raised her eyes to Treyford, but he appeared equally as lost.

'What do Richard's journals say of this?' asked Mr Alden finally. 'He kept detailed notes of all of his research. Have you consulted them?'

A brief stab of hope flared to life. 'I have not. I do not have his journals.' She looked again to Treyford. 'The same thought actually occurred to me yesterday during the long drive. So much has happened, I forgot to ask you. Might you know what happened to the journals?'

Treyford frowned. 'You should have received Richard's effects a month or more ago. It took me several weeks to plan the journey to England and prepare to leave my work, but I had his things sent on ahead.'

'I did receive a few boxes of gear and books,' Chione recalled, 'but no journals and not many personal items. Is it possible that not all of the boxes have reached us? Were they all posted together?'

'I do not know for sure. Aswan packed them and saw to the shipping.' He shrugged. 'We can ask him when we get back to Oakwood.'

Even such a small step helped Chione to feel better. At least it lent her hope for further progress. 'All the more reason we should be getting back quickly.' She stood, happy to have an excuse for decisiveness again. 'Mr Alden, I don't know how to thank you.'

He stood as well and pressed the lacquered box into her hand. 'The pleasure has been mine. I cannot tell you how happy I am to have met you at last.'

Chione blushed at the frankly appreciative look he gave her.

'You are all that Richard boasted of and more,' he said warmly.

'Thank you for being such a good friend to him,' she said. 'I hope I may count you as mine, too?'

'I insist upon it,' he said.

Treyford stepped in and distracted the scholar by offering his hand. 'You know the direction of Oakwood Court, should you recall anything else?'

'Indeed I do.'

Chione saw a glint of humour in Mr Alden's eyes. She looked to Treyford, but he did not appear to share it.

'I wish you both the best of luck,' the scholar said.

The warning sting was lodged in the base of Trey's neck again. He kept his step light and his senses on alert as he hustled them both back through the darkened streets. But he struggled to keep his thoughts focused. They kept determinedly wandering back to the chit at his side.

Bad enough that he'd kissed her. Truly kissed her, this time. Yes, he'd had an excuse; a couple in the midst of a tryst was the only sort who would be regarded as an ordinary fixture in such a situation, and the act had also hidden their identities quite thoroughly. No, what bothered him was how much he had enjoyed it. Immensely—Good God, but he'd enjoyed it immensely. It was a sad truth—one virginal kiss from Chione Latimer had rocked him more thoroughly than even the most erotic nights spent with the skilled women of the East.

Once she had entered into the spirit of the thing, Chione had melted into his embrace. He'd branded her with the heat of his desire and the sweetness of her innocent need had flowed into him, filling up cracks and crevices he hadn't known were empty. When that pox-ridden clerk had interrupted them, Trey had literally wanted to throttle him.

Heaven help him, but he knew better. He knew firsthand the dangers that came with allowing that sort of passion to rule your life. He'd seen with his own eyes the bitterness that comes when it inevitably fades, and he'd made a vow never to find himself in such a miserable spot. And yet, even knowing the futility and risk of such a thing, still he longed to kiss her again. God help him, but he wanted more.

She'd bewitched him. With her beauty, yes, but beautiful women were found the world over. Chione Latimer had so much more. Passion, loyalty and the rare ability to give of herself. She was unlike any woman Trey had ever met. Certainly she bore no resemblance to his vacuous, self-absorbed mother.

Her defence of her family had touched him tonight. Always, and in defiance of seemingly insurmountable odds, she placed their welfare ahead of her own. She cared for them, laboured for them, strived mightily to keep the remnants of her happy home together.

But at what cost? He thought of her longing to start anew in America and wondered what other dreams had Chione sacrificed for her family. Had she hoped to meet a man there? One who would not mind an Egyptian mother and a notorious family? One who would offer marriage?

He thought of the smitten look on Alden's face tonight and frowned. Why not? Trey might have forsworn a legshackle, but any number of other men would be lucky to take a woman like Chione Latimer to wife.

Trey's own temperament was without doubt the wrong sort to ever contemplate a lifelong commitment. Every significant relationship in his past had proven that he was capable of neither giving nor inspiring that sort of devotion.

In contrast, Chione appeared to be designed for it. She was far too lovely to wither away a spinster, too full of warmth to remain for ever childless. It was a certainty that no child of hers would ever question his mother's love.

Perhaps, then, that should be his goal, though even the thought of her with another man caused both his fists and his stomach to clench.

Perhaps, then, it was time that they both faced a few hard truths.

No matter the physical response she evoked, and perhaps especially because of the other, more complicated feelings she inspired, nothing could come of it. The sooner they finished this wild goose chase, the sooner he could be gone, away from temptation and the futile contemplation of what could never be.

And the sooner she could move on as well. Before long she must face the fact that Mervyn was beyond their reach. Perhaps Trey could help convince her it was time to think of herself as well as her family.

Abruptly he realised that the street had ended, spilling them into the wider area of the marketplace. It was deserted, the open spaces forlorn in the faint moonlight. Trey steered Chione to the shadows behind the empty stalls and together they circled quietly towards the George.

He breathed a sigh of relief when they entered the courtyard of the inn. Back safe. He spared a brief thought for Renhurst. Since he and the girl had gone unmolested, he had to assume that trouble had indeed followed the viscount. He hoped the man was up to the challenge.

The yard of the George was quiet, the galleries empty. Trey steered Chione towards the stairs, but as they reached the first step he paused. Before he could talk himself out of it, he grasped her arm and pulled her to a stop.

'Miss Latimer, I will, of course, ask Aswan about the whereabouts of Richard's journals, but I hope you realise the likelihood that they will contain anything useful is extremely low.'

She frowned up at him. 'We don't know that. You heard Mr Alden; he said Richard kept detailed notes.'

'Did Mervyn's journals contain anything helpful?'

She didn't answer.

He sighed. 'It's a long journey back. We'll both have plenty of time for contemplation. I hope you will begin to realise that we are nearing the end of your quest. You've done your best, not even your grandfather could fault you. But soon it will be time to think about a new chapter in your life.'

'I don't understand.' She gazed up at him. 'You want me to give up?' She pulled away, every line of her broadcasting her incredulousness. 'I thought you understood what Mervyn Latimer means to me. I can't give up. I won't admit to failing him.'

'You haven't failed him. Can't you see?' Trey was in uncharted waters here. Lord, he hoped she would throw him a line. 'You've done your best for him, for his children, even for his faithful servants. But you must know when it is time to stop. Stop and think—have you done what's best for you?'

She looked utterly blank. 'I have no idea what you could mean.'

'Mervyn loved you no less than those children. Wouldn't he want what is best for you?' He straightened. 'In any case, it seems doubtful that you can continue on much longer the way you have been.'

'Treyford, it's been a long day.' She began to fish in her reticule for her key. 'I'm not even sure what you are talking about, and I'm too tired to argue with you.'

But Trey had to finish this now. He might never get up the nerve for such a conversation again. 'I am talking about thinking in new directions. I want you to think about doing what is best for everyone—including yourself.' He was fast becoming exasperated. 'I heard Renhurst mention the children's grandmother. Where does she reside?'

'In Portsmouth.' She sighed. 'Why?' He saw comprehension at last in her eyes, followed quickly by anger. 'Do you think to tell me I should give Will and Olivia over to her?' She laughed, but it was an ugly, bitter sound. 'Never, not as long as I draw breath.'

'What reason could you possibly have…?' He paused. 'Oh. Unless…. Is she poverty-stricken as well?'

'Poverty-stricken?' she gasped with indignation, but then she flushed. 'No, she is comfortable enough.'

'Then your reason is?'

'She might have pounds and pence, my lord, but she also has all the warmth of a snake. She is cold and distant and de-manding. The children don't know her, nor is she truly inter-ested in them. What interests her is the money they might bring her way. What she hopes for is influence. Enough influ-ence over the children so that she might gain some control of Mervyn's shipping company and estate.'

'Is it so bad a trade? Let me play devil's advocate for the moment. What of nannies and governesses and tutors? Will could go to school, make friends of a similar age.' He wanted to touch her, hold her tight, force her to listen. Instead he gripped his hands tightly at his sides. 'He wouldn't have to fish for his supper.'

'He wouldn't have anyone to love him, either!'

Trey snorted. 'I assure you, many an English child has survived without love. It is practically an unwritten rule, is it not? It is the established custom among the wealthy to ignore their offspring until they are of age.'

'Just because it is done does not make it right. Yes, do look at the children of the aristocratic and the wealthy. How do they turn out? Selfish, for the most part, and lazy. They don't contribute anything to the world around them.'

They had been speaking in whispers, but her voice raised a notch as she grew more vehement. 'Yes, every child deserves security, but emotional security is just as important. We must feed their bodies, their minds and their souls as well. Then they can grow confident, trusting, ready to give back to the world they inhabit, rather than just taking.'

'But must it be you?' Trey asked. 'Are you the only one who can do this for those children?'

'No,' she said and now it was triumph ringing in her tone. '*Mervyn can.* He raised me with love and caring. They deserve no less. Do you understand at last why I cannot just abandon this search for him?'

'I do understand why you feel that way,' he huffed. 'But you must eventually face the facts. There is a very real possibility that Mervyn is dead and we will never know why or how.'

He turned and walked away a few steps in frustration. 'The more I hear, the more I cannot accept that you must sacrifice so much of yourself. I never said you must abandon the children. They deserve a happy home and the chance to realise their potential—but so do you. Will you be content dedicating yourself to their needs and ignoring your own?'

He could see in her stare that she was no closer to comprehending him. They came at this issue from absolute opposite ends of the spectrum. But then her head went up and he saw her eyes narrow in suspicion.

'Are we talking of my needs or yours, my lord?'

'Excuse me?'

'I'm beginning to suspect that it is your freedom you worry about.' She stepped closer and lowered her voice. 'Those children are a gift, not an obligation. Perhaps you are unable to see that. But then, not everyone is as eager to escape responsibility as you are.'

Her words stirred to life the embers of old wounds. 'Would you care to explain that statement?' he asked carefully.

She lifted her chin. 'You are an earl, a peer of the realm,' she said with a flourish of her hand. 'Surely you have lands, estates, a duty to the people who depend on you, and indeed to the laws and subjects of England.' She stepped closer still and glared directly into his face. 'When were last at your seat, my lord? Do you know the condition of your tenants? Are they thriving? Suffering? Have you once sat in your place in the House of Lords or concerned yourself with the difficulties facing this nation?'

Rage flickered along veins, fuelled by ancient hurts he'd thought long buried. He closed his eyes. Idiot. When would he learn? A pretty face, a sweet smile and he'd done what he'd known he should not. He'd got involved, offered opinions, took a step into the chaos that swirled around this slip of a woman.

Silent, lips braced against the torrent of angry words that threatened, he walked back to the stairs. Gesturing, he waited for her to proceed ahead of him.

She went, and kept quiet until they reached her room. There she turned to him, her back against the locked door. 'Don't worry, Treyford,' she said in a subdued voice. 'I will not hold you any further. You've more than fulfilled your promise to my brother, and you've been a tremendous help to me. I thank you.' She raised those incredible eyes to his and, like the first day he'd met her, he could see once more sorrow and pain reflected there. 'When we get back you must feel free to make plans to return to your work.'

Trey turned to go. He took a step towards the door of his adjoining room. Then he stopped. He shook his head. Why, with this woman, did he always act against his instincts? He turned back. Already she fumbled with her lock.

'Miss Latimer.'

Her furtive movements stopped, but she kept her face to the door.

'I have a fine and trustworthy man of business. He hires estate agents and caretakers and the myriad number of people required to look after my interests. They all fare far better under his kind and interested guidance than they would ever do with me.'

He breathed deep. 'I am a hard man. I admit it. Hell, most of the time I embrace it.' His sigh was long and heartfelt. 'Tonight, however, I find myself regretting it.'

She turned to face him, her expression blank.

'I hope you will believe me, Miss Latimer, when I tell you that tonight, for once in my life, I was not looking out for my own self-interest.' He raised a brow in self mockery. 'If I appear ignorant and bumbling, it's because it is what I am. I have no experience in caring for anything except my own sorry hide. I'm unsure how to share concern or offer advice.' He allowed the bitterness he felt to creep into his voice. 'And since I do it so ill, I don't plan to repeat the attempt. Please forgive me.'

He turned away. But he hadn't taken more than a step when she caught his hand, held it close, cradling it against the warmth of her bosom. He could feel the rapid beating of her heart; see the uncertainty in her face.

'I'm sorry,' she whispered. 'I don't know what it is. In your company I lose…something.' Her head tilted back and she stared upwards, as if searching for answers in the dark recesses of the corridor. 'I don't know why, I only know I am not myself when I am with you. Or maybe it is that I am more myself—and it frightens me.' She ducked her head back down, staring at their clasped hands for a moment, before raising her gaze finally to his. Behind the dark curtain of her lashes shone both remorse and something close to despair. 'I shudder to think of the things I have done since I've met you. I've shouted, lectured, practically blackmailed you into doing my bidding, and now I've attacked your character.'

Never in a thousand years would Trey dare tell her how similarly she affected him. He reached out and ran a finger along the exotic bones of her face. 'That's not all you've done,' he said roughly.

She put her hand up to his, encircled his wrist with a fragile grip, and leaned her soft cheek into his caress. 'No,' she whispered, the word thick with emotion, 'not all.'

Everything inside Trey screamed for him to drop his hand, back away and run. All the perils he'd faced in a long and adventurous life were as nothing compared to the danger represented by Miss Chione latimer.

Again, instinct failed him. His heart was pounding, his breath coming fast. He answered the mute appeal in her eyes by closing his own. He slipped his hand further, buried it in the ebony tangle of her hair and covered her mouth with his.

Fire. It was the answer to all of her uncertainties, the reason why her body inevitably betrayed her mind when Treyford was near.

Djinn were creatures of fire. As humans were created from earth and the angels of air, so *djinn* craved heat and warmth and flame. Something inside Treyford—his soul, perhaps—blazed with the heat of his passions: for life, for the past, for his work. But right now she knew that the highest flame inside of him burned for her.

It escalated, calling irresistibly to the *djinn* Chione had buried so long ago. And she answered. She remembered what he'd taught her earlier, slanted her mouth and returned his kiss, hot and demanding.

Foolish. Chione well knew the dangers of exposing herself, acknowledged the risk of giving in to such undisciplined passion. But all the gods help her, she just didn't care. Parting her lips, she invited him inside. The thrust of his tongue sent her need spiralling out of control. *Yes.* She was wild with wanting, fierce with it. She reached up, wrapped her arms around him, pulling him even harder against her. Extraordinary heat, exotic scent, the hard feel of his body pressing her against the door. Heaven.

He tore his mouth from hers and traced her jaw with his kiss. She arched into him as he seared the sensitive skin of her neck with his hot, seeking mouth, marking her as his. Chione shuddered. *God, yes*—she was his. The hidden part of her had always known it. The rest of her was swiftly reaching agreement.

His fingers were hard at work, frantically unfastening the many buttons of her pelisse. Desperate for his touch, Chione reached up to help. In a moment it was done, and his hands were inside, cradling her, caressing her, teasing her nipples into hard, eager peaks. Her breath exploded from her as he bent down and suckled her, right through the many thin layers of her gown and her undergarments. The heat, the wetness, the hard flick of his tongue, all of it combined to shoot molten rivulets of desire through her body, stealing her breath, weakening her knees.

He must have sensed her unsteadiness. He ran a caressing hand over her hips, and down her leg, lifting it gently until it was curved about his hip. He leaned his body into hers, pressing her into the door, lending her stability even as he rocked the hard length of his erection against her.

Chione moaned. The unfamiliar position opened her body

in the most intriguing way. She felt at once eager and excruciatingly vulnerable. But there was no turning back now. His hand was inching its way in tiny, teasing circles towards the most intimate part of her. She arched into him, bracing the other foot and settling her shoulders firmly against the hard support of the door behind her.

Without warning that support disappeared. Chione tumbled backwards into her own room as the door was snatched suddenly open from within. Too surprised even to cry out, she landed hard on her back.

A great whoosh of breath left her lungs. Aghast, she stared up, saw hands reaching for Trey, pulling him away before the door slammed home once more, shutting her away from him. She gasped, fighting for air.

Strong hands grasped her quickly from behind and crushed her back against a massive chest. One hand clamped firmly over her mouth, gagging her with the strong smell of garlic and tobacco. Panicked, she struggled for the room to breathe, for freedom. Her captor barely noticed. Just like that she was caught, without a struggle, without even a cry of alarm. If Chione hadn't been so frightened, she would have been disgusted.

Such was not the case on the other side of the door. She could hear grunts, a crash, then a repeated thudding sound, as if somebody's head was slamming repeatedly into a wall.

Her captor listened as well. He still held her fast with only one arm—the other he trailed over her breasts, down her belly. 'I am to bring you unharmed,' he rasped in her ear. 'Hassan has ordered it to be so. Disobedience is dangerous, but if you fight me, I will be happy to forget what I am told.'

He spoke with a heavy accent. Chione bucked away from his searching grasp, her mind racing.

'I am going to take my hand away. If you scream, I will enjoy making you stop.' He squeezed her even tighter for a moment before he eased his hand away. Then his hand gripped her wrist and cruelly twisted her arm up behind her back. 'Do not scream.'

She shook her head.

Something heavy hit the door with a great crash. A small, high window let in just enough moonlight for her to see the wood rattling on its hinges. The man leaned around Chione to take up a piece of rope. The move gave her a first look at him, but he wore both a turban and a cloth wrapped around his face.

As he released her arm a gasp of relief escaped her. Both her wrists, though, were caught tight in one of his massive hands. He turned her so that she faced him, still gripping her hard. 'Tonight the interfering Englishman dies.' She could hear the satisfaction in his voice. 'Nothing will save your lover now.'

Chione shook her head and strained away, a sudden idea growing. 'No,' she said. 'He is a demon—he cannot die!' She pulled away, not towards the door, but away from it, towards the back wall of the tiny room. 'Do not let him in here! He is an *ifrit*!'

He was startled enough to let her go. '*Ifrit?*' Then he gathered himself. 'Impossible! He is English. What do the *inglizi* know of the *ifrit*?'

Chione glanced fearfully at the door again. 'He knows the secrets of the ancients. Perhaps they have given him his powers.' She cowered into the corner. 'Do not let him in! He has the eye! You have angered him greatly. We will be dead in an instant.'

The doorknob rattled. The entire door shook again. 'Chione!' Her name rang out in a powerful bellow.

Her captor had forgotten her. All of his fearful attention was focused on the door. Chione grabbed the water pitcher. No— too light. As was the basin.

'*Ifrit* or not, he can be killed,' he muttered. With swift and deadly precision he moved to one side of the doorway, his sword out and gleaming in the low light. 'We will see how he likes the taste of my steel.'

With a tremendous crash the door fell in. Treyford strode over the wreckage. Chione screamed a warning. He jumped aside only just in time to avoid the heavy downward stroke of the sword. The blade did not rise again. Instead its owner followed it down, landing sprawled across the wooden door, pieces of the heavy porcelain chamber pot scattered around his head like a halo.

Chapter Ten

His chest heaving, Trey looked up from his fallen attacker and straight into Chione Latimer's distressed gaze. All the colour had drained from her golden complexion. Almost without thought he reached out a comforting arm to her.

She didn't respond. Eyes wide with horror, she was staring down at her handiwork. 'Is he…dead?'

Trey squatted next to the prostrate man. 'No. He'll be fine, except for one hell of a headache.' He rested an arm on his bent knee and shot her an amused glance. 'Prehistoric knives and chamber pots,' he said with a shake of his head. 'Remind me to stay in your good graces.'

Her shoulders sagged. Alarmed, Trey jumped up and enfolded her in his arms. 'My God, are you all right?'

She nodded weakly against his chest. 'Are you?' she asked faintly. 'I thought…I was afraid they had…'

'No,' he soothed. 'I'm fine.' From somewhere he dragged up a reassuring grin. 'Besides this fellow, there are two more outside. One is knocked out cold. The other was tossed down the stairs by a nice strapping lad who saw the fight, didn't like the odds and came to my aid. The rest of them fled once everyone began to stir.' He sighed. 'We'll have to come up with something better next time. Picking them off one by one is hardly effective.'

'Next time…' she began, but then she stopped. 'Wait! He said his orders came from Hassan. Do you know him?'

Perplexed, Trey shook his head. 'No. An enemy of your grandfather's, perhaps?' He looked down at the man sprawled on the floor. 'He's crafty, whoever he is. Do you suppose they followed us and Renhurst too?'

She stepped away and looked up at him again with frightened eyes. 'The boy—Cedric's nephew!'

For half a second, Trey's heart stopped. He stared at the crowd beginning to mill outside the door and shouted 'Cedric!'

'Here, sir!' the answering call came. 'Vandals!' Cedric's voice spat, growing closer. 'Thieves and rogues. Nothing to worry about now,' he blustered to the gathering people. 'The constable will deal with this lot. Tie 'em up good and tight, boys!'

'Cedric!' Trey called again.

'Yes, sir!' The crowd parted. 'Here I am.'

'Your boy, Cedric,' Trey said in a lower voice. 'Has he made it home?'

'Home safe, sir.' Trey breathed his relief and noticed Chione's matching sigh.

'And his packages are safe as well,' Cedric continued. 'All taken care of.'

'Thank you, Cedric,' Chione breathed. 'I could never have borne it, had anything happened to him.' She shuddered. 'And thank heavens you had the notion, Treyford, for him to take the artifacts and slip away before us.'

'Yes, well, I have a slippery mind,' he said wryly.

'Sir!' Cedric's barkeep was kneeling over the man Chione had struck. 'This one's starting to stir.' He grinned. 'Shall I give 'im another bash in the noggin?'

'Let's just get them to the constable, lads,' Cedric said.

'Heaven knows what he'll do with them,' Trey said. 'Find out what you can from them—but I doubt it will be much.' He paused, suddenly struck by a notion and spoke an Arabic phrase out loud. 'Chione, doesn't something in that mean gold?'

She thought a moment. 'Box of gold? No, I think golden box.' She looked his way with dawning horror. 'Do you mean that they knew of it?'

'Damn. It sounded so. Certainly I heard those words more than once.' He huffed in frustration. 'Either they heard all that we said or they know more than we do about this damned mystery.'

'But if they heard—they'll be after the journals. They'll head back to… Trey, the children!'

Bleakly, Trey turned back to the innkeeper. 'Cedric, rouse your stables. We'll need the coach. We'd best be off right away.'

Their need to travel quickly eliminated all but the most cursory conversation. Chione confessed to herself that this was a relief rather than a hardship. She needed time alone to think, to gather her wayward feelings into some semblance of order, and, most importantly, to pack away again the passionate aspect of her nature. The curious thing was that she didn't find herself trying very hard. At last she reached the conclusion that, for good or ill, Treyford had irrevocably awakened her unbridled half. Her sensible self very much feared that it would be for ill, but the *djinn* was out of the lamp now, and there was no forcing her back in.

Many times in the past her passions had manifested themselves negatively. Anger, jealousy, betrayal—Chione had sometimes frightened herself with the intensity of her feelings. Painful experience had taught her to resist the seductive pull of her fiery nature. It was nothing like that now. This time she had something truly pleasurable to focus on.

Scenery slipped by unnoticed and afternoon stretched into

evening as Chione's thoughts lingered on the Earl of Treyford. With flushed cheeks she relived the heat of his lips, the exquisite feel of his hands on her body. He'd touched her everywhere and it hadn't been enough. Even now she quivered as she remembered his fingers playing her like a harp, sending lush vibrations to her very core. He'd been at once firm and tender, and she had been nothing if not eager.

She forced herself to consider the wisdom of dwelling upon the sweetness of those forbidden moments, when she knew full well that hurt lurked just around the corner. Without a doubt Treyford would be leaving. Chione had enough experience with men of his character to know that he would be gone sooner rather than later. Hadn't she already thought that. Treyford was like the men in her family—exactly the sort of man she had pledged not to become involved with. Could she forsake her own vows and leave herself open to that pain again?

At last, as the light faded, the coach rolled to a stop. Chione and Jenny Ferguson had the chance to stretch their legs while the horses were changed. Treyford had pushed himself hard, driving for such a long stretch, and once they were ready to get under way again, positions were switched. The coachman climbed back on top. Jenny decided to brave the cold night air for a chance to keep him warm. Treyford, clearly exhausted, crawled into the coach and shot Chione a weary grin. 'We're near to Trusham, and making good time,' he'd said hoarsely. In mere moments, he'd been asleep.

Only Heaven knew how. Chione smiled at his unknowing form, curled up awkwardly on the opposite bench. They'd hit a particularly rough stretch of road and the jerking of the carriage was anything but comfortable. Treyford had his head propped in the corner, but with each new bump his head slipped lower, until finally his chin would hit his chest and he would startle, bouncing back upright to start the process over again.

Chione at last took pity on him. Timing her movements

with the jostling of the carriage, she slipped over to his bench, slid up next to him and eased his head over on to her shoulder. For a moment all was well. Then she encountered the same problem. Every bounce sent his head sliding down and towards her bosom. Fighting laughter, she gave up. She moved further away and gently settled his head comfortably in her lap.

Ah. The weight and heat of him felt good. She heaved a sigh, relishing the wide curve of his shoulder pressed against her hip. This was not fire, but warmth. It felt comfortable, intimate.

The rhythmic rise and fall of his chest soothed her, while at the same time the stir of his breath against her skirts excited her senses. Chione felt oddly suspended, caught in a moment out of time. Outside the chill wind blew and trouble awaited. But here existed peace and warmth. Sanctuary.

Without conscious thought her hand raised, her fingers hovering over the thick tangled length of Treyford's hair. How she longed to touch him. She wanted to run sensitive fingers over his ear, along the bristly line of his jaw. And more—she wished she could touch his soul, soothe his skittishness, ease away all of fate's tangles that lay between them.

Unbidden, her mother's voice echoed in her head.

'Stay free, if you can, of passion that exists without a deeper foundation.'

How well she remembered the love, the concern that had hidden behind the warning. Her father had been dead by then—murdered by a villain seeking knowledge of the Lost Jewel—and the frantic flight her mother had embarked upon with two children cut short. Eshe had been captured, bartered, sold, tossed around like meat at a butcher's stall. Chione and the toddling Richard had been left in the street like dogs.

But Chione was her mother's daughter. She'd heard where the men had said they meant to take Eshe, and doggedly she'd followed, her baby brother in tow. Her mind instinctively shied away from those horrid days. Mostly vague impressions remained—endless heat, pitiless eyes, the incessant crying of her hungry brother. Only two truly sharp memories remained to haunt her dreams; the first time she had stolen a loaf of bread to keep them from starving, and the kind smile of the farmer and his wife who had taken them in, fed them and given them transport to the small city of Asyut.

There she'd succeeded in tracking down her mother, ensconced in the household of a Frank, a foreigner. Eshe had cried over them and praised her daughter to the heavens for her strength. The Frank hadn't minded them, as long as they stayed out of his way, and they had all settled quickly into a routine. Chione had been happy to mind her brother all day, keeping mostly to the gardens, and she'd curled up contentedly with him on a pallet in the kitchen during the night. But the evenings belonged to the three of them, those precious hours between the foreigner's dinner and the time he took himself—and her mother—to his bed.

It was in the evenings that they talked, of common things, and of life, and of dreams. That night Eshe had been combing Chione's hair with long slow strokes when the sharp knock on the door and the perfunctory summons had come. Chione had taken the sleeping Richard into her arms and asked the question that had been haunting her.

'Does he hurt you, Mother?'

Her eyes had been cast down to the floor. She'd been afraid to see the truth of it in Eshe's eyes. But a calloused finger beneath her chin had forced her to lock gazes with her mother.

'I do not give him the power to hurt me, young one.'

Chione had not answered, only wrapped her baby brother tighter in her arms. Eshe had correctly interpreted the gesture.

'Do not confuse what he does to me with what I had with your father. Your father and I, we had a great love—the sort that poets sigh over and all the world aches for.'

Her tone had been fierce, but then her gaze had drifted away from Chione, concentrating on something that her daughter could not see.

'No, my dear one, this Frank does not hurt me, but neither does he move me. We feel nothing for each other.'

She'd grown silent for a moment and pensive.

'Perhaps that is the danger, though. Memories of your father—they fill my heart with joy. What this man does is empty, heartless. He does not harm me, but perhaps he does…bring me down, rip me from the heights I shared with your father.'

The impatient call had come again. Her mother had gone then to answer it, but turned back as she reached the door.

'You are strong, like me, little one. Some day you will also be a lovely young woman. I tell you now to stay strong, Chione. For my sake I hope you will remember that desire is nothing without finer feelings. Without love, it cannot lift you to the heavens.'

With Treyford Chione did indeed feel lifted to the heavens. What if he was the only one who could take her there? No other man had ever affected her so profoundly. Her eyes drifted closed. What would her mother think of a passion in which the deeper attachment was only one sided? No doubt she would scorn such a connection.

Chione sighed. She was less inclined to do so. What she felt for Treyford, she was beginning to realise, was true. But she must also face his fundamental truth. The earl was unable—or unwilling—to return such feelings.

She sighed again.

'You are not going to cry, are you?'

Though his voice was soft, Chione jumped. 'How long have you been awake?'

He shifted around until he could look her in the face, though he didn't lift his head from her lap. 'Since you moved over here.' His smile was tender.

'You're a rogue.' But she said it without heat. 'I'm sorry—you need your sleep. I only sought to help.'

'You did help. I think this has been better for me than sleep.' His gaze was smouldering, his tone concerned. He reached up and tucked a wayward lock behind her ear. 'What were you thinking of, that made you feel so sad?'

She flushed a little. 'My mother. I was remembering something she tried to teach me. Something I don't seem to have learned very well.'

The shadow of some strong emotion passed over his face. 'At least she made the attempt,' he said. 'That counts for something.' He twisted back around into his original position on her lap. 'You don't mind, do you?' he asked quietly. 'It's been a long time since anyone really touched me.'

'I don't mind,' she whispered. His words set off her longing once more, and the aching need to comfort him. But Chione knew that he would not welcome such emotions. She thought instead to lighten the atmosphere. 'I don't think I believe you in any case. Richard alluded to your many conquests in a few of his letters, you know. I confess, at the time I always wished he would include some of the details.'

'None of them were worth the ink,' he said shortly. 'Tell me, what was your mother like?'

She smiled. 'Amazing. She was incredibly alive. Vibrant with it. Perhaps you know what I mean? Richard was the same, living each moment to its fullest.'

'I do know. I think that is perhaps the first thing that drew me to Richard. He was the only partner I've ever worked with, you know.' He sounded pensive. 'The only person I could tolerate in such constant contact.'

'Eshe, my mother, was impatient with people as well. Did Richard tell you that she ran away from her family as a young girl?'

'No, he didn't.' He sounded intrigued. 'That's most unusual for an Egyptian girl, is it not? Do you know why she left them?'

'All she would ever say was that they refused to live in the world. She was determined to learn more of it before she settled down to marriage and family.' Chione stopped, unwilling to follow the thought any further.

The silence stretched out for long moments. A comfortable, companionable silence. Chione jumped a little when he broke it.

'And what was it that had you so melancholy? What was it that your mother tried to teach you, and failed?'

She realised that when he spoke, she could feel it. And somehow it was the most intimate thing she'd ever experienced. Vibrations travelled from him directly to her thigh and further, unsettling her almost as much as the question itself.

She swallowed. 'So many things. She was a very wise woman.'

'As is her daughter.'

Chione knew he meant it. There was a strange sort of intimacy to this position—bodies touching, but unable to read each other's expression. Without facial cues Chione had to rely on his tone and the total relaxation of his body against hers. She sensed how rare this was for him. It was without a doubt a first for her. It was also freeing, as if she could say things she might otherwise not, forge ahead with questions that any other time she would have hesitated to ask.

'And your family?' she asked. 'Did your mother labour as fruitlessly as mine—trying to impart the mysteries of life?'

He tensed, and she could sense the struggle he tried to hide. She kept quiet and after a moment he continued.

'Unfortunately, my mother was not as wise as yours.' He paused. 'Wisdom has never been counted a fashionable accomplishment, you understand.'

'Was she a great society lady, then?'

'For a number of years, yes.' He shifted a bit, but didn't turn. 'Are you not familiar with the Stafford family scandal?'

'No. Indeed, I didn't know there was one. I do apologise.'

'I thought everyone in England knew of it.' His tone was bitter.

Perhaps that explained his distaste for his homeland. 'I am a merchant's daughter, living in the wilds of Devonshire. Society's gossip is nothing to me.'

'It is a sordid little tale, in any case.'

A lock of his dark hair had snagged on a button of her pelisse. Gently she untangled it. Unable to resist any longer, she gave in to the intimate atmosphere and her own temptation. Blissfully she dug her fingers in and chased the highlights through the thick layers that drifted across her lap.

Treyford let out a sigh of intense pleasure and went boneless against her. For several long minutes silence reigned as she indulged them both.

'She used to do that, you know. I always loved it.' His voice hummed against her, low and reflective.

'Before she went down to dinner, or out for the evening, my nurse would take me down to her. She was always so beautiful, in her rich gowns and sparkling jewels. She would smile at me, hold me close a moment and stroke my hair. I always thought she smelled like an angel.' His words sounded meditative. 'She was happier, then, when I was very young.'

'What changed?' Chione asked in a near whisper.

'Everything. My parents had had a volatile courtship, a grand passion. My mother had been meant to marry another. She was not officially betrothed, but the understanding existed. But then she met my father. They fell instantly in love, and they were not discreet. Her father ended up having to pay reparation to the other man, but I suppose he thought nabbing an earl for a son-in-law was well worth it.'

He sighed. 'I don't know what happened. I was young. One minute I lived in a happy home, the next I did not.'

'How sad.'

'Yes, it was sad, and somehow…frightening. I don't recall

specifics, you know. It is all jumbled into an image of horrendous accusations, loud voices, scurrying servants and endless sobbing.'

His voice trailed away and Chione thought he had finished, but in a moment he began to speak again. A chill went down her spine as she realised how his voice had changed. He sounded hollow, detached, as if he spoke of something that had happened to someone else.

'The last fight was the worst. They caught me unaware. I had brought some of my painted soldiers downstairs to the drawing room, hoping my mother would come in eventually. I remember the glorious battle I had set up. The French were arrayed on the bench by the pianoforte, the English, of course, had the high ground on top of the keys. Victory for our boys was imminent when at last my mother did come in.'

It was several long moments before he went on. 'She didn't see me through her tears. She went to the sofa in the far corner, almost as if she were hiding. I understood why a moment later. My father followed her into the house. He passed the drawing room by at first and went upstairs. But soon he was calling her, screaming her name. So angry—I had never seen him in such a rage. I hid beneath the pianoforte while they argued. It was…ugly. I huddled there, feeling as if each vicious word tore another piece of my world away.'

The image horrified Chione because she knew precisely how it felt. How painful it was to have security and comfort ripped away. How hurt and anger sometimes rushed in to fill the empty spaces of your heart and left you for ever changed. Her own heart ached for that devastated little boy and for the bitter, wary man in her lap.

'I found out later just why he was so angry. My mother had taken up with my uncle—his own brother.' His shoulders hunched a little, the bones digging into her thigh. 'I imagine you know what a travesty that is considered by the English.'

Chione did know. She could imagine the resulting scandal-broth.

His chest rose and fell on a massive sigh. 'My mother packed her things. She came in for moment to kiss me goodbye. She said she would send for me, and then she was gone. I never saw her again.'

Sadly, Chione thought that the lessons Treyford's mother had taught him were not the ones she might have wished.

'My father died a few weeks later. An accident,' he said bitterly. 'I was left to the care of my uncle—the same uncle who had torn them finally apart.'

His voice trailed off. Chione sensed there was more to the story—but she doubted she would ever hear it. She closed her eyes and let her head fall back. Even this little bit of information illuminated much about Treyford's character. He manipulated his life so that he would never again be that vulnerable little boy. Who better to sympathise with that than her?

It became suddenly easier to understand his moods and his restlessness. Incredibly, it was largely her doing. She had him well and truly trapped and he retreated emotionally because he could not do it physically.

His breathing had deepened, the rise and fall beneath her hands had become more rhythmic. Chione thought he had finally fallen asleep. In a burst of clarity she realised how difficult it had been for him to reveal so much about himself. It touched her, but it also reminded her of the bitter truth. Treyford might give in to a moment's passion, but that was likely all he could ever give.

He wanted her; that she could not question. But Chione doubted whether he could bring himself to pursue her—not without encouragement. By her reckoning, this left the ball firmly in her court, but also left her to answer one burning question. Could she accept his desire knowing that nothing more would follow?

Chione rather thought she could. Her heart rate ratcheted at the thought of finishing what they had started. Yes, it was unconventional, but truly, it was almost a relief to have no expectations beyond the physical. Treyford was not likely to ask awkward questions. A man with secrets of his own; he was unlikely to probe hers. It would be liberating, really. She would be free to relax as never before. No need to reveal the ugliness of the past, no need to sustain her consuming role, no need to feel guilty about living a lie. She could unleash her passionate nature with impunity. Treyford would not be around long enough to be harmed by it.

She rested her gaze tenderly on the tousled head in her lap, felt the tension in the shoulder her hand rested on, and she knew. For the first time she would forsake Eshe's sage advice. She would savour what the fates allowed her. Perhaps it would turn out to be nothing more than the desire Treyford poured over her with his touch. For certain it would be short lived. But she was going to reach out and take whatever he felt he could offer. It might not be the grand romance that her parents had, but, like her mother, she would have memories for the cold and lonely times ahead.

Trey had drifted off under the ministrations of Chione's clever fingers. He awoke some time later to find her gone back over to the other bench, Ferguson's niece huddled there with her, and the carriage stopped for another change of horses.

Purposefully not meeting Chione's eye, he scrambled out of the carriage, circled around the back, then stood there in the cold morning air, scrubbing his hands over his face and cursing himself for a fool.

He winced when the driver came up from behind and gave him a friendly slap on the back. 'Sleep tight, my lord?' he asked with a wink. 'Or did ye take advantage of the dark as I did with wee Jenny?'

'Should have done,' muttered Trey.

But the driver looked suddenly chagrined. 'My apologies, sir. I didn't mean no disrespect to Miss Chione.' He straightened. 'Nor to my Jenny. T'was naught but a kiss or two we shared, and my intents is honourable.' He grinned. 'Mrs F. would be having my hide, otherwise. And 'tis clear that neither of them is *that* sort o' girl, iff'n ye knows what I mean.' He ended with a broad grin and sauntered off to check the traces.

Trey watched the man go and envied him his certainty. The only thing Trey could be certain of was his own idiocy. And perhaps of the fact that somewhere buried under Chione Latimer's calm and competent exterior, there did lurk *that* sort of girl. Exactly the sort of girl to set his blood afire and make him forget all the principles that had governed all of his adult, blessedly unfettered life.

After a nod from the driver he climbed up on to the box, took up the ribbons and eased the fresh horses from the crowded inn courtyard. Once they had left the town behind he let them go and found his thoughts straying right back where they didn't belong: on the ever-more-prickly problem of Chione Latimer.

Yes, he'd long suspected that a well of passion existed underneath her tranquil exterior. He'd enjoyed teasing her occasionally, pricking her temper, rousing her to a spirited debate. But, good God, he'd never imagined she might gift him with such an uninhibited response, and he'd been shocked at the tower of answering passion her hunger had unleashed in him. He'd sprouted a hammer between his legs, iron hard and clamoring for her grip. Hell, he'd been so lost that he'd almost taken her right there against the door.

Unintentionally, his hands tightened on the ribbons. One of the horses threw up his head in protest and Trey forced himself to ease up. Madness. Outright idiocy. What else could one call it? Ravaging an innocent girl on English soil ranked right up there with the stupidest and most perilous things he'd ever done. And not just any girl, but one caught up in exactly the sort of tangled web of relationships that he abhorred.

By God, he should be grateful that those thugs had been lying in wait. Had it been Cedric who interrupted them, it would be Trey stuck in a trap of his own making instead of three stubbornly mute bandits mouldering in the constable's strong room.

And then, last night he'd compounded the problem, exceeding even his own capacity for stupidity. Good God, he hadn't mentioned his mother to a living person in nearly twenty years. The ease he felt with Chione, the comfort he took in her touch, her conversation—it grew ever more addictive. And dangerous.

Marriage. It was what she probably contemplated, what he might have been forced to—what, if he had any honour at all, he should consider even now. He shuddered. Only his high regard for her allowed him to even entertain such a thought.

Such a marriage could never be anything but a trap. For her as well as him. Trey was not capable of giving the sort of intimacy she would expect, nor could he bear to be stuck in any one place for long. England would be the death of him in mere months. Neither could he ask a well-bred girl like Chione Latimer to give up her family, or subject her to the hardships of his itinerant lifestyle.

No—a union would be misery for one of them at the start and a disaster for them both before long. How could it not be, when resentment and petty jealousies came on the heels of the best alliances? How much worse would it be for a pair so mismatched? Trey was not eager to find out. He'd had a lucky escape. He would make the most of it and get away while the exit still lay clear.

Chapter Eleven

The memory of the rest of that journey would not be one Chione cherished. Frightful scenes drifted through her mind's eye: the house looted or burned, the children held hostage. Her nerves were in a ragged state when at last they pulled up the drive to stop in front of the house. Eagerly, Chione peered through the open window and breathed a heavy sigh of relief. Everything looked to be in order from the outside.

But then the carriage door opened to a familiar leering grin instead of to Eli's welcoming smile and Chione's heart dropped to the gravel below.

'Higgins, you are here,' she said stupidly. Mrs Stockton's impertinent footman. But if he were here, then that meant…

'Aye, miss, but not for long.' Only slightly lower he muttered, 'With any luck.'

Chione ignored the impertinence. The cloying taste of dread lay heavy in her mouth as she hurried into the house. She didn't even wait to speak to Treyford. A threat to her family had indeed manifested itself, but it had come from an entirely unexpected source.

Inside all lay quiet. The downstairs rang empty and deserted. Even the kitchen was vacant. Panic rose as she raced up the stairs to the schoolroom. Afraid of what she would *not* find, she eased open the door.

They were there. Chione sagged in relief to see Mrs Ferguson grouped at the window with Olivia and Will. Then her brain began to function again and she took in the reality of the little tableau.

The housekeeper held a bowl and a rag. She sat next to the boy on the sofa, bathing the reddened wheals that crossed his thin shoulders. Will's face was turned away from her. Next to him, on the floor, sat Olivia. She stroked his hand, a look of profound sorrow on her little face.

A whisper of a sound—some dreadful cross between fury and sorrow and regret—escaped her. Olivia's sharp ears caught it. At once her head came up and her eyes lit with joy.

'Shone!' she shouted. In an instant she had flown across the room and flung herself into Chione's arms. 'Shone! A bad lady came! She hurt Will.'

Will's head had whipped around. He sat up, manfully fighting back tears. 'It's Grandmama, Chione,' he said thickly. 'She arrived the day after you left.'

Clutching Olivia close, Chione quickly crossed the room and enveloped the boy in a careful embrace. Swallowing heavily, she asked, 'What happened, Will?'

He couldn't answer. He buried his face in her gown and shook with silent sobs.

Mrs Ferguson answered for him, the thunderous look on her face growing even darker. 'She accused him of shirking his studies,' she spat.

'I didn't!' Will erupted with red-faced, boyish indignation. 'I only went to help Eli in the kitchen gardens. I saw him struggling with the seedlings from my window.'

'She did *this*,' Chione said in a dangerous voice, 'because you helped in the garden?'

'No—she called him in for a lecture when she saw him out

there,' the housekeeper said. 'Said he needed to learn what is suitable for a boy of his station.'

'A boy of my *fortune*—that's what she said.' Chione had never heard so scathing a tone from her dear Will. He'd lost his innocence, his precious faith in the world, and she ached with guilt even as she mourned its loss.

He looked pleadingly at her now. 'She said that Papa is dead, and that I must learn to act as befits his heir. I told her he's not dead! He's missing—but he'll come back! She said I was insolent and had to learn not to talk disrespectfully to my elders.'

'And she struck you?'

'No,' interjected Mrs Ferguson. 'She had her woman do it.' She shook her fist. 'Aswan put a stop to it, but I swear—t'ain't finished. That one will soon know what comes from beating an innocent child! I'll break her fine, haughty nose for her, see if I don't!'

Will leaned back into Chione's embrace. Searchingly, he looked into her face. 'He'll be back, won't he, Chione? Papa's coming back, isn't he?'

'I pray so, Will.'

'The bad lady locked Livvie,' Olivia piped up. Her tone was proud.

Chione stroked her hair. 'Locked you, my darling?'

'Had a right fit about little Miss's wanderin',' Mrs Ferguson said darkly. 'Said she was too young to be outta the nursery. Locked her in, and with no nurse!'

'I can well imagine the state of the nursery.' Chione tried to summon a smile, but it wouldn't come.

'She's dismissed Eli, Chione!' Will said, still distraught. 'And she tied Morty up in the stables.'

'Has she, then?' Chione could hear the danger in her own voice. 'Well!' she said. She kissed both children and stood. 'I think it is time I greeted our guest.'

'What will ye do?' the housekeeper asked.

'How many times has the old woman told me I was no better than a spiteful stray cat? Now I have it in mind to show her my teeth.'

'Chione, dear! Do sit down. How glad I am to see you back.'

Chione had found Mrs Stockton in the suite of rooms that Mervyn had shared with his second wife—Mrs. Stockton's daughter, Marie. She'd obviously made herself at home. Ribbons, feathers and something that looked like cattails covered the table in front of her and the floor close by.

'I think I shall stand, Mrs Stockton.'

The woman had aged in the years since Chione had last seen her. Always slender, she looked painfully thin now, almost skeletal, with bones protruding through fine skin. She shrugged one prominent shoulder now. 'You will suit yourself.' She held up the bonnet she was trimming. 'How do you like it?' She sighed in satisfaction. 'I do believe I could have made a smashing milliner, had Mr Stockton not snatched me up to make me his bride.'

Chione did not reply and the other woman looked up at her. The chiselled lines of her face had deepened, but the dark eyes burned just as intently.

'Oh, do sit,' she said, 'otherwise I shall have a crook in my neck.' She sighed deeply and frowned, deepening the grooves that lined her mouth. 'There's no use ringing for tea, not in this house, but *we* can at least be civilised. I don't mean to complain the minute you return—but your servants! Such a stubborn, prideful lot. Four days I've been here and not a word would they speak of where you'd gone or when you'd be back.'

'Why are you here, Mrs Stockton?'

She smiled, but the expression was a stark contrast to the cold glitter in her eye. 'My dear Orville insisted!' she said with a wave of her hand. 'My son is technically head of the family now, Chione.'

'Perhaps he is head of your family, ma'am,' Chione retorted. 'He has nothing to do with mine.'

'You know he holds your interests close to his heart, my dear. And of course he wished to hear of his dear sister's children. He thought that now you've had a taste of dealing with all of this on your own, you would be willing to accept a little help.'

She set down the bonnet and sat back in her chair. 'Orville is quite the fashionable young man now, Chione. Did you know that his closest friend is the son of a baronet?'

'No, I did not.' Chione's tone conveyed how little she cared.

Mrs Stockton narrowed her gaze. 'He could have his pick of any number of *ton*nish young ladies, you know. But he thinks only of you.' She leaned forward. 'My dear, he is ready to share your burdens.'

'Thank you, but I can manage my burdens on my own. You may wish to write and tell him I said so before you begin to pack your things.'

The woman stood. 'I should have known better than to expect good manners from you.'

'Yes, you should have, when you barge in where you know you are not welcome.' Chione raised her chin. 'What claim do you have on manners? Angling for an invitation is not the same as receiving one.'

'You left me no choice. A good thing it is, too, that I did not wait. For what do I find but you gone—who knows where!— and my grandchildren left in the care of servants...' she lowered her voice to a malicious whisper '...and *heathens*!'

'Will and Olivia were well looked after by people who genuinely care for them. I understand this is a difficult concept for you to comprehend.' Chione allowed some of the spite she felt to leak into her words. 'In addition, our friend Mr Drake agreed to look in on them every day during my *short* trip.'

'That jumped-up innkeeper? I sent him on his way quick

enough.' She folded her arms and stared down her long nose at Chione. 'Have you no idea what sort of acquaintance is suitable for these children? They have a place in this world and it is time that they learned it.'

Chione snorted, a distinctly unladylike sound. 'Perhaps a viscount will be considered suitable, ma'am? Lord Renhurst has been close to our family for years. He also pledged to keep watch on the children if he returned from his business before me.'

'Yes, yes, he was here,' Mrs. Stockton said dismissively. 'I received him civilly enough, but it quickly became clear that, though his title is respectable, he is not the sort that will do us any good. He speaks more like a farmer than a man of society and influence.'

She huffed her exasperation. 'Listen well, girl. Mervyn Latimer robbed me of my chance when he stole my beautiful girl away. But he's gone now, and I've heard how my grandchildren have been forced to live.'

Chione bit back her anger. 'We have done well enough.'

'Ridiculous!' the old lady spat. 'Look at this place!' She gestured about her. 'But then I shouldn't have expected you to comprehend me.' She raised a superior brow. 'Even a dusty, deserted house and a diet of porridge is a step up for you, isn't it?

Chione cringed.

'Will should be in school by now,' the old woman intoned, 'keeping the sort of company that will do him good later in life. Just look what Oxford did for Beau Brummel, or look what Joseph Banks did with his father's money and a good education!'

She turned her back on Chione and strolled back to her place at the table. Picking up the unfinished bonnet, she said, 'Things are changing. Boundaries are not what they used to be. Will some day will be head of an immense shipping company, but he could also be so much more. The boy has wealth, and good looks. All he needs are connections.' She tossed her head proudly. 'One of my own dear friends just happens to know a member of the board of admissions at Cambridge. Think of it, Chione. There is no telling how far he could go.'

'With you trailing right along in his footsteps, no doubt.' Chione could not hide her disgust for the woman and her cease-less ambitions. 'I am sorry that your plans for Marie were thwarted, sorry that Mervyn Latimer was not high enough on the social scale to satisfy you. But those two loved each other. They were happy.' Her shoulders slumped in defeat and she turned away. 'I am sorry that was never enough for you.' She took several steps towards the door before turning back with a hardened gaze. 'Just pack your things and go. I will not have you using these children for your own gain.'

'Hold on a moment.' Mrs Stockton's mollifying tone had vanished. Now her voice rang with command. 'I am not finished with you, young lady.'

'I am finished,' Chione threw over her shoulder.

'Perhaps you will be, before I am through.' The bitter old woman pressed her lips tight in irritation. 'Do you think I shall sit back and let you decide the fate of my grandchildren?'

'It is what you have always done before,' Chione replied flippantly.

'I haven't wasted my time alone in your house, Chione,' Mrs Stockton said, gloating. 'You will accept Orville's suit and you will bow to my wishes concerning Will, or I will expose you.'

Incredulous, Chione turned. '*Expose* me?' The worst of her secrets were buried deep. The chances of them being unearthed now were highly unlikely. But an ominously cold spot of fear rolled down her spine and made her stop.

'That is what I said.' Mrs Stockton crossed to a delicate lady's desk near the window and withdrew a stack of papers from a drawer. Crossing back, she flung them triumphantly on the worktable, heedless of the fripperies underneath. 'You will do as I say or I will tell the world that it is *you* writing these vulgar little serial stories!'

The small knot of fear inside of her relaxed. 'Will you?' The corner of Chione's mouth turned up.

'Yes, I will! What do you think will happen when your readers discover it is a *girl* stuck in the back of beyond penning their sensational tales?'

'Well, I imagine it might cause quite a stir.' Chione shrugged. 'One might even call it a scandal.' She paused and tapped her teeth with a finger. 'I should think that everyone who has never read one of my stories will suddenly want to. My readership will double, even triple, perhaps. My publisher will renew my contract. I'll receive more money, and, if I'm lucky, perhaps a bit of acclaim.'

She narrowed her eyes and took a menacing step towards the evil old woman. 'Then I predict I will feel an urge to stretch my talents. I think I shall wish to pen an article for the society pages.'

Chione raised her brows in question. 'What do you think your lofty friends would say once they heard of your father's wig shop, Mrs Stockton? What will they think of a merchant's wife's plans to lift herself as far and as fast as she can? Will they shake their heads at a woman who goes where she is not invited, stays when the mistress of the house is not at home, disparages her acquaintances, and dismisses her servants? Will they offer the cut direct to the woman who locks a little girl alone in a room and has a young boy beaten on the flimsiest of excuses?' Almost casually she reached out and picked up the sheaf of papers. 'Shall we find out?'

Her opponent was white-faced, but far from beaten. 'How dare you threaten me, you insolent little guttersnipe? My father might have been a wigmaker, but he was a loyal, solid Englishman. We cannot say the same of your dark-skinned heathen mother, can we, my dear?' She crossed over to the door connecting to the bedchamber and opened it. 'Reynolds,' she called, and her sturdy dresser came into the room. 'Go out and call for Higgins. I have put up with this chit for quite long enough. The two of you will take her up to one of the servants' rooms in the attics and lock her there.' She sneered at Chione. 'The tides have turned, young lady. You will do as I say or I will leave you locked up there until you agree. If that fails, then I shall lock Higgins in with you for a day or two, and then we shall see what becomes of your high-and-mighty airs.'

She laughed at the shock that Chione knew showed in her face. 'It is over. Who shall come to your aid? Your house-keeper?' Her smile broadened.

'I shall,' came a deep, reassuring rumble from somewhere behind her.

There had never been any real chance of the old woman suc-ceeding in her threats. Chione knew that. Yet she also couldn't deny the nearly overwhelming relief that flooded her at the sound of that voice. Trembling a little, Chione turned to see Treyford approaching. He took her arm in a steadying grip and together they turned to face the surprised Mrs Stockton.

'Who are you?' the woman demanded.

'I am a witness to your failings, Mrs Stockton,' he answered easily. 'I suggest you follow the lady's advice and pack your things.'

'Chione,' the old witch said imperiously, 'I demand to know who this man *is*!'

Chione had to clear her throat. 'He is a colleague of Richard's—' she began.

'I am a friend of Miss Latimer's,' Treyford interrupted. 'One of many who might have thwarted your scheming, I might add.' He eyed Mrs Stockton with distaste. 'But since you seem to place a value upon these things…' He drew himself up, his face like thunder. A little flutter went through her as the sheer size and strength of him struck Chione anew. 'I am the Earl of Treyford, madam.'

The older woman flinched and abruptly sat back down.

'And now I shall have a turn at making demands,' he said in a dangerously low voice. 'I demand that you gather up your possessions and your damned impudent servants and be out of this house within the hour. I demand that you set your scheming mind permanently away from this woman and her charges.' He drew a hand across his mouth as if wiping away a bad taste. 'By God, but you make me sick. What right do you think you have to come into this house, making threats and doing harm to those two innocent children?'

'What right?' she answered weakly. Then she straightened her spine. 'I have a blood right! I am the grandmother of those children.'

'A grandmother who hasn't seen the boy in years? Who by all accounts has never before laid eyes on the girl?' Treyford scoffed. 'I should think you have waived any rights you might once have had.'

The woman's servant stepped forward and whispered something fervently in her ear.

'What?' Mrs Stockton's eyes widened, first in horror, then in sudden delight. Chione saw it and a foreboding chill grew in her breast.

'Yes, now I recall it,' the old woman cackled. She stared intently at Treyford a moment, then her expression turned to one of scorn. 'Well, I find I do not care an iota what you think, my lord. I cannot believe I did not make the connection right away. Treyford! A name that lives in infamy. The original scandal was a disgrace, of course. But you have only added to it, have you not? Rapscallion! Rake! Wanderer! Adventurer!' She turned a sneering expression on Chione. 'Exactly the sort I would expect you to take up with.'

She stopped with a gasp and an unholy glee dawned in her

eye. 'Is *this* who you have been gallivanting about the country-side with? Oh, good heavens, but you could not have gifted me with anything more perfect! And to think that I meant to sacrifice my Orville…' She breathed deep and a small, triumphant smile played about her lips. 'But now there is no need! You've ruined yourself with this rakehell!'

But Chione had heard enough. She was trembling in fury. 'Stop right there! I will have no more of you or your insults. Get out of this house. Now!'

The hag laughed in triumph. 'Gladly! And I will go straight to the nearest magistrate.' She gestured to her maidservant and sauntered to the connecting door. 'Those children will be mine before the day is out!'

Chapter Twelve

Trey watched the door close on the scheming old hypocrite before he glanced down at Chione. Startled, he reached and took her hand. 'Chione?'

She was no longer trembling. Instead she stood, pale and unnaturally still. 'Chione, are you all right?'

She breathed deep and held it a long moment.

'Yes,' she said, turning to go. Outside the doorway she braced a hand on the wall. Following, Trey could see that her gaze was unfocused.

'Chione?' he asked again.

She looked at him. 'I thought about what you said, Treyford, long and hard. I considered the possibility that you were right, and Mervyn is gone.' Her breath hitched, but it was not quite a sob. 'And still I knew we had to continue. Much as I hated the thought of chasing after the treasure, I knew we were doing the right thing. Even if we found the worst, at least the children and I would know. We could grieve and move on—without being caught up in an endless cycle of hope and despair.'

Trey winced. Those troubled eyes—why did they always stab him to the quick? A single tear spilled over her lovely face and Trey shifted restlessly on his feet.

'I convinced myself—I was secure in the knowledge that we've been pursuing the right course, the only course. And I was wrong! I've accomplished the very thing I've been fighting all along!'

'It will be fine, Chione,' Trey soothed. 'I'm sorry I ever caused you to doubt yourself. Now that I've met the woman, I'm sorry I ever brought her up. We won't let her take the children.' He frowned. 'Not after what I heard today.'

'I never even stopped to consider that she might use such a thing against me, or ever even know we'd gone. And she doesn't even know the worst of it! What if she discovers the rest?' A note of hysteria crept into her voice. 'I've lost them, Treyford! She'll take them and it is all my fault!'

She turned on him with surprising swiftness. 'And it's your fault, too! You and Mervyn and Richard, and even my father! All the men in my life who talk of far-off lands, exotic and mysterious, when all along the true appeal is just that it is far away!' She gripped his arm with surprising strength. 'Well, I've had enough! You've all swept me into this nonsense and look what has happened! I love those children, Treyford. I can't bear to lose them!'

Trey had seen Chione face hardship and danger without a flinch. She'd faced this entire ordeal with scarcely a tear. Now, for the first time, he saw her control snap. Terror washed over her in an almost visible wave. Her body convulsed, her fingers digging tighter into the muscle of his arm before slipping away. Trey watched, helpless, horrified, as she sank, sobbing, on to the floor.

Despising his own weakness, he stood frozen a long moment. He couldn't think past the terrifying sound of her grief. Finally he shook himself free of inertia, reached down and scooped her up. Cradling her shuddering form close, he strode down the hall. 'Mrs Ferguson!' he called.

No answer. He called again, pacing up and down. He had no idea where to take Chione and she was in no condition to tell him. Still awash in tears, she had curled herself into his embrace, a pitifully small, heartbreakingly despondent bundle in his arms. Finally he went to the stairwell, took a deep breath and again called the housekeeper's name.

As the last echo faded there came the sound of a door slamming on the next floor up.

'Quite the pair o' lungs on ye, haven't ye?' he heard her call back. The housekeeper reached the landing above and poked her head over the rail. She caught sight of Chione and gasped. 'What did the wicked auld baggage do to her?' She beckoned. 'Quick, before the bairns see her.'

Trey was already walking up the stairs. 'She's threatening to take the children,' was all he had to say. 'The local magistrate, who is it?' he asked.

Her face grew even graver. She held Chione's door wide to allow him to enter with his burden. ''Tis Lord Renhurst…' she paused, then added significantly, 'but ye canna count on him to side with Chione. He was more than a bit liverish when he got back, and talking of finally doing his duty.'

He laid Chione tenderly on the bed. She turned away, still curled into a ball. Trey sighed. Just when were they going to get a bit of luck to go their way in this mess? By his calculations they were long overdue. 'Where the hell is Aswan?' he asked the housekeeper.

Perching herself on the bed next to Chione, she shrugged. 'Haven't the faintest. That one stays gone for hours, then pops up where there was nobody a moment before.' Her thick fingers were running tenderly through Chione's hair.

'If you see him, tell him not to disappear again. I have need of him.'

He turned to go, but she stayed him with a calloused hand on his arm. 'What will ye do?'

Trey knew what he wanted to do. He wanted to run, as far and as fast as he could.

'I don't know,' he answered and turned away.

How had he got here? To a place where people looked to him for answers, expected him to right the wrongs in their lives? This was exactly why he had *left* England.

Viciously he kicked the front door open and headed for the stables. It was too late for him to run. He was embroiled, entangled. Damn Richard for sending him right back where he never wished to be.

The doors of Renhurst's impressive home were opened by the butler and Trey was escorted to Renhurst's spacious study. The older gentleman stood braced behind his desk, a frown upon his face and his arm done up an elegant black silk sling.

'Treyford,' he said without a smile. He did not come out from behind the desk, instead indicating that Trey take the seat across from him. It was at that moment that Trey truly began to worry.

'Renhurst,' he said, with a nod in greeting. 'I must assume that you met up with our miscreants as well? Is it serious?'

'No, damn you, it's not my arm that's serious.'

'What happened?' Trey asked carefully.

'The bastards made their move in Chudleigh. I was there waiting for you, and wondering just what was taking you so cursed long.' Renhurst frowned and took his seat. 'Woke up in the dead of night to find one of the devils searching my bags. Picked him off with my pistol, but was overrun by a regular swarm of them. Good God, what a mêlée! My groom knocked a couple out and your hired man sunk his knife in one. Then the inn roused and they retreated. Took their wounded with them, but left us the gun-shot one. Had to pay to have him buried outside the churchyard.'

'We had nearly the same sort of trouble,' Trey said, sinking into his chair.

'And Chione? Is she well?' the viscount asked sharply.

'Yes, of course, she is fine.' He quickly outlined all that had happened.

When he had finished, Renhurst leaned forward in his chair. 'And is that *all* that occurred?'

Trey stared. 'Of course.'

The viscount sat back. 'Because I tell you, Lord Treyford, that I was not pleased to receive your message and learn that the two of you would not be meeting me as planned. I was even less pleased to hear that the pair of you would be journeying in another direction altogether. Alone.'

Trey straightened and glared at the man. 'We were not alone. Just what is it that you are insinuating, Renhurst?'

'I'm insinuating nothing. I am telling you outright that I am as angry as a wet hen.' He sank back into his seat and cradled his arm. 'Lord, I am too old for this. What was I thinking, letting the pair of you embroil me in such a mess? Clearly this is more serious than we have believed.'

'It is serious,' Trey agreed, 'but not insurmountable. And we've other trouble that must be dealt with first. The Stockton woman is running mad in Chione's home. We've got to get rid of her.'

'Yes, I am aware. It's all part and parcel of the entire foolish situation.' He shook his head. 'Clearly I have been remiss in my duty. I've let Chione's pretty ways—and my own foolish hope that Mervyn might just show up—sway me.' He glared at Trey. 'Well, that's done now. One way or the other, I mean to see the girl settled.'

Before Trey could ask just what he meant, a sudden commotion in the hall outside distracted them both.

'Don't be ridiculous, you oaf, of course he will see me.'

With a sinking feeling, Trey recognised the querulous voice.

Mrs Stockton's slight form appeared in the doorway. She carried a satchel under one arm. When she saw Treyford she stopped dead, causing the butler to nearly run her over. Then she looked to Renhurst. 'I will have my way, my lord, or I swear I will take this all the way to Chancery Court.'

'Oh, do come in, Mrs Stockton,' Renhurst growled. 'I've already been looking into this matter. Chancery Court *should* take up this sort of thing, but since Mervyn has not been declared dead and the children are neither orphans nor wards, it falls into my jurisdiction—and I swear by all that's holy, I'll have it ended today.'

'It is your duty to give me those children, Lord Renhurst.' The woman minced into the room, moved the other chair at the desk as far away from Trey as possible and sat, her bag at her feet.

Renhurst cleared his throat. 'Now then—' he began.

'Hold a moment, my lord.' Trey stopped him. 'You need to send for Chione. She has a right to be here.'

'What the girl has,' Mrs Stockton interjected, 'are my grand-children. And I want them.'

'No, Treyford is right,' Renhurst agreed. He rang for the butler and instructed him to send someone to fetch Miss Latimer.

'She's probably halfway here by now, in any case, the inter-fering chit,' sniped Mrs Stockton.

'Enough of that,' warned Renhurst. 'This is an official pro-ceeding. Your spite has no place here.'

'Well, surely you have seen the way they are living,' the woman protested. 'All alone in that dusty tomb of a mansion with only two decrepit servants? It is a situation of which I cannot approve.'

'It's a bit late to be voicing that opinion now,' Renhurst objected, 'when you might have done something about it any time in the past two years. You've never had them for a visit, or come here to see them. Not so much as a Christmas ham have you sent, and believe me, it might have been put to good use!'

'I could not interfere while it was still possible that Mervyn might return,' she retorted. 'But now that it seems that the old

An Improper Aristocrat

dastard has met a fitting end—' She stopped at the look of sudden anger on the viscount's face. 'That is, you must know that I've never felt welcome! Even now I am here uninvited and have been treated most rudely!'

The magistrate rolled his eyes.

'I tell you, I came here with the best of intentions. My son Orville meant to offer for the girl, then they would all be under my…ah, our, protection.'

Trey started when Renhurst nodded in agreement.

'That is, actually, not such a bad idea. I've long told the girl that a good marriage would be the simple solution to her problems.' He glanced askance at Trey. 'That opinion has only been strengthened by recent events.'

Trey sat forward, but the viscount had turned back to Mrs Stockton, a speculative expression in his gaze. 'It does seem as if you've left it a little late, though. The girl's been struggling on her own for some time now. And I've never heard of any special regard between her and your son.'

'Orville is young. He was not ready to take a bride before now,' Mrs Stockton said primly.

Renhurst's fingertips met in a steeple in front of him. 'Orville Stockton? It seems as if I'd heard that name somewhere. Yes, I recall it now, some contretemps with Lord Sharpe's daughter, eh?'

'A mere misunderstanding,' she said hurriedly. 'My Orville sent me here in good faith to offer marriage, only I arrived to find Chione mysteriously gone and the children left in highly questionable hands. Not a word would anyone tell me of where she had gone, and when I searched the house, I found this!'

She pulled a stack of papers from her satchel, on top of which sat a bound copy of a set of serial stories.

Renhurst took them. Upon looking them over, he laughed. 'All this tizzy because the girl reads adventure stories? It's hardly surprising considering her family history, and, in any case, I confess I've read 'em myself on occasion.'

'If you will examine the papers closely, you'll see that she does not read them. She writes them!' Mrs Stockton declared damningly.

His brow furrowed, Lord Renhurst made a closer examination. 'Hmm. By George, I believe you're right.' He looked up, met Trey's gaze, and laughed. 'So that's how she's been doing it? And she never said a word!' His eyes crinkled further. 'I suspected she had begun to sell off Mervyn's things.'

'It's no laughing matter, it is a disgrace!' Mrs Stockton said, outraged. 'The girl has practised a deception on the public, and I dare say, on her neighbours and her community as well.'

The magistrate frowned at that. 'Well. It's not exactly seemly for a woman, but hardly fatal, either. Especially for girl in her circumstances.' He leafed through the volume for a moment. 'She does a dashed good job of it too, I say.'

Mrs Stockton sat silent, clearly taken aback. Obviously she had expected the viscount to be more repulsed at her revelation.

Trey spoke up. 'From what I understand, Chione only took up writing to keep food on the table and clothes on the children's backs.' He frowned at the old woman. 'It's a step she might not have had to take if Mrs Stockton had shown some interest or support before now.'

'What would you have me do?' Mrs Stockton had resorted to a pitiable role now, it seemed. 'My beautiful daughter gone before her time, and my annuity from Mervyn Latimer halted?'

'It is my understanding that you have a very generous inheritance from your late husband. Had you wished, I'm sure you might have seen your way to helping.' Renhurst's disgust for the woman rang out clearly now.

'And Mervyn Latimer might have kept his personal finances clear of Latimer Shipping's,' she spat back. 'My Harold worked too hard to see his money go to—' She stopped suddenly.

'His grandchildren?' Renhurst asked.

The woman's face twisted. She could obviously feel success—and her chance at Mervyn Latimer's company— slipping through her fingers. 'None of this changes the fact that Chione Latimer has proven herself no better than a lightskirt! The girl has ruined herself!' She pointed a bony finger in Trey's direction. 'With him!'

Renhurst cast a disapproving frown at him. Trey merely glared at the woman and gave a sad, little shake of his head. How had he ended up here? Perhaps the Egyptians had been correct. Perhaps his quest to uncover the past had offended the ancient gods. Perhaps this situation he found himself trapped in was their revenge—tangled relationships, half-truths, chaotic events—his own personal version of hell on earth.

He'd brushed the notion of the gods' displeasure aside when he'd first heard it. After all, the smirking native who had proposed it sat tending a fire built from scavenged bits of his own ancestors and their sarcophagi. But it might bear a bit of rethinking, given his current circumstances.

Before he could speak, however, there sounded yet another commotion in the hall.

The door opened and Chione came in, brushing past the long-suffering butler. 'Miss Latimer, my lord,' the man said with a speaking look at his master.

'Yes, yes, it's fine, Hodge,' Renhurst said with a roll of his eyes. 'But no one else, do you hear? I don't care if 'tis Liverpool himself come to tea.'

'Very good, sir.' The door closed with a click in the dead silence of the room.

Chione hadn't moved. She stood stock still, looking taken aback at finding the lot of them there before her. Trey caught the smallest droop of her shoulders, saw the incremental widening of her gaze. For a moment he feared her reaction. He watched with baited breath, knowing that an emotional outburst would cause the worst sort of damage.

But she recovered. Trey watched, transfixed, as her chin lifted, her shoulders went back and she stood, the very image of determination in the face of adversity. In that moment he suffered an elemental shift. She faced down her enemies, as beautiful, proud and remote as an Egyptian goddess come to life, and Trey knew deep in his soul that he would never again be the same.

This, then, was the reason he found himself here. On shaking knees, he stood. Belatedly, the viscount did too.

'I hope my arrival comes before you have all decided my fate,' Chione said. She sounded completely self-possessed. Trey suddenly wished he felt as steady as she sounded.

'Oh, do sit down, Chione,' Renhurst grumped. 'When a complaint like this arises, it's my duty to listen. You're here now. You'll get your say.'

Trey pulled a seat into the spot between Mrs Stockton and himself. Chione took it, and cast a contemptuous glance upon her relative.

Mrs Stockton returned her cold regard. 'I was only just telling the magistrate of your disgrace, Chione.'

'My *what*?' She raised a disbelieving brow and Trey breathed a sigh of relief. Thank the gods for intelligent women. If Mrs Stockton had expected a tearful, repentant Chione to make her case for her, she'd underestimated the girl.

'Oh, no,' the older woman snorted. 'Don't think you'll be getting out of this, dear girl.' She turned to Renhurst again. 'The girl has been gone for days, and not a word would anyone breathe about where she might be. Today she waltzes in, dishevelled as a common port whore, in the company of a man renowned for his womanising and itinerant lifestyle!' She paused to breathe deeply. 'I won't have it! I do not wish those children exposed to her moral decay. I want them out of that house and turned over to me today!'

Chione's tawny skin had paled, but she glared at Mrs

Stockton with murder in her eye. Trey barked out an incredulous laugh and Renhurst turned to him, his brow raised in question.

'Lord Renhurst knows where Chione has been and why, you wicked old baggage. He helped us plan the journey! As for her being ruined, we took along Ferguson's niece as a companion.' He turned to Renhurst. 'Can you imagine that anything objectionable could befall Miss Latimer under the watchful eye of a Ferguson?'

The old woman looked disdainfully at Trey. 'Are you daft, man? A hired maid is not a suitable companion.' She directed a baleful glare at the magistrate. 'And in any case, you can't trust her word. The girl will say anything that her family tells her to say!'

'This is Devonshire,' Renhurst objected. 'Not London. Not Portsmouth. Do not think to paint the good local people with your own dirty brush, Mrs Stockton.'

'Chione is practically penniless,' the woman said flatly. 'The children dress in little better than rags. They eat peasant food, and little enough of it. Worse, she fills their head with nonsense. After all this time, she is telling those children that Mervyn Latimer is still alive.'

Renhurst appeared surprised. 'That is perhaps not the best course, Chione.'

'Such a thing is not beyond the realm of possibility,' Chione said. 'My lord, the children and I remain cautiously optimistic. Is there a crime in that? Even if we are wrong, you may tell me which is worse—believing in a lost cause or being beaten for it?' She sent a hate-filled look in Mrs Stockton's direction. 'I wish you could see Will's back, sir. He looks like a sailor caught pilfering rum, not a boy hoping his father still lives.'

'It's true,' Trey affirmed. 'And in a decision such as this, I think you should be made aware of Mrs Stockton's propensity for harsh punishments. I myself heard her threaten Miss

Latimer this morning. She said she meant to lock her in a room with her footman for a few days. As a cure for your high-handed ways, was it not, Miss Latimer?'

'Of course, I didn't mean it,' fluttered Mrs Stockton. 'I merely meant to frighten the girl.' She shrugged and turned to appeal to Renhurst. 'Perhaps she cannot help it. You've had experience with her. Surely you know how she is; always going beyond the line of what is pleasing for a young, *English* lady.'

Chione gasped. Trey sat up straight in his chair. Lord Renhurst banged a hand on his desk.

'I'll have none of that sort of talk here, madam. Miss Latimer has been known to us all since her girlhood. She's never acted anything but a lady.' He raised a hand as the older woman started to protest. 'No, I've heard enough. I'll decide the salient points of this issue.'

He stood and went to one of the mullioned windows. For several long minutes the room filled with an oppressive silence while he gathered his thoughts. Finally, he spoke.

'This is a most uncomfortable decision to be forced to make. The welfare of the children must be paramount.' He turned to face the motley crew assembled before him. 'It is clear that I have been remiss in my duty. I should have seen this situation resolved long before now, but I suppose it was easier to assume that all was well enough.'

He cast an ironic look over their little group. 'Until today I have never heard a word spoken against Chione Latimer.' His face softened when his gaze moved on to Chione. 'Without doubt she has already demonstrated years of loving concern for Will and Olivia.'

He cast a disparaging brow upon Mrs Stockton. 'You, madam, have only demonstrated your own churlish small-mindedness today. And yet…'

He crossed to the desk and sat once more, a frown of concern clear upon his brow. 'Mrs Stockton does have the resources needed to care for two children. I hope she has a level of maturity that could guide her,' he said with a meaningful look. 'And I'd hazard a guess that she harbours some ambitions for the children—' He held a hand up as Chione made a sound. 'No, Chione, that is not necessarily a bad thing.'

'It is when it is not tempered by love for them, my lord,' Chione said, very pale.

He compressed his lips thoughtfully. 'You may be correct about that. But you may also rest assured that I intend to take a special interest in these children, until news of Mervyn Latimer is uncovered, or until they come of age. This is a difficult decision, and I must give a thought to their future to help me decide.'

'No,' whispered Chione.

'Your own future is uncertain, Chione. Despite my belief in your best intentions and conduct, I cannot deny that your reputation will suffer once word of your journey gets about.' He cast a disgusted look at Mrs Stockton. 'As it no doubt will.'

The woman suppressed a confirming smirk. Trey suppressed a stab of hate and something that felt remarkably like fear.

'There is no notion of what might have happened to Mervyn,' Renhurst continued, 'and no end in sight to the squabbling that has beset the directors of his company. Your attempts have been valiant and praiseworthy…' he gestured to the pile of manuscript pages '…but Mrs Stockton can send Will to school. She can dower Olivia. She can see to their futures.'

Chione had begun to shake. An eerie calm had descended over Trey. Very deliberately he reached over and took her hand.

She shook him off. 'Please,' she whispered.

'The situation cannot continue. It would be best if you married, Chione,' the viscount said flatly. 'Would you consider taking Orville Stockton?'

'You cannot be serious,' she said.

'I am deadly serious. Enough to have even given thought to

Mrs Ferguson's wild scheme of marrying you to me. I can do no less to see Mervyn's family settled.'

'There is no need for these theatrics.' Trey's voice emerged firm and calm, an accurate reflection of the total calcification of his soul. 'If Chione's prospects are the only thing keeping you from granting her custody of the children, Lord Renhurst, then you may rest easy.' He raised her hand in his. 'You may all wish us very happy, for she has already consented to become my wife.' Trey felt Chione stiffen, heard her quick intake of breath, but he dared not meet her eyes. He stared hard at Renhurst instead. 'I trust the prospects of the Countess of Treyford should be more than adequate to provide for two children?'

Profound relief showed on the viscount's face. Mrs Stockton looked ready to explode.

'Of course, of course!' Renhurst agreed. 'I confess, I had hoped it would turn out to be so! The perfect solution to all the various difficulties of the thing. May I be the first to congratulate you both?'

Trey inclined his head. Mrs Stockton made a strangled noise that everyone ignored. Chione sat frozen and silent.

'Well, then! I do pronounce that legal custody of William and Olivia Latimer be given to the Earl of Treyford and to Miss Chione Latimer, the soon-to-be Countess of Treyford. Such a decision assures the children of both a loving home and a secure future. And so I do order it be done.'

Renhurst stood then, and crossed over to a bell pull. 'Now, we must have something to toast the betrothed pair,' he said happily.

Trey stood. 'I appreciate the sentiment, but if we have finished, I have some pressing business to attend to.' He cocked a brow at the viscount. 'Will you see Chione home for me? I know she would like to fill in the details on the outcome of our travels.'

He fixed a piercing eye on the still dazed Mrs Stockton. 'Chione is to be my wife. Olivia and Will I regard as my own until Mervyn Latimer is found. I protect what is mine, madam. I trust you will be gone from Oakwood within the hour.'

He bowed over Chione's hand without ever looking her in the face and then strode from the room.

Chapter Thirteen

Chione sat by the fire in her bedchamber, drying the heavy cascade of her hair, staring at the flames with a leaden gaze. The welcome heat combined with the hardship of travel and the emotional turmoil of the day; together they should have been an irresistible burden, pushing her towards sleep. Yet her mind refused to rest.

She has already consented to become my wife. The words—the lie—echoed relentlessly in her head.

With one sentence Treyford had routed them all. Then he had left and no one had seen him since.

Chione had never been so shocked in her life as when he had baldly made his announcement. She was still surprised and intensely grateful. He had not run off and left her to face her difficulties alone, although she strongly suspected that was exactly what he had wished to do. He had saved her, saved the children, and only she knew how great a sacrifice he had made. She could not rest until she saw him, thanked him, told him how sorry she was for the pain such a step had caused him.

With some dismay she thought back to her resolution to accept whatever sort of emotional liaison that Trey could offer. Whatever else might come of it, she feared this impromptu engagement would put an end to that. Chione knew with a certainty that Treyford would now be closed against her. He'd been spooked, and even if he did go through with the betrothal, and—her mind whispered the word—*marriage*, then she strongly suspected that he would be gone within months. He'd go back to his adventuring, and she would be left alone, again.

Part of her recoiled at the idea; it was most assuredly *not* what she had hoped for. She sighed. It only reinforced the folly of permitting herself to dream.

A larger part of her mourned the lost opportunity with Trey, pined for the warm connection, the sense of intimacy that had begun to grow between them. She could not deny, though, that it was a price she was willing to pay. He'd gone so far past any expectation that either she or Richard had had of him. She would do her best to ease his anxieties, tell him she was ready to deal with this situation in any manner he wished.

So she sat while the fire died down, her hair dried, and her nerves balanced on a knife's edge. And still he did not come.

Trey left Thornton Castle on foot and walked the coastal paths of Devon for hours. He fiercely ignored the beauty of the landscape, focusing all his attention on the violence of the Atlantic crashing into the cliffs so far below, allowing the endless conflict to reflect his own emotional turbulence. Unfortunately, it could not do much to ease it.

Trey breathed deeply and tried to calm himself. He'd faced far worse in his life. He'd escaped not one, but two Turkish prisons, outmanoeuvred a malevolent pasha bent on making him a eunuch, and once he'd narrowly escaped being sacrificed to a primitive tribal goddess. Surely a mere slip of a woman could not lay him so low.

Truthfully, there was a part of Trey that thrilled in excited expectation at the thought of marrying Chione. She was so profoundly unlike any of the women he had known before. Not an innocent, nor yet a seductress. She had an unearthly self-assurance, a quick wit, an appreciation for the absurdities of life and the courage to fight against the injustices. If ever there was a woman he could trust—it was she.

His heart rate ratcheted up again and he knew he'd reached the crux of the matter. This was the thought that had him quaking in his boots. He didn't think he could do it—let her in. He'd been alone his entire life, by preference, purpose and design. He didn't know how to trust.

But he wanted to. And that was the thought that truly terrified him.

It was a long walk back to Oakwood Court, but not long enough for him to sort out his conflicted feelings. When he arrived it had grown late and the house lay in darkness. Trey thought everyone was abed until he got to the stairs. There he found Aswan, with Olivia in his arms, both admiring a portrait of an extravagantly dressed Tudor gentleman.

Olivia's little finger pointed to the painting. 'Codpiece,' she said.

'Cod peeese,' said Aswan. 'Codpiece.'

'Good God,' choked Trey. 'What are the two of you about so late?'

Olivia looked about in delight. 'Draybird!' she cried, holding out her arms imperiously.

Trey took her from his servant. 'Olivia,' he said in greeting, 'how is it that you cannot get my name right, nor half your family's, and yet you know the correct terminology for a codpiece?'

She nodded and pointed. 'Codpiece.'

'I suspect I shall have to speak with your brother about this.'

'The little miss wanders at night, *effendi*,' Aswan said, unruffled. 'I watch her.'

'Yes, I understand how thoroughly you have guarded these children, Aswan, and I thank you.'

The Egyptian bowed. 'It is an honour, *effendi*.'

The girl yawned and laid her head on Trey's shoulder. He handed her over. 'Is Miss Latimer abed?'

Aswan nodded. 'She is in her bedchamber, but not yet asleep.'

Trey raised a brow.

Aswan let loose with a rare, shining grin. 'I watch. I also listen.'

'I'll keep that in mind,' Trey said, clapping him on the back.

Trey hesitated outside Chione's door a moment, gathering his courage before he knocked.

Once he did, the portal opened immediately and she looked out, her brow clearing as she saw him. Trey had to suppress a smile. Only a woman of Chione's great beauty could look so tempting in a frayed dressing gown wrapped tight up to her chin. Then he swallowed. Good Lord, her hair was down. It fell straight, shining dark to her waist. A powerful wave of lust hit him at the sight and he had to fight to concentrate on her words.

'Treyford!' she said. 'I am so glad to see you back. I had begun to worry.' She paused, regarding him with a long steady gaze, then deliberately she stepped aside and motioned him in.

He returned the thoughtful regard, acknowledging her decision to admit him into her room and all the potential ramifications of it. Swiftly he made his own choice and stepped in. It was the least he owed her.

'What?' he asked lightly. 'Did you think I'd do myself in rather than marry you?'

She smiled. 'Actually, I considered it, along with any number of other vividly morbid scenarios.' She shrugged. 'It is one of the drawbacks of being a storyteller. It seems I'm always imagining the worst possible outcome of any given situation.'

A fire smouldered in the grate. Exhausted, but acutely aware of their isolation, Trey dropped into one of the chairs before it. 'We'll make a good match, then,' he said, 'because I am for ever imagining a way *out* of the worst possible outcome.'

She took the other chair. Trey couldn't take his eyes off of her hair. It hung, thick and glorious, glinting in the dim light. A fall of velvety night sky brought to earth. His fingers twitched.

'Shall we?' she asked, and the tension in her voice brought him back to attention. 'Make a match of it, that is? I thought perhaps you only said that to rout Mrs Stockton.'

'Did it? Rout her, I mean?'

'Oh, yes.' Her tone rang with no little satisfaction. 'When you walked out I thought she would have an apoplexy. I've never seen anyone so red in the face. Nor heard such vitriol spilled. She's not happy, but she's gone.'

Trey frowned. The healthy glow of her skin was nearly as distracting as her hair. 'But if we did not marry, if the old witch discovered the betrothal was a sham, she'd be right back here. With twice the spite.'

She sighed. 'Very likely.'

'Well, then.' Trey sat, shoulders slumped, heavy with exhaustion. His conflicting emotions were tearing him in two. Residual fear lingered on one side, along with the conviction that Chione deserved so much better than anything he could give her.

But the other side—oh, the other side of him thrummed with nearly irresistible desire. It pooled heavily in his loins and at the same time whispered temptingly in his ear. He was very much aware of her, perched nervously on the matching chair. They were here, alone together in the dark of night and, somewhat absurdly, they were betrothed. She wasn't dressed, yet she'd admitted him to her bedchamber and now she sat, gazing at him with her siren's eyes—a fascinating mix of knowledge and innocence, need and nervousness.

'Treyford.' Her voice was gentle, as if she knew what

writhed inside of him. 'I wish you to know how very grateful I am. I hope you realise that I never expected—'

'I do,' he interrupted. 'It was not your doing.'

'I want you to know I'll do whatever I can, handle this in any way you wish. We can declare that we don't suit, or I shall say that I've found another—'

'Stop,' he whispered. 'Let the world believe as they wish. I don't care. But between us, let's have the truth.'

Eyes wide, she nodded.

'The truth is, I don't know what I wish for. Nor, I suspect, do you. How can you when you are caught up in such circumstances? Let us agree that the betrothal will stand until we find Mervyn...and then we will discuss our options.'

'Thank you,' she said quietly.

He let loose with a sharp bark of laughter. 'God, don't thank me. It's a bad bargain you're getting at best.' He sighed. 'I suppose that I should have thought of it at the outset of all of this, but...' A terrible sadness washed over him. 'The issue is not what I wish for, Chione, but what I—' He sank his head in his hands, then, distraught, he forced himself to look up, to face her. 'I can't do it,' he whispered. 'I can't be the kind of husband that you deserve.'

Her breath caught. Above the worn collar of her wrapper he could see her pulse begin to jump. For a long moment she stared, then abruptly she shook her head. 'You've done so much for me.' Determination flared in her eyes. She stood, crossed to him and knelt at the foot of his chair. 'There are some things that perhaps I should tell you, but I do not want you to worry, Treyford.'

Trey couldn't help himself; he reached out, touched an ebony lock of her hair, followed it down past her curves. Then he brushed a caress across her cheek. 'So soft. So incredibly beautiful.' He took his hand away. 'I can't bear the thought of hurting you, Chione. But I will. It is inevitable.'

She gazed at him through the lush curtain of her lashes, reached out and took his hand. 'I won't ask for what you cannot give.'

Her words sprang a lock hidden inside of him. Somewhere, buried deep, a lonely weight shifted from his soul. She understood, at least partially. Perhaps she only said the words out of gratitude, but right now *he* was the grateful one—thankful for her insight and the caring generosity of her spirit.

Wordless, he gripped her arms and pulled her into his lap. She gasped again, her breath coming quickly as he settled her firmly across his thighs. Trey ran an appreciative gaze over her flushed cheeks and widened eyes. She looked a little frightened, but more intrigued. He groaned as she wiggled her rump experimentally, then bent down and covered her mouth with his.

Insistently, urgently he kissed her, claiming her with his mouth and with his tongue. She opened to him, following where he led and moulding her mouth to his. Her arms curled up behind his neck, her fingers sending shivers down his spine. Greedy, he wrapped her in his embrace, drank deep, and sucked the clean scent of her into his lungs until he thought he would gladly drown in it.

She felt tiny when he ran his hands along her sides. How could she be so fragile and so strong at once? For she was tougher than he, he knew it for a certainty. Deeper he kissed her, thrusting with his tongue and fighting off the clear, cold truth. God, he was a fool. All along he'd worried that he would not be able to let her in. Now harsh reality hit him hard. The truth was he didn't know how to keep her out.

He pulled back. In the dim light of the dying fire the look she gave him was soft, accepting, welcoming. Suddenly he stood, taking care to keep her close. 'I wish I were different. I wish I could be what you need.' He groaned and stooped down a bit, resting his forehead on hers. 'God help me, I most especially wish I did not want you so damned much.'

She smiled. 'I am glad you do, for where would that leave me?'

Trey stared. 'Do you want me, Chione?'

'I…I do.' Her gaze faltered and fell away. 'Perhaps I should not, but I cannot help myself.'

Heart pounding, Trey put a finger to her chin and pulled her face back to his. She came easily, closing her eyes, pressing herself against him and lifting her mouth to be taken. He obliged them both, driving deep, needing the taste of her to force out every niggling fear and doubt. And it worked. She clung to him, matching kiss for kiss, until he thought their souls must be touching.

Finally, impatient, Trey tore his mouth away, moving on to the sweet hollow beneath her jaw. Chione let her head fall back and he took advantage of the opportunity, snaking loose the tie of her wrapper and pushing the garment from her shoulders until it sank to a puddled heap at her feet.

She wore a simple shift beneath, cut low with slender straps, baring her long neck and a delightful expanse of golden flesh. Beneath the fine linen her nipples strained, already taut against the soft fabric. He filled his gaze with her, and then his hands. His heart rate quickened, and at his temple a pulse began to beat.

With a groan he reached down, swept her off her feet and into his embrace. Chione squeaked, then nuzzled his neck, pressing soft kisses beneath his ear. Growing bolder, she licked her way along his jaw. His mind raced as they reached the bed, imagining all the other places he wanted her tongue, and he nearly exploded right then and there.

He set her down on her feet and she breathed his name. 'Treyford.'

Slipping his fingers beneath the straps of her shift, he leaned in close and began to run a slow caress up and down, from her shoulder to the enticing softness of the top of her breast. 'Chione,' he said, low and urgent, 'I want you to call me by my name.'

Her eyes had closed in ecstasy at his teasing touch, but now they flew open. She smiled and crept warm fingers up his chest, then began to slowly undo the buttons of his waistcoat. 'Trey,' she said softly.

'No.' His hands stilled. 'My real name.'

She stopped. 'I'm afraid I don't know it.'

'I know,' he said simply. 'Not many people do. For a long time I've preferred it that way. But I'm going to tell you,' he said huskily, 'because when I bury myself inside you I want to hear you call my name.'

His words made her tremble. 'What is it?' she whispered.

'Niall,' he said.

Her fingers spasmed into his waist. 'What?'

'Niall.'

'How do you spell it?' she asked, her eyes wide.

He told her.

'And you do not pronounce it in the northern way? Neal?'

'No—my mother thought it more original the other way. I gather my father was not fond of it.' He tensed a little. 'Does it bother you?'

'No,' she said slowly, 'it is only that—do you remember when Renhurst told you the meaning of *my* name?'

'Yes. Chione—daughter of the Nile. It is beautiful.'

She smiled. 'Thank you. That is a widely accepted translation of the name, but Eshe, my mother, always told me that she meant the older translation for me.'

Trey waited.

She flushed. 'Lover of the Nile.'

He laughed and her blush deepened. The flush of colour entranced him. His desire rushed back, so fast and hard it took his breath away. He kissed her again, but this time it was a long, slow plunder. His hands circled restlessly over the swell of her breasts and then he couldn't wait a moment longer. He pulled at the worn, old shift impatiently and heard a tearing sound as he swept it over her head.

'My shift!' she cried in dismay.

'I'll buy you a hundred,' he growled, 'but I have to see you.'

Lord, but she was beautiful. Full, high breasts, each crowned with dusky, wide areolas and tipped with a tiny nub of nipple. The contrast enthralled him. He reached out, ran his flat palm over them and, when she gasped with pleasure, he squeezed her nipples gently between his fingers.

'Oh, good heavens,' she said.

He smiled, then paused, trying to remember if sex had ever been so light-hearted, so *right*. Purposefully he sat her down upon the edge of the bed. He knelt in front of her, as she had done earlier, and set his mouth to her breast. She gasped and arched to him, and for long, untold moments he suckled her, first one breast, then teasingly moved to the other, until they were both breathing hot and fast and nearly undone with desire.

At last Trey could wait no longer. With one last teasing flick he let Chione's nipple slide away and he stood. 'Move back to the middle of the bed,' he urged.

She complied, the dark curtain of her hair falling forward and covering her like a silken cloak. Trey began to undress with eager fingers, his gaze feasting all the while on her enchanting curves, her luscious long legs and the dark thatch of glistening curls at their apex.

In turn, Chione's gaze followed his fingers, and her obvious fascination with his body made him surge even harder yet. When his hands went to the waist of his trousers, her expression changed slightly. She was still intrigued, but there was something defiant there, too.

'You do not mind if I…?' He gestured to his trousers.

Her chin went up. 'I'm not scared.'

'Good God, no. I just wanted to be sure…' He trailed off.

'I'm sure,' she said, rising to her knees and coming closer. 'In fact, I wish to help.'

He jumped at the light touch of her fingers on his belly. 'I think I'm the one who's scared,' he said. He ran his hands down the silky skin of her back and over the sweet curves of her behind. 'You are a goddess,' he whispered, 'an ancient dream come to life.'

At last she found what she sought. The woollen fall of his trousers was pushed aside and he sprang free. A low, appreciate grumble tore its way out of him as she stroked it with delicate, searching fingertips.

'My God,' he groaned. 'You're everything I've been afraid of my entire life.'

She smiled—the self-satisfied smile of a woman discovering her own sensual power. Then she grasped him with her other hand. Trey gritted his teeth, rocked back on his heels and let her explore until he could take no more.

'My turn,' he said, climbing on to the bed and pulling her down beside him. He trailed a finger down her quivering body, parted her swollen folds and slipped into hot, slick paradise.

Now she moaned in pleasure as he stroked her, spreading, rubbing, teasing her to breathlessness. Her fingers tangled in his hair as he suckled her again and let his fingers work magic. When he at last slid a finger into her she cried out in helpless surprise.

'Niall,' she gasped, and the sound of it was a hot brand to his heart. 'You are making me want…need…something.'

Trey kissed her again and laughed low. 'Don't worry, Chione. I'm going to give you what you need.'

He braced himself above her and kissed her hard. Her head went back when he parted her velvet core. Gasping again, she writhed in wild abandon as he eased himself against the slick heat of her desire.

God. He had to slow down, to bide his time. He had meant to pleasure her to the brink of madness before he sought his own, but her artless, uninhibited response was driving him there instead. There could be no waiting.

Carefully he eased into her. It was the brink of heaven he was poised upon, nirvana, every sort of bliss ever imagined by man. But beneath him Chione had stilled.

'All right?' he croaked. God help him, but it was all he could manage.

'It hurts,' she said, frowning up at him.

'I'm sorry.' He could feel her body adapting around him as she shifted beneath him. There was no help for it. He groaned deeply and slid home.

'Yes,' she moaned, arching her back. 'That's better. Please.'

He answered her inarticulate plea, moving slowly, stroking high and long, building the ache and the longing, destroying doubt and fear. At first she merely hung on, wrapped around him and clinging like a vine, but then she began to understand the rhythm. She braced herself and thrust up to meet him, tilting her pelvis and inviting him in. Trey's urgency grew, his hunger swelled until it was bigger than he or she, and instead became something beyond themselves, something they could only experience together.

Trey couldn't wait. He reached down to where their bodies joined and found the secret nub of her pleasure. The effect was instantaneous. Her eyes flew open and her body tightened around him. He thought his heart might burst with the effort of holding back.

'Let go, Chione,' he urged hoarsely. 'Just let it happen.'

'I don't…I don't know…if I can.'

'You can, you will. We'll both go together.'

And she did. Her body shattered around him, milking him with the strength of her rapturous response.

It was beyond bearing. He was harder than he'd ever been in his life. No matter how many times he'd done this before, with Chione it was different. She'd changed him, bound him with ties that he had never wanted, but which somehow freed him to find new heights of exquisite passion. He let loose, driving into her with abandon until his climax took him by storm. For endless moments he rode the wild currents. Gradually they gentled and he drifted down, floating peacefully into a rolling wave of contentment.

Chapter Fourteen

Chione awoke slowly the next morning, boneless and warm. Naked. And alone. A stealthy rustle sounded somewhere behind her and then the soft click of a door. She sat up, but Trey had gone.

Telling herself firmly that he was making a nod to the proprieties and not running away, she burrowed back beneath the covers. For several minutes she lounged, reliving the glories of the night before. It had been eye opening and amazing, but, despite her brave words, she had been a little frightened.

When Trey had urged her to let go, her first thought had been that he didn't know what he was asking. Somehow it had become more than just loosening a natural restraint. He'd been asking her to abandon a role that had saved her life. And it was a role, a persona that she had adopted to fit with her new life: calm, resolute, restrained. A good little English girl, whose name was the only exotic part about her. She'd thought she couldn't let it go, for it would leave her open, vulnerable, exposed.

Then the truth had hit her. She could, because Trey had already seen past the facade. He was the only person who had ever looked deeply enough to glimpse the emotional, uncertain, volatile creature within, and from the very first he had accepted her, welcomed her, pushed her out of hiding and into the cold light of day.

It was her, the real Chione that Trey had been making love to. The Chione who had scolded, scorned and rejected him. The Chione who had turned to him in her hour of need, trusted him, kissed him, talked with him. Loved him.

So she had done it. She had let go and allowed Trey to take her to the heavens. It had been a lovely trip.

But now her feet were firmly back on earth, and unease began to set in. Last night she'd done what her practical, grounded self had sworn never to do. She'd given herself to an adventurer, linked her fate to an emotionally distant man who was likely to always be gone—in head, in heart and in fact.

And he still did not know the truth about her. In Exeter he had scolded her for putting her family's interests ahead of her own. How would he react to find that she wasn't truly part of this family? Could he understand how ties of love and gratitude bound her as tightly as those of blood? She was afraid to find out. What if it angered him enough to abandon this uncertain betrothal?

The thought spurred her into activity and she leaped out of bed to wash and dress. But mundane activity could not banish her distress, or change reality. She was at war with herself and required a greater distraction.

She breathed deeply and left her rooms. She thought she would take breakfast with the children. Just knowing it was a possibility soothed her. This was why the emotional turmoil was worth it. Will and Olivia were safe now, their futures secured. It was enough. It had to be.

Trey's manservant was leaving the nursery playroom as she approached.

'Aswan,' she called as he closed the door behind him. Always she felt a little uneasy around him. He rarely spoke to her, but she knew that he watched her a great deal, and with a startling intensity.

'Aswan, have you spoken with Lord Treyford this morning?'

'I dressed him,' he replied. 'But there was little enough speaking.'

'Oh. Do you know where he is now?'

'He has gone to the village with young Will. He says only that he will require a mount since we are to stay a while longer.' Undeniably there was a question in his gaze.

'Yes, well. I am sorry that Lord Treyford did not give you the news himself,' she began.

'News?'

'Yes. We—Treyford and I—are betrothed.'

'I do not know this word. Bee-trothed.'

Chione could feel heat rising to flush her cheeks. 'We are to be married.'

'Married?' For the first time he met her gaze squarely, eye to eye. 'Mated?'

A little intimidated, Chione nodded.

'So,' he said in a musing voice. Then he collected himself and gave a little bow. 'May I wish the…young Miss Latimer much happiness?' He turned and started down the hall. Chione could hear him muttering under his breath. She called out to him again.

'Aswan, did Lord Treyford speak to you about my brother's journals?'

He turned back, curiosity alight in his face. 'No, young miss, he did not.'

'Treyford told me that you were the one who packed Richard's possessions and had them shipped home. We were wondering if you could tell us if perhaps some of the boxes have not yet arrived? I never received his journals and some of his other personal effects are missing as well.'

He took a step back towards her. 'I have seen the boxes in the *effendi*'s rooms. I hope the young miss will not mind, but I noticed that one or two were not there. I thought perhaps you had kept them close to you—' he watched her '—or perhaps that the thieves had taken them. But you say that you have never received these crates?'

'No. Everything I have received is there.'

An indecipherable gleam shone in his eye. 'Ahh. Yes. I will investigate this, young miss. You have my word.'

'Thank you. There is no regular post in Wembury, but the man who travels to Knighton twice a week to the post office might be able to help you.'

'Thank you.' He bowed once more.

'And, Aswan, I wish to thank you for the care you have given the children while we were gone.'

He looked as if he might speak, but then he bowed again, abruptly turned and left. Chione watched him go, and then she entered the playroom.

She was still there, reading to a drowsy Olivia, when Will and Morty returned, a look of suppressed excitement on the boy's face.

'Good morning, Will.' Chione spoke low and gestured to the nodding child in her lap. 'Did you and Lord Treyford enjoy yourselves?'

'Oh, yes, Chione!' he answered in an excited whisper. 'Trey let me help choose his mount—a strapping, good-natured grey—and he says that it is time I had a horse of my own!'

'Did Lord Treyford return to the house with you?'

'No. He sent me on home alone. He said he had business to attend to.' Will had grown more solemn. 'Trey told me that he means to marry you, Chione.'

'Yes,' she said with a semblance of a normal tone. 'I think we will all be very happy together, don't you?'

Slowly, Will nodded. He walked over to the window seat where Morty had retreated and perched beside her. 'Does this mean we'll stop looking for Papa?' he asked. His fingers ran idly over the dog's ears.

'Of course not,' Chione replied, surprised. 'In fact, I think

Lord Treyford is the best person we could choose to help us, don't you?'

'Yes, I suppose that is right,' he said a little more hopefully.

Chione could see that he was still unsettled at the idea of yet another change in his young life.

'I'll tell you what,' she said, shifting the sleeping Olivia in her arms and standing carefully. 'Why don't you practise your sketching by drawing us Lord Treyford's new mount? Then, when you are finished, we'll have another look at the *Aeneid* and you can tell me what you remember of the Trojan Horse.'

As she'd hoped, the resumption of such an ordinary occurrence as lessons soothed him. 'All right,' he agreed. 'Do you know, Chione, that Trey was mightily impressed that I already knew so many of the finer points to look for in a saddle horse? That's what he said—mightily impressed.' His chatter continued as he took out his sketchbook and Chione breathed a sigh of relief as she went next door to put Olivia down.

The first thing Trey noticed when he entered the parlour that afternoon was that horses were still the dominate topic of Will's conversation. He sat next to his sister, who was astride a rocking horse, her mouth full of buttered muffin and her eyes as big as saucers as Will regaled her with what sounded like the tale of the Trojan Horse.

'Imagine your horsey fifty times as large, Livvie,' the boy enthused, 'and stuffed to the brim with fierce warriors!'

'Ooooohh,' breathed Olivia.

'Ye watch what ye be fillin' her head with,' Mrs Ferguson grumped from the fire where she was toasting the muffins. 'Odds are it'll come spillin' out at the least likeliest moment.'

Morty noticed his entrance before anyone else. The dog got to her feet with a happy bark and came to welcome him. Trey gave her a thumping greeting and let his gaze slide past the dog to Chione.

She betrayed herself with only a slight start and a faint colouring of her cheeks. Trey smiled at her and acknowledged the housekeeper and the children. He had gleaned before that this heavy tea more often than not served as dinner for the family so when Chione gathered herself enough to ask him to join them, he accepted.

He took a hot muffin from Mrs Ferguson with thanks and tried to conduct himself normally—a nearly impossible task. Like a boy in the grip of calf-love, he hadn't been able to get the image of Chione out of his mind all day. How was he supposed to converse like a gentleman when he had an intimate knowledge of the beauty beneath that stark grey gown and a nearly constant urge to run his hands over it?

He'd awakened early this morning with a need to escape, to breathe free air and spend some time alone. But he'd changed his mind when he'd found Will gingerly descending the stairs. Fury had flared fresh as he watched the boy's careful stride and he'd immediately invented an errand to distract him from his pain. To Trey's surprise, he'd enjoyed himself almost as much as Will had. The boy was clever, eager to learn and apparently quite horse-mad. When he'd begun to tire, Trey had sent him home and had gone on alone to meet with Drake.

There had been much news to exchange with the innkeeper, little of it good. Trey had thanked him for his help with Cedric and filled him in on their trip. Grimly, he had heard what Drake had to report. Locals were talking of strangers in the area, some with questions about the Latimers. Mervyn Latimer's sloop appeared to have been broken into. Drake had sent a few of the guards Trey had hired out to scour the hills around Oakwood. He had taken Trey to view what they had found.

Trey had stood in the sheltered nook and looked out at the clear view of Oakwood Court. The spot was well used. And, according to Drake, it was one of several, each with a different perspective on the house below. Trey had poked at the log dragged over as a seat and felt a spasm of worry.

'Hassan,' he had mused. 'Who the hell are you?'

He'd been in danger more often than not, it sometimes seemed, but this was different. This threat was like quicksilver, slipping through his fingers each time he got a grasp of it. Like a nebulous cloud it hung over the woman and children he had just made himself irrevocably responsible for. He'd remembered the captivating mix of Chione's fragility and strength beneath him last night and the stick he'd been exploring with had snapped in two.

'Did you bring the grey home tonight?' Will's question broke in on the memory.

'Yes, I did.' It took an effort for Trey to get himself focused on the present. 'The gelding is ours now, all right and tight. Perhaps after tea you would like to come with me and make sure he's comfortably settled?'

'Oh, yes,' the boy agreed, eyes shining.

Trey looked to Chione. 'I didn't find Eli in the stables when I got back.'

He noticed her breathing quickened as she answered. 'Aswan took him off this afternoon.'

Trey raised a brow in question.

'I talked with him about the journals this morning.' She shrugged. 'Perhaps they went off to the post office?'

'I'll heat some water so ye both can have a bath when ye get back,' Mrs Ferguson interrupted. 'There's no need for the pair of ye to smell of horse, too.'

Trey laughed. 'Thank you, Mrs Ferguson.'

The housekeeper heaved herself to her feet. She directed a sharp look at Will. 'Don't dawdle in the stables. I'm puttin' the water on to heat.'

As she left Chione leaned over and placed a hand over his. 'Thank you,' she said softly. 'For everything.'

Trey ran his gaze over her face and didn't reply. For a long moment they sat, simply watching each other, enjoying the mounting tension, until a brisk knock sounded on the parlour door. Eli poked his head in.

'Aswan's got a parcel for ye, Miss Chione. Where do ye be wantin' us to put it?'

'Good heavens, but that was fast,' she replied.

'Is Aswan with you, then?' called Trey.

The door opened wider to reveal the servant standing there. 'Yes, *effendi.*'

'I'll need to speak with you when you are done with that.'

'Yes, *effendi.*'

'However did you find it so quickly, Aswan?' Chione asked, rising and going to investigate the box he held.

'I merely began looking in the right place, young miss.'

'The right place would o' been at the post,' grumbled Eli. 'They said there that they gave this over to a woman a week or so ago. A woman who said she was travelling on to Oakwood.'

'A woman?' Chione asked. 'More of Mrs Stockton's meddling, no doubt.'

'I don't know,' Eli said doubtfully. 'Were it she, she would have brought it here to open it.'

'Where did you find it then?'

'We asked in some o' the pubs in Knighton. Found a young scrapper who spotted a fire lit at his granddad's empty fishing shack. No one there when he arrived, but he found some things that sounded like what we were looking for. He took what hadn't been put to the fire yet and sold them to the pawnbroker. We got back what we could.'

Trey saw Chione look uneasily at Aswan's expressionless face. Then she glanced back at him. He nodded imperceptibly in her direction.

'Thank you so much, both of you,' Chione said. 'Will you just take it along to the library? I'll get started right away.'

Trey stood. 'Come along, Will. We'll drop off Olivia in the kitchens. She can help Mrs Ferguson while we are out in the stables. Aswan, I'll speak with you when we get back.'

Chione gratefully followed the men to the library. This was just what she needed—something to keep her mind occupied. She was very happy not to have to sit in her room tonight and wonder if Trey would come. And if she repeated that to herself, she might just come to believe it.

Chione opened the box with eager hands. She stilled when she discovered the objects lying loosely wrapped at the top. Two miniatures: one of Mervyn Latimer and one of his lovely wife, Marie. Both were smoke stained. Tears gathered as she drew the paintings out, but she fought them back.

A few of Richard's journals were indeed underneath, along with some of his drafting equipment and a singed book or two.

She did cry, then, for all that she had lost and perhaps a little for all she feared she might never gain. But shortly she dried her eyes. She took up the latest of Richard's journals, settled herself comfortably on the worn chaise, and set to work.

Chione told herself it was natural to begin with her brother's budding relationship with Lord Treyford, but she couldn't deny the eagerness with which she sought out any mention of his name. They were few enough at first. Richard had begun this new journal as he set out for Egypt. The first pages were filled with short notes regarding the journey; the first entries of any length began when he reached Alexandria.

The excitement with which her brother had returned to Egypt surprised her. He had thrilled to each new sight, sound and experience. Just reading about their homeland filled Chione with a vague dread. She skimmed ahead, looking for a mention of Trey.

At last she found it; a brief mention of Richard's first meeting with the infamous earl. A few pages later, a slightly longer description of their decision to work together. Disjointed bits about their trip up the Nile followed, but when they reached Thebes and established a more permanent base in the Valley of the Kings, the entries became more detailed.

Chione drank in several descriptions of Richard's growing respect for Trey. She smiled when Richard approved of Trey's treatment of their workers and laughed when he once despaired of the earl's reluctance to discuss anything personal.

She grew more serious when she discovered several mentions of Richard leaving their site for a day or two, searching for something that he never named outright. She knew it must be the scarab when she found the entry written just a week before his death.

Found s. today. Nearly shamed myself by crying like a woman. But will not give in to despair. The thief who sold it to me could not—or would not—say where he obtained it. I did learn that C. G. B. is in Egypt. Coincidence? Will watch him closely.

Chione drew a shuddering breath. It had to have been the scarab. But who or what was C. G. B.? A similar entry a little further on only raised more questions.

Drovetti in Thebes today, and in the company of C. G. B. Neither happy to see me. I am getting close.

Even more troubling was Richard's last entry.

Drovetti knows. I will find him.

Chione stared at the words for a long time. The last words Richard wrote before he had been killed. He'd been close to finding Mervyn, she knew it. And he'd been killed because of it.

'Have you found something?'

Chione jumped and looked up to find Trey standing in the doorway. His voice sounded soft, but a hard glitter shone in his blue eyes as he closed the door behind him and entered the room.

'Something, yes, but not what we need.' She sighed. 'It's frustrating. Richard's notes are very cryptic. I think I know what he means, but I can't be sure.' Heart pounding, she waved him down to sit beside her and showed him the last entry.

'Drovetti?' he asked. 'Drovetti knows what?'

'Where Mervyn is, I had supposed.'

Trey looked sceptical. 'I highly doubt it, Chione. Drovetti is the French consul in Egypt. His focus is firmly on besting England's consul-general, Henry Salt. Drovetti spent the months when I was there travelling the Nile looking for more treasures to send to France. Unless Mervyn is sitting on top of an impressive artifact, I can't see him caring one way or another.'

Chione did not argue with him. 'Did you speak with Aswan?'

'I did. Our Egyptian is a man of many resources, my dear. It appears that while the bandits have been watching us, Aswan has been learning a bit about them.'

'Are you sure that is all that there is to it?'

'Completely sure. You know, Aswan came to our dig with Richard. He always seemed devoted to the lad, and he's shown you and the children the same devotion.'

'I can't deny how wonderful he's been with the children.' Still, there was something more to Aswan's story, Chione knew. Perhaps she would begin to watch the servant as intently as he watched her.

She picked up another journal. 'This one covers the time before Richard left for Egypt. It mentions Mr Belzoni more than once. Have you ever met the man?'

'The circus strongman turned intrepid traveller?' Trey looked amused. 'From what I saw he is quite a skilled excavator. He certainly beat Drovetti to some prize antiquities, but, no, I have not had the pleasure. Why?'

'It looks as if Richard spent time with him in London before he left. I think he felt as if they had a good deal in common. Belzoni gave Richard advice on how to handle himself in Egypt. He even gave him some letters of introduction to smooth his way. It appears that in return, Richard helped him catalogue his artifacts and prepare them for exhibition.'

Trey squinted in remembrance. 'Yes, Alden did mention that Belzoni's exhibit had opened to great success, didn't he?'

'I had forgotten!' Chione suppressed a shiver of excitement. 'Could he be the C. G. B. that Richard mentions? Do you think we should go to London and speak with him ourselves?'

'We might. Let's give you a chance to get through those journals first, though.' A grim look passed over his face. 'I know I scoffed at the notion of finding anything in these before, but now I'm asking you to do your best, Chione. This mess is far from over.'

Cold dread seized Chione as he told her what Drake had shown him today.

'They are not done with us yet,' he finished.

She straightened, allowing anxiety to coalesce into determination. Gripping Richard's journal tighter, she shot him a blazing look. 'I'll find it.'

The flare of approval in his eye warmed her. 'That's the spirit,' he said softly. 'We're not done with them yet, either. And while you are looking, we'll all have a chance to adjust to our new—circumstances.'

The 'we' he used caused her heart to trip faster.

Reaching out, he put his hand over hers. His finger traced a tiny circle on her skin. 'I couldn't ask earlier,' he breathed. 'How do you feel?'

'Fine.' She breathed deeply and confessed, 'Scared. Confused.' She did not reveal the predominant emotion she'd clung to all day. *Hopeful.* 'How do you feel?' she asked with a twist of her mouth.

He laughed. 'I've been bombarded with more emotions in the past twenty-four hours than I think I've experienced in my life,' he said a little helplessly. 'But right now?' His circling finger began to creep up her arm. 'Lost. Found.' He'd reached her shoulder and he began to lean in, his eyes fixed ruthlessly on her mouth. 'Desperate to touch you again.'

Her eyes widened just as their lips met, then slid closed on a moan of homecoming. His questing fingers found her breast and she leaned into the caress, wordlessly asking for more and knowing with a sudden certainty that that was what Trey meant to her. Home. Her other half. For most of her life Chione had known something was missing. She'd thought it must be her heritage that made her feel so, or the dark secrets of her past. She'd tried so hard to be what she was not, seeking to hide her insufficiencies from the world. But all along she'd only been missing him.

Trey deepened his kiss and Chione's ability to form a coherent thought vanished. This time she banned fear and gave herself over to simply feeling.

He kissed her sweetly, with a tenderness that replaced last night's urgency and incredibly, aroused her even more. His fingers moved lightly over her; butterfly wings that sought out buttons and ties until he had her bodice down, her stays undone, and her shift about her waist. And all the while he kissed her. Deep, soul-stirring kisses, nipping, teasing kisses, and every sort of kiss in between, until he had her leaned over the low back of the chaise and her naked breasts thrust up at him entreatingly. Her nipples were hard, yearning for his touch, and at last, with a look of rapture, he took his mouth from hers and worked his way slowly down.

An eternity later his mouth closed over her nipple. He gave her aching breasts the same treatment he had given her mouth. He licked, laved, sucked, and even bit her with a gentle pressure. Chione wanted to scream. A molten trail of pleasure, of endless, joyous *need* trickled from his mouth to pool between her legs.

She couldn't help it. This was Trey—her Niall—making her feel so right. Passion built inside of her until she had to give it voice or die. She gasped, shuddered, and moaned his name aloud.

He raised his head and met her gaze with a blazing blue triumphant one. 'God, Chione, I wish there were words for what you do to me.'

For a moment she shared his triumph, marvelling at how giving him pleasure intensified her own. Then she forgot everything as he raised the hem of her gown.

The heat and the longing she felt grew as his fingers travelled past her stockings, over her garters and on to the naked skin of her thigh. He touched her centre and she was lost.

She was wet, drenched with need, and soon so was he. His fingers slid like magic over her most sensitive spots and the tension inside of her loomed suddenly large.

But then his hand disappeared from where she needed it most and he slipped down from the chaise to the floor. She whimpered her confusion. His movements were jerky as he pushed her skirts up further and his voice sounded hoarse when he spoke. 'Wider,' he urged. 'Open your legs, love. I have to taste you.'

Her body obeyed before her mind could wonder and his questing tongue soon answered in any case. Chione gasped. 'Niall—what are you…?'

'Shh.' He eased her back down. 'Let me, Chione.' He flashed her a wicked grin. 'I promise you'll be glad you did.'

She was. His tongue was hot and it went unerringly to all the places that craved it. He teased her unmercifully, far past the point of restraint. Chione's hips bucked wildly and she buried her fingers in his hair, clutching him hard and surrendering all control until she exploded in a thousand different directions.

She came back to herself abruptly when Trey loomed above her, filling her to the hilt in one hot, hard thrust. She cried out, holding him tight with arms, legs, and muscles she hadn't even known she'd had.

'Hang on,' he said in a strained voice above her. 'This isn't going to take very long.'

It didn't. And this time, after the explosion, Chione very much feared that a few of her essential pieces had unknowingly bonded with his.

Chapter Fifteen

Chione breathed deeply. The half-forgotten smell of warm honey and dates drifted to her on the breeze. She'd forgot how astonishingly cool and clear the morning air could be in Egypt. With a start she realised where she was. Or where she wasn't. In the garden of the Frank, outside the home of the man who had owned her mother.

A dream, she told herself firmly, staring down the gravelled path that led to the house. *It's only a dream*. Suddenly Trey was on the path, stalking towards her. This was not the languid, satisfied man who had walked her to her rooms and kissed her thoroughly goodnight a few hours ago. This Trey looked angry, resentful. She caught a brief flash of hurt on his face before he reached her and stopped, an icy glare spearing her to the soul.

'You could have told me,' he rumbled, his resentment echoing like thunder. 'Why didn't you tell me, Chione?'

She came awake with a jerk, and drew a shuddering breath. Her mother had told her that her mind would speak to her in dreams. There was no mistaking what it was saying. It didn't feel right to share her body and not her whole soul. Chione just did not want to hear.

Seeking distraction, she climbed out of bed and threw back

the curtains. The softer, early morning light of Devonshire flooded in, obliterating her vision of Egypt. She wished that the spectres of her past could be so easily forgot, and her guilt in not sharing them with Trey. Taking up one of the journals that she'd brought to her room, she settled in the window seat.

She was working her way backwards and now was ready to give her attention to the journal that chronicled Richard's thoughts as he prepared to leave for Egypt. The tone in these pages was more eager expectation than grim determination. The familiar easygoing voice at once comforted her and made her miss her brother all the more.

She sharpened her eye and read closely when she first saw Jack Alden's name, but she could find no mention of Mervyn, Richard's search for information on the legend of the architect's daughter, or of his acquisition of the golden box.

There was rather a long section on his meetings with Mr Belzoni. Her brother appeared to have been very impressed with the former strongman and his ambitions. Belzoni wrote out several letters of recommendation to various *kashifs* and others he thought might be useful in Richard's work, and in return Richard seemed to have helped him catalogue his artifacts. Stuck in the pages were copies of several inventories that her brother had written out. The first one appeared to be a list of objects with short descriptions. Despite herself, Chione was interested.

Mummified fingers
    Forty-three in all. Belzoni reports the remainders of the bodies have disintegrated into dust.
Papyrus
    Lavishly decorated, three and twenty feet long—the longest in Europe!

Some of the objects were marked; these appeared to be the ones that Belzoni meant to include in his exhibit. She had to assume the others would be sold. She was folding the lists to put them aside when abruptly she stopped.

She gasped. It was true; she'd seen her name, at the bottom of the first list.

Wooden Statues-Two
Each four feet high, with a circular hollow, as if to hold a scroll or papyryus. Chione might be particularly interested in what the scroll contains.

The mark was there. The statues were in London—in Belzoni's exhibition.

Chione was out of the window seat so fast she tripped over the small pile of journals. Scrambling to her feet, she tore out of her room and into the hall. When she reached Trey's room she did not stop. She burst through the door, surprising both Trey, who stood in front of a long mirror, and Aswan, who was handing him a starched neckcloth.

'I've found it!' she gasped. 'We've got to go to London!'

They were travelling again, but in a completely different manner from the first trip Chione had taken with Trey. Instead of four people in a fast-moving coach, they had a caravan the size of a regiment and nearly enough people to form one.

Chione had absolutely refused to travel without the children again. Both Eli and Mrs Ferguson had refused to be left behind. Jenny came to help with Will and Olivia and to keep an eye on the coachman. Aswan held sway over the large number of armed outriders that Trey had hired.

There could be no attempt at stealth this time, not with two carriages, a luggage wagon, Will's pony and the dog. But though they were a large group, they were not unwieldy and they made surprisingly good time.

Chione could not help but notice how much happier Trey

appeared since they had left Oakwood Court. The challenges and excitement of travel suited him. He lost the faint hunted look he had been carrying and appeared completely relaxed. The obvious change only added to Chione's burden of guilt. Clearly Trey was not a man meant to be tied down.

Just as clearly, she was not a woman who could slide easily into the role of countess. One look around at their rag-tag entourage proved that, as did Chione's ever-increasing worry about her past. Her mind kept wandering back to her confrontation with Mrs Stockton, to the cold stab of fear she'd suffered when the harridan had announced that she'd discovered Chione's secrets. She hadn't, of course, but what if, in seeking revenge, she stumbled across the truth? It was unlikely, but not impossible.

Chione wondered repeatedly if she shouldn't just tell Trey about herself right out, but her imagination won out over her resolution every time. She would picture his shock, imagine seeing shame in his eyes when he looked at her instead of warmth and desire, and she would delay. As the trip continued, it became easier to push back her vague feelings of dread and focus instead on keeping Olivia from falling out of the open carriage window.

For their last night on the road, Trey stopped his little caravan in Maidenhead. He chose Mr. Lovegrove's Red Lion rather than the more famous Bear Inn, for he thought all the coaching traffic in and out of the Bear might provide an opportunity for their adversaries.

The tang of freshly oiled tack mixed with the solid smells of horse and hay as Trey inspected the hacks available for hire. Across the way Eli groomed the tired grey with loving hands and Will slipped Charlemagne a carrot and a quick caress. Morty had curled into a contented ball near the door, but Trey was aware when her head perked up. She sampled the air and gave a soft woof.

Trey exchanged glances with Eli, then nodded meaningfully towards Will before he stepped away from the job horses. 'Will,' he said casually, 'I thought I saw Charlemagne favouring a back foot when you put him away. Why don't you check it out and give all of his shoes a good going over, too? I'm going to speak to the stable master about this pair of chestnuts.'

The boy agreed and with a last silent warning look to Eli, Trey crossed to the stable door, where the dog now stood at attention. It had grown dark and the stiff breeze had driven nearly everyone indoors. As Trey watched, an ostler took a horse from a newly arrived traveller near the inn's main door. As the boy and the horse grew closer, Trey saw the dark figure of a man finish speaking with Lovegrove. Yet instead of following the innkeeper inside, the newcomer turned towards the stables.

Trey ducked into the shadows and called for the dog to follow. She came willingly, yet stood alert at his side. The ostler passed into the stable. The man still came on. Trey murmured a stern command and stepped into the light.

The stranger stopped short. 'Treyford! Here you are, then! I've caught you at last!'

'Alden,' Trey said in surprise. 'Jack Alden.' He stood still while the scholar thumped him enthusiastically on the back. 'What are you doing here?'

The man took Trey's arm and pulled him towards the stable door. 'I've come to warn you.'

'Warn me?' Trey soothed the dog, who had begun to bristle when Alden took hold of him.

'Yes, you and your companions are being followed.'

'Oh?' This Trey already suspected, and, in fact, hoped was the case. He just wanted to get his little caravan safely installed in London before their adversaries struck. When the situation escalated again, he wanted to have the upper hand. 'What is it exactly that you've seen, Alden?'

The scholar breathed deeply. 'I'll start at the beginning,

then, so you won't think I've gone off half-cocked.' He smiled. 'I'm on my way back to London. My brother's wife is due to present him with a child soon, and I expect I'll be needed to provide him moral support. Or at least enough brandy to get him through her ordeal.'

Trey managed a smile.

'In any case, I had left Exeter and stopped for the night in Glastonbury. On settling the bill the next morning, I heard a man mention your name. Very casually, to be sure, but it was clear he was hoping to find out if you'd passed through there.'

'Did you know this man?'

'He could have been anyone's lackey, save for his unusual accent. The innkeeper had no information for him. I paid my shot in record time and followed him outside.' Alden's tone grew more serious. 'A rag-tag group waited outside, such as I've never seen. But it was seeing their leader that made me decide to follow.' He eyed Trey carefully. 'I suspect, with a career like yours, you've made an enemy or two, but I confess, were it me, I'd think twice before crossing such a man.'

'Tell me,' said Trey.

'Two score and ten, perhaps? Difficult to tell behind the impressive beard. He was dressed as immaculately as any English gentleman, and sported an elaborate turban. Don't take me for an old woman, Treyford, but it was his eyes that were most disturbing. They were dark, but somehow…flat. Inhuman, I could almost say.'

The mysterious Hassan? Trey wondered. 'And that was in Glastonbury?'

'Aye. Ten or so of them, near as I could tell. They've trailed carefully behind you ever since. Until this afternoon. I overtook them in Twyford. They were gathered at the King's Arms and it looked to me like a council of war. I'd say you'd better prepare yourself for some trouble.'

A surge of anger and frustration welled in Trey's chest. So

close. They were but a day's short travel from London. He stood a moment, indecisive. Should he gather his odd regiment together and run? Or was this it? Had it come already to a last stand? He bit back his irritation. He needed time.

'You know,' Alden said slowly, 'what you need is a distraction.'

'It would be ideal,' Trey agreed tersely, 'but how?'

'Most of these men appear to be Egyptian, or Turkish perhaps. By all accounts they are a superstitious lot.'

'They can be,' Trey agreed.

'Perhaps we can spook them, give them a little something to worry about? And you could use the delay to get your people out of here.'

Trey grinned. 'I like the way you think, Alden.'

The man smiled back, ruefully. 'Yes, well, I have to say, life has been quiet since my brother settled into domesticity. It will be good to shake things up a little, and, I confess, I look forward to putting all that study to a good use.'

'Well, I'm happy to oblige,' laughed Trey. 'I'll send my man Aswan with you. If anyone could put the fear of ancient gods and modern Englishmen into their souls, it'll be the pair of you.'

His tired and bedraggled caravan arrived in London early the next morning. Despite their exhaustion, the children hung out the window, enthralled by the teeming streets, the tall buildings, the joyful noise and noxious smells of so many people and animals living cheek by jowl. Will, in fact, seemed almost disappointed when they reached the more genteel environs of Soho Square. Trey supposed to an eager boy's eyes it lacked the dangerous romantic appeal of London's more treacherous districts.

'Not to worry, Will,' Trey called. 'London has more than its share of adventures for you to get into.' They came to a halt in front of a suitably impressive home. Trey dismounted and slapped the grey affectionately as Eli came over to take it in hand.

The ornate door still stood closed. Trey put down the step and handed the women and children out of the carriage. Jenny and Olivia stood hand in hand on the pavement, gaping at the handsome row of townhouses. Will and Morty faced the other direction, both staring longingly at the grass and gardens in the Square.

'May I take Morty over to stretch her legs?' asked Will. 'She doesn't like being confined to the coach.'

'We're none so fond of it either,' muttered Mrs Ferguson as she accepted Trey's help in descending.

'Of course, Will,' Chione answered, 'but you'll have to wait until we can get the key.'

'No need.' The boy gestured at another lad crossing the street, ball in hand. 'We'll just tag in with him.' He set off, the dog frisking at his heels.

'Oh, dear,' Chione said, surveying the still silent house. 'I do hope Pilkens got the letter I sent ahead.'

'I only hope the old barnacle's still alive,' Mrs Ferguson said. 'He always was an odd duck, I don't figure close to two years sittin' in an empty house has done him any good.'

'Now, don't you begin by pestering him,' Chione chided. 'I offered the poor man the chance to come to Oakwood Court when we closed this house up.' She raised a brow at her house-keeper. 'Strangely enough, he declined.'

'I said he was odd, not stupid,' Mrs Ferguson answered. She picked up her bag and laboured up the short stairs, Jenny and Olivia following.

Trey laughed and exchanged a glance with Chione. Seconds ticked by while the rest of the world receded. For this moment they were alone, alive and enjoying the inevitable pull, the intangible call of desire. Not urgent, just the private joy of a promise to be fulfilled. Then the coachman called for Trey and the spell was broken.

Chione looked across the square to where Will had gone and then back at the house.

'Go on in,' he told her. 'The outriders are waiting for me. I'll deal with them and the luggage and keep an eye on Will.'

She smiled. 'Thank you.'

Trey sent a couple of his hired men to the mews with the remaining riding horses. The others he set to unloading baggage. He shared a quick word with the coachman and went to the front to check the straps on the lead team. Calling a reassurance, he walked down the street side of the coach and team.

That was when he saw it—a grubby hand at the end of a reaching arm, snaking from beneath the baggage wagon to snatch a small portmanteau.

Trey did not react. He finished his conversation with the driver, then strolled down to the cart. He stopped very casually next to the large front wheel, bent down, reached right through the spokes and grabbed the scruff of the boy underneath, who was quietly trying to creep away with his prize.

A startled yelp rang out and a massive struggle ensued. 'Get off me!' The boy flailed like a fish on a line, but Trey pulled him in close to the wheel, reached his other arm around and hauled him out and over to the curb.

The scrawny lad glared at Trey and at the gathering circle of curious men. Obviously deciding that resistance in the face of such odds was futile, he abruptly ceased struggling and changed his tactics.

'Don't turn me in, guv,' he pleaded, his eyes welling with unshed tears. 'I wouldn't a nicked it if me bruther didn't need 'is medicine.' He sniffed. 'Comes turrible dear, it does.'

Trey laughed. 'Little brother needs medicine, eh? That's one I haven't tried myself. Full marks for inventiveness, lad.' He kept his hold on the boy and squatted down to look him in the eye. 'That bit work often for you?'

The dirty creature shrugged. Trey noted how thin the

shoulder in his grip felt, nearly as insubstantial as the patched and worn jacket that covered it. 'What's your name?'

His answer was an unintelligible mumble.

'What's that?'

'I said, it's Bartholomew,' he spat.

'Ah.' Trey gazed down at his captive thoughtfully. 'Church orphanage, was it? Born in August?'

He nodded.

'Well, it could have been worse. Had you been born in October, you might have been named after St Jude.' He ran his gaze over the boy again. 'Are you still living there?'

He looked away.

'Where are you staying, lad?'

The boy shrugged those thin shoulders defensively. ''Ere and there.'

'You might be able to help me, then. I need a likely lad while we are here in London. Someone with their wits about them, someone who knows the streets and has a watchful eye. He'd have to know when to keep quiet and be able to blend into the background, perhaps even be willing to do some fetching and carrying. Do you know anybody who might fit the bill?'

He gave Trey a measuring look. 'Is yer business above board, or shady-like?'

'Strictly above board, I swear.'

'Too bad,' the lad scoffed. 'I got a few contacts.' He heaved an exaggerated sigh. 'But iff'n ye be needin' someone right away, I s'pose I could do it for ye.'

'That would be convenient,' Trey agreed. 'Tell me, do you have a brother or are you on your own?'

A slight shake of the head was all the answer he got.

'I'm going to let you go, then. You can run off, if you like. But there's a warm bed in the stables and a shilling a day to be had if you take the position.'

His eyes widened. 'I'm yer man, guv!'

'The name's Treyford. And if you work for me, there's to be no more "nicking" anything. Are we agreed?'

He nodded.

Trey tossed him a coin. 'Run on back to the stables and tell the man with the peg that I've given you the job. He'll see you settled.'

The boy pocketed the coin. He looked Trey over and shook his head. 'Ye must be daft, yer lordship.' With a cheeky wink he was off, running down the street to make the turn that would take him back to the mews.

Trey grinned at the watching men. 'Let's get this unloaded quick, then, before I get taken in again.'

Laughing, they went back to work. Trey turned, and saw Chione still poised on the top step. He'd had no idea she'd witnessed the incident, but even from here he could see her tremulous smile and the tears trapped in her thick lashes. He paused, drawn up short by her unexpected reaction, but she only nodded at him, turned and went in.

Trey shrugged and went back to work. When the baggage was unloaded, he left the opening of the house to Chione. He quickly arranged a watch schedule for his men, and then he set off for Piccadilly.

Belzoni's Tomb had closed for the day. Trey was unable to wangle his way into the Egyptian Hall, but he did purchase tickets for the following day, and after parting with a good bit of coin, he managed to 'discover' the explorer's town address.

Unfortunately, the rooms in Bayswater were empty. Trey left a polite note asking if the Italian explorer could meet with him at his exhibit the following day. He walked back to an employment agency along the Strand, where he persuaded the owner to delay his dinner to go over his files of household servants.

What with one thing and another, it was once again late in the evening when he arrived back home and most of his motley crew had gone to bed. His watchmen were alert, but reported no signs of trouble. Trey climbed the stairs with weary feet, only to pause on the second floor and wonder where he was to go.

Fortunately he'd only been there a moment when a door down the hall opened. Chione backed out with a quiet tread. She turned, saw him and gifted him with a tired but brilliant smile.

Trey's heartbeat ratcheted up alarmingly. He looked away, a little wary of the intensity of his response.

'Brace yourself,' she whispered as she came closer. 'Incredibly, our entourage has grown again since you left.' She stopped, very close. He could smell the sweet scent of her hair. 'We've a new cook bedded down next to the kitchen, a nursery maid in with Olivia…' she nodded towards the door she had just left '…and a chambermaid upstairs, who, she says, the employment agent threw in for good measure.' She tilted her head. 'And of course, there is your urchin asleep in the stables.' She paused. 'It's a scary prospect, is it not?' Her tone was sympathetic, but there was a definite challenge in her raised brow.

She was teasing him. And she was right; the thought of being responsible for even more people should have bothered him. The fact that she knew it should have bothered him even more. Perhaps later it would. Now all he could think of was the taste of her mouth, the soft slide of her skin beneath his. He pulled her in close and kissed her, hard and demanding, using his rising excitement to blot out any incipient anxiety.

It appeared her mind ran in a similar direction. She fisted her hands in his hair and kissed him back with matching ferocity. When finally he released her she reached up, cupped his cheek with her hand and turned him, forcing his gaze to meet hers.

'Thank you,' she said fiercely. 'Thank you for everything you did for that boy today.'

Puzzled at her reaction, he nodded. 'One person at a time, remember?' he asked.

She did. She smiled through watery eyes and something inside of Trey gave way, crumbling before the emotion he saw there. She stood on her toes, pulled his face in to hers and kissed him with soft lips.

He groaned and they were gone, mouths and hands roaming wildly. Trey felt that in some way Chione was offering him something more than her body. He ran his hands over her back, pulled the sweet curve of her bottom tighter to him and wondered if he had the courage to take it.

He never got the chance to answer the question. A door opened and long, loud throat-clearing commenced, interrupting their embrace.

'Betrothed ain't married!' chastised Mrs Ferguson. 'Both of ye get to yer rooms. Alone!'

They broke apart. Laughing, Chione slipped away. She stopped, pointed him towards a door and gave him a little push. Obediently, wondering just what the hell he'd got himself into—or more importantly, what Mrs Ferguson had got him out of—Trey went.

Chapter Sixteen

A brisk wind invaded London early the next morning, clearing the fog and making the way clear for a glorious, sunny spring day. Unfortunately, neither Trey nor Eli had the opportunity to take pleasure in it. They sat in a coffee house in Piccadilly, across and down a bit from the Egyptian Hall. The exhibit had only just opened. Mrs Ferguson and Trey's new protégé had just entered.

Trey looked and saw a hackney carriage pull up in front of the Egyptian Hall. As he watched, Chione and Will climbed out, both dressed in plain, serviceable clothes. He had to admit, they did look like a boy and his governess out for a morning's romp. They approached the pillared entrance of the Egyptian Hall and Trey stood.

In a leisurely fashion he and Eli made their way across Piccadilly and towards the Hall. The bright morning light did not flatter the place any more than last evening's dusk had. Certainly it stood out from its neighbours, with its pylon shape, its stucco front and its figures of Isis and Osiris flanking a first-floor window. If the statues were more Greek, and the overall design only vaguely Egyptian, then Trey was sure that the average Londoner would scarcely know different.

Ah, but the inside was another matter altogether. Belzoni

had obviously gone to much trouble and expense to remodel the entire place. They entered the first area, which the pro- gramme proclaimed to be 'The Room of Beauties'. The flick- ering gas light burned low, the atmosphere was hushed. It was meant to convey the moment that the strongman had first entered the tomb, likely the first person to see these sights in three thousand years. The room was large, nearly twenty feet long, Trey guessed, and a very close approximation of the real tomb. Every wall was lined with gorgeous figures in relief, just as in the Valley of the Kings.

Although the hour was early yet, a good number of people were inside, taking in the wonders in nearly mute fascination. Trey separated from Eli as planned. As he moved farther into the room he spotted Mrs Ferguson ensconced on a bench next to a mummy case, knitting in hand. The boy Bart stood next to her, completely absorbed in the grisly figure. Trey smiled wryly. The mummy was not nearly so horrifying as the thought of what Mrs Ferguson might do with a set of knitting needles.

He could see no sign of Chione or Will, and though he took his time exploring the dark shadowed corners, he did not see a wooden statue with a hollow back. Signalling to Eli, he moved on to the next room.

This was an even larger area, named the 'Entrance Hall' by the Italian. Four pillars, adorned with scenes of Pharaoh being welcomed by the gods, dominated the centre of the room.

Still Trey did not see Chione. Carefully he made his way through the crowd. He edged his way past a group of people and gave a violent start. A woman stood in the corner, poised over a glass case filled with medals and decorative ornaments. A woman with dark hair and beautiful, intense features. Not Chione. Madame Fornier.

His stomach churned and his mind flashed back to the image of her standing naked before him, his hands roaming over her flesh. Flushing right to the roots of his hair, he glanced about, searching for Chione. He breathed a little easier when he did not see her and debated his next move.

All of his instincts told him that she did not belong here. The lady's presence was entirely too coincidental. He would have to approach her. Pasting a smile on his face, he advanced in her direction.

'Madame Fornier,' he said in a low voice. She did not look pleased to see him. 'What an unexpected delight. I had not heard that you meant to leave Egypt.'

His caressing tone had reassured her. She smiled into his eyes. '*Ah, Monsieur le Earl!* I did not think to see you in London,' she purred. 'Alas, many things have changed since last we met.' She shot him a quizzical look. 'I heard of your partner's death. A sad blow.'

'Yes,' Trey agreed, suddenly curt.

'We, too, have suffered misfortune. My husband—he has fallen from Drovetti's favour. And so we have been forced to take up a new business venture.'

'I am sorry to hear of it,' Trey said. 'But I hope your new position is as…satisfying…as the old?'

She moved a step closer. Trey kept his gaze locked with hers, though he knew they were in danger of attracting unwanted attention.

'Oh, no, my lord,' she spoke in a whisper now and with a pout on her lovely face. 'Only to you will I confess that I have not been satisfied at all since our last encounter.'

Trey raised her hand to his lips. 'Now that is a tragedy indeed.'

She watched him through half-lidded eyes. 'Perhaps you will help me with this trouble?'

'Perhaps I shall.' He took a step back and resumed a more normal tone. 'But, please, tell me of your new business.'

She sighed. 'My husband has entered the service of Captain Batiste. Perhaps you have heard of him? He is a well-known traveller and has shown an interest in Egypt as well.'

'I'm sorry I have not, but I wish you much success.'

'Thank you,' she simpered. She gestured to the exhibition around them. 'Monsieur Belzoni does not know what a great service he has done us. So many people have arrived early in London for the coronation. Belzoni's book and now his exhibit have once again stirred a great interest in Egyptian artifacts. We have done very well, selling some of our collection at a good profit.' She glanced about, slightly irritated. 'I was to meet a potential buyer here today, but I am afraid he has decided not to keep the appointment.'

'How rude…' Trey smiled lazily '…and how incredibly stupid.'

'I shall not wait any longer.' She tilted her head and smiled. 'But that does leave me with a great deal of free time this morning. Perhaps, if you are free also, we could spend it together?'

'I am heartbroken to say that I have an appointment also this morning, and it is one that must be kept. Would you forgive my refusal and grant me the privilege at another time?'

'For you? Of course. Our lodgings are in a dreadful area of Shadwell, but my husband is very rarely there.' She leaned in and pressed her bosom against him intimately as she kissed both his cheeks. 'I promise, should you visit, I will make you very comfortable indeed. *Adieu, Monsieur le Earl.*'

'Goodbye, *madame.*'

He watched her take her leave. She sashayed right past the combined force of Mrs Ferguson, Bart and Will, who all stared as she went by. Trey waited a few moments before he approached them himself.

'I take it you saw the lady?' he asked.

'Cor, guv! Who didn't?' Bart said appreciatively.

'I want to know where she goes from here, Bart, but I do not want her or anyone else to know you are trailing her. Can you do that?'

'Easy,' he scoffed.

'Do you have the money I gave you this morning?'

The boy nodded.

'After her, then. And be careful, lad. Do not get yourself in trouble. If something doesn't look right, leave it, and get yourself home quick.'

'Aye, guv.'

He turned to go, but Will put a hand on his sleeve and turned to Trey with pleading eyes. 'Please, Trey. I want to go too.'

There was more in his face than just a boy's lust for adventure. Mervyn was the boy's father, after all. After a moment's hesitation Trey glanced wordlessly at Bart.

The former street urchin knew what he was silently asking. He glanced at Will and he nodded.

'Fine, then, but Eli will go along.' Trey sighed. 'If something happens to you, your niece will skin me alive.'

'Thank you,' said Will fervently. Eli nodded at Trey and then they were gone.

Trey turned to Mrs Ferguson. 'Do you know where in blazes Chione has got to?'

The housekeeper nodded and gestured with her chin. 'She's making friends.'

Trey turned and saw an immensely tall man framed in an arched doorway, talking to someone in an animated fashion. By the height and breadth of him, it could only be the infamous Belzoni himself. The large man took a step aside and Trey caught sight of his audience. Chione, very pale, stared back at him with narrowed eyes.

'The *ushabti* figures of blue faience are indeed very beautiful,' the Italian explorer said as they entered what he called the Entrance Hall. 'We also found some of wood, and stone. There were an immense number of them stored in a room with the slaughtered carcass of a bull.' He chuckled. 'Clearly, with so many of the little servant figures buried with him, Seti did not intend to waste his afterlife on manual labour.'

'Who could picture Pharaoh fetching water or cooking a meal?' asked Chione inanely. Her brain had ceased to function the moment she had seen that strange woman pressing herself obscenely against Trey. She'd known he'd had a multitude of women in the past, but somehow she'd been so preoccupied with the search for Mervyn and dealing with the present reality of her unexpected betrothal that she had just pushed the idea of the future away. She was very much afraid that a glimpse of it had just hit her hard. She clenched her fists. She fully planned to hit back.

But not at this moment. She was here with a purpose. Now she had to concentrate on finding her brother's clue. Chione focused her attention back on Belzoni and his conjecture on what a pharaoh's lift might have been like. He paused when she laid her hand on his massive arm.

'Mr Belzoni, I see Lord Treyford across the room. Shall I introduce you?'

'Of course,' he agreed readily.

Trey had already started towards them. They met in the centre of the four pillars.

'Lord Treyford,' Chione began, 'may I introduce Mr Belzoni? He has been showing me some of the *ushabti* figures he found buried in the tomb.'

The great Italian bowed low.

'Richard Latimer spoke of you often, sir, and praised your collection of antiquities so highly that we could not possibly stay away,' Trey said.

'Ah, I have already offered the lady my sincerest condolences. Richard was a kind boy and an excellent scholar.'

'He spoke of the extensive work you did, copying the reliefs of the tomb in wax and reproducing them here. What a huge undertaking that must have been. Would you do us the honour of escorting us through yourself?'

'It would be my pleasure.' The big man did seem truly delighted. 'We must go upstairs to the galleries to see the true sequence from corridor to burial vault. But first, have you seen the models? I have the Second Pyramid and also Abu Simbel.'

Chione trailed in the men's wake, listening to Trey marvel over the Italian's stories of his explorations and the insights that had led him to so many discoveries. Her own attention was divided. She kept her eye out for the wooden statues, and for Eli and Will and the rest of them. She glimpsed the housekeeper, but her interest in the men's conversation peaked when Belzoni began to talk of his feud with the French and even with England's own consul in Egypt, Henry Salt.

'In your travels, sir, have you ever made the acquaintance of my grandfather, Mervyn Latimer?'

'No, miss.' The Italian shook his head. 'I did not have the pleasure. Your brother mentioned his many exploits. He sounds as if he was a great man.'

Chione ignored his use of the past tense. 'Did Richard ever speak to you of his interest in the Pharaoh's Lost Jewel?'

Belzoni stroked his chin. 'Once. We had a lively debate on the subject.'

'And will you share your opinions, sir?'

'Of course.' He glanced at her thoughtfully. 'I will tell you what I told your brother. The pharaohs of Egypt have been robbed of thousands of jewels over thousands of years. What is one more? No—if there is such a treasure—and I have my doubts—then I would guess it is something more valuable than gemstones or gold.'

Trey looked sharply attentive. 'Such as?'

'An important scroll, perhaps? A map to the tombs in the Valley? Or a key to finally translating hieroglyphs? An Egyptian once told me he had heard it was a map to a lost city of treasure, but he was a thief, himself. Who can tell which is the truth of it? I would guess it must be something out of the ordinary for the legend to persist so long.'

'That is a very interesting theory, Mr Belzoni. I shall think on it.' Trey glanced at Chione before continuing. 'In his journals Richard described some of the amazing artifacts he helped you catalogue. I've seen some of the most interesting ones he wrote about, but haven't seen two wooden statues he mentioned— hollowed out to hold scrolls? Are they included in your exhibit?'

'Yes, of course. They are not so magnificent as my statues of Sekhmet. I hope you will not be disappointed.'

Chione's heart began to race as Belzoni led them to a shadowy corner of the gallery. There stood the statues, just exactly as Richard had described. Two sheets of rolled papyrus had been tucked into place. Trey walked around them, eyeing them critically.

'Not very fancy, perhaps, but definitely useful, are they not? Especially to a royal scribe or some such person.' He looked to their host. 'I have not seen your Sekhmets, sir. Where are they?'

'Downstairs. They are truly lovely. I shall take you there.'

'If you will excuse me, gentlemen, I think I would like to finish admiring these reliefs you worked so very hard on, sir.' Chione struggled to keep her tone even.

Trey nodded. 'We will meet you downstairs when you are finished, Miss Latimer.'

'Of course.'

Struggling to stay calm, Chione strolled on. She watched the gentlemen exit downstairs, then had to wait until an obviously courting couple followed. Finally, her pulse racing, she went back to the statues.

Glancing furtively about, she drew out one sheet of papyrus. It was blank. Uttering a prayer, she reached for the second. She unrolled it carefully, and nearly collapsed in relief when she glimpsed her brother's handwriting.

To find the coffer, Chione must face her greatest fear.

Clutching the scroll to her, she slumped against the wall.

Trey was standing with Belzoni when Chione came downstairs. He took one look at her pale face and drawn expression, uttered a sound of concern and hurried to her side.

'Did you find it?' he asked quietly, reaching out a steadying hand.

'Yes.'

'You have it?'

She nodded.

'Mr Belzoni,' Trey said as the explorer approached, 'I am afraid that Miss Latimer is feeling unwell. Unfortunately her carriage is not due back for quite some time. Do you think you could procure us a hackney?'

'Yes, yes, certainly. There is a bench right here, my dear young lady. Please sit while I see to it.'

'Thank you, you are so kind.' The look she gave Belzoni was truly grateful. 'I suppose, after the trials of our journey, I should have rested today. I was just so eager to see your treasures, sir.'

The explorer beamed. 'But it is not worth risking your health, my dear. I hope a rest will put you to rights.'

It was not long before Trey was able to bundle her into a hackney carriage. They bade their genial host goodbye and pulled away, but Trey had given the jarvey orders to wait at the corner. In just a moment, Mrs Ferguson climbed in.

'Where is Will? And Bartholomew? And Eli?' Chione said, looking around from the corner she had curled herself into.

Trey explained.

'You sent Eli to watch over them? What if he can't keep up?' She looked paler still, and suddenly furious.

'Bart knows what he is about,' Trey said.

'And young Will deserves a chance to do his part,' Mrs Ferguson piped in.

'I warned them both about not taking chances,' Trey continued. 'They will be fine.'

Chione looked even more upset at being overruled, but she turned away. She sat staring out of the window while the rest of them exchanged silent glances. Trey began to wonder if perhaps she truly was ill.

'Well…' Mrs Ferguson eventually broke the silence '…what of it? Did you find what you were looking for?'

They looked to Chione, who never turned from the window.

'May we see it, Chione?' Trey asked gently.

She pulled the tightly rolled papyrus from her pelisse. Trey read it, and then passed it on to the others. They all stared at each other once more in puzzlement.

'But what does it mean?' Mrs Ferguson finally asked.

'I think only Chione can answer that,' Trey said.

'I don't know!' she finally burst out. 'I have no idea. Damn Richard! How could he bring us so far and not be clear in the end?'

'Must be something,' the housekeeper said pragmatically. 'A childhood fear? Something he would ha' remembered? Snakes, maybe? Or spiders?'

'No, I've never been frightened of such things,' she answered irritably. 'Richard would know that. I don't understand. Perhaps someone else switched the scrolls.'

'Who?' asked Trey. 'If those thieving bandits had discovered and interpreted the clue, they would not have bothered to leave a fake. They'd have taken the damned coffer, whatever it is, and gone back to Egypt.'

'Well, there's been no sign of them,' she returned. 'Perhaps that is what happened. I don't know.'

In fact, Trey had indeed had word of their adversaries. Last night Aswan had frightened a year off of the life of one of the guards by 'risin' out o' the dark like a haunt in the dead of night.'

The former dragoman had come bearing good news. As with most predators, the bandits had focused on their stealth and their target and never once considered a threat from elsewhere. He and Alden had turned the tables on the bandits and now the hunters had become the prey.

One by one, the scholar and the Egyptian had begun picking the villains off. Aswan knew multitude ways of silencing a man, and they now had four of the thieves tucked away with Bow Street, and full knowledge of where the rest of the increasingly nervous band was quartered.

Unfortunately, Trey did not feel that now was a fortuitous time to share that information with Chione. He watched her face redden with embarrassment and even anger when Mrs Ferguson cast a dark look his way and suggested that men were what frightened Chione most.

'That makes no sense at all,' Chione snapped.

'That boy always did love a puzzle,' the housekeeper moaned. 'Why didn't he just tell us straight out where the damned thing is?'

'He left a clue only Chione could decipher,' Trey said. 'Otherwise anyone at all could have come along and found what we have searched so hard for.'

'I don't wish to discuss this,' Chione bit out. 'I need time to think.' Trey could not ever remember hearing her use such a sharp tone.

The carriage fell silent, but they did not have to endure the uncomfortable atmosphere for long before they arrived in Soho Square. Chione stalked into the house without uttering a word to anyone. Ferguson followed. Trey retreated to the stables to wait until Eli returned with the boys.

* * *

'The woman went straight to a boarding house in Shadwell,' the groom reported. Trey told him what had occurred after he left. They sent the boys back to the house, then stood in the courtyard of the mews and shook their heads at the capriciousness of women.

'Can't recall when I've ever heard of Miss Chione in such a taking,' mused Eli. 'Don't look good, does it?'

'If it is her greatest fear that has her in such a mood, I'm not sure I want to face it either,' Trey agreed.

Eli sighed.

'Wait—' Trey stopped, struck by a sudden thought. 'Eli, have you ever heard of a Captain Batiste?'

Slowly the old salt turned, surprise alight in his face. 'Aye. Knew him as well. Where did you be hearin' o' him?'

'From the lady you were following. Did you know her? Madame Fornier, or her husband? They were minor agents for Drovetti in Egypt when I was there, collecting antiquities for him.'

'No, never heard o' the pair o' them. But Gustavo Batiste? He's a bad character.'

'How so?'

'Mind if we sit?' Eli asked, pointing to a bench along the wall.

They crossed over and settled on the bench. 'Ah,' Eli sighed, 'that's better. Batiste,' he mused. 'Hadn't thought o' him in donkey's years. Used to captain one o' Mervyn's ships, he did. They were friends, o' sorts. Had a lot in common. He loved exploring new places, being first somewheres, jest like Mervyn did. But they had a fallin' out. Mervyn fired him. Furious he was, but he got him another ship and struck out on his own. They were rivals afterwards, even though Batiste could never really compete on the same level as Latimer Shipping.'

'What did they argue over, do you know?'

'Man was a slaver. He was runnin' with a light crew, havin'

converted half the crew quarters to slave holds. Mervyn found
out when one o' Batiste's men came to him. Turns out Batiste
was dumpin' the poor buggers overboard whenever they
spotted a ship of the line, to keep from paying the fines—right
steep they would a' been, too, at a hundred pounds per head.
Lordy, I ain't never seen Mervyn so mad as he was that day.'

'He does sound a nasty character.'

'Aye, best avoid him,' Eli said, rising and heading away
to his room.

Trey slowly followed him into the house. He could not help
but wonder what the Forniers might be doing for such a man
as Eli had described. Their presence here at this time made him
extremely uneasy. Things were coming to a head, Trey could
feel it. He had to find a way to get Chione talking about her
greatest fears.

Chapter Seventeen

Something had happened to Chione when she had read her brother's words on that papyrus. The creature inside of her— the *djinn* who had left her hiding place behind and begun to blossom under Trey's careful tutelage—had roared in sudden anger and fright, and then promptly disappeared.

Chione had been left feeling suddenly small and alone, burning with a strange combination of terror and hateful defiance. When Trey had spoken so gently to her in the carriage she had wanted to scream at him, to jump from the moving vehicle and run until her breath gave out and she lost the dark swirl of emotion churning inside of her.

Instead, hours later, it still churned and Chione did not know how much more she could take. She'd gone straight up to her room and although she had been glad to hear of Will and Bart's safe return, she had refused each gentle nudge to come down. Now the afternoon had lengthened into evening and the house gradually grew quiet. Chione slipped into the darkening corridors and began to prowl.

From the family bedrooms to the attics, past the kitchens where the servants were having their dinner, and even to the wine cellars, she stalked. She could not contain herself or the terrible anxiety besetting her. Window to window, room to room, she watched and waited and tried desperately not to think. She saw the guards changing shifts, one at the front of the house, one at the back. She nodded and kept going. She found Olivia in the stairwell and firmly tucked her back into bed in the nursery.

Inevitably, and at last, she found Trey. Or he found her. He ran her to ground in the dining room, a location she capitalised upon by keeping the long table between them.

Clearly, this exasperated him. 'Enough, Chione,' he barked. 'You're as edgy as a cat. We need to talk.'

'I don't wish to talk.'

'Yes, that is becoming increasingly clear. The real question here is why don't you wish to?'

'Because I am exasperated and frustrated, that's why,' she answered sharply. 'You know how I feel about the Jewel.' She struggled to keep the anger out of her voice. 'It dangles there, just out of reach. Men chase after it, dancing to its tune like puppets. And after a lifetime of vowing to ignore the song, I gave in. I started the dance and now the music has suddenly stopped!'

He raised a brow. 'So you are ready to give up looking for Mervyn? Just like that—you'll accept that you'll never know what happened to him?'

'No! Of course not.' She sounded unreasonable. She didn't care—she *felt* unreasonable, and she didn't know if she was more annoyed with Trey or herself. She turned away from him, running her hand along the sideboard.

'That does seem to be what will happen if we don't puzzle out that clue.'

'It's not a clue—it's an unanswerable question! How could Richard do that? Lay the blame for failure so firmly at my door?' Pain gripped her, and a sorrow so profound she thought she might crumple to the floor beneath its weight. But there was resentment inside of her too, and anger, and they gave her the strength to stay on her feet—and on her side of the table.

'No one is blaming you, Chione. We haven't even tried to answer that question yet.'

'I have tried. I've racked my brains all day. I cannot recall any silly childhood terrors. I'm not afraid of water, heights or dogs. *This* is my biggest fear—not finding Mervyn. After that would come fear of losing the children, but you've taken care of that. If I had to choose another, it would be not having enough money to care for all of us, but you've dealt with that as well, haven't you?' She gave a belligerent wave of her hand.

'Perhaps that is it, then,' he said quietly, leaning his hands on the dining table. 'Perhaps you fear losing control. But I am not a conventional man, Chione, nor are you in any way typical. I am not going to dominate you. I would never even wish to.'

She gave a bitter laugh. 'You couldn't be more wrong if you tried. Haven't you learned that most basic principle, even in all of your travels? Control is an illusion, Trey. It doesn't exist. All we can do is hang on, do our best, and pray that some good will follow the bad in this life.'

He looked surprised, but not angry. 'Is that really how you feel?'

'It is what I know. What I've known since I was eight years old and my world fell apart.'

He pushed away from the table and she started, moving back a step. She didn't know what was wrong with her. This was Trey—she knew she could trust him. But she also knew that if he touched her she would fall apart.

He stared at her as if he could see the strain ripping its way through her. Abruptly he sat down. 'Let's just talk then, all right? We'll speak of an entirely different subject.' He waved at the chairs along her side of the table. 'Sit.'

'I was wondering,' he began, 'if you had found a mention of a Monsieur or Madame Fornier in Richard's journals?'

'Madame Fornier?' she asked testily, sliding into a chair. 'Is that the woman who draped herself all over you today at the exhibit?'

'Yes, have you heard of her before?' His voice was frustratingly even.

'No, nor have I seen her mentioned in Richard's journals, but I haven't made my way back through all of them.'

'What of a Captain Batiste? Eli tells me Mervyn knew him. It seems the Forniers are working for him now.'

'Yes, I know of him,' she said. It was difficult to think, to focus on anything outside her own misery. 'He is a merchant captain. He used to work for Mervyn. They had a friendship, a partnership of sorts, but it went bad. I was young, but Richard told me that Batiste was jealous of Mervyn. He wanted what Mervyn had and he wanted it without delay. Eventually it ate away at their relationship.'

'Yes, Eli told me the story. It was just a thought. Something doesn't feel right, and I'm trying to figure it out. I'm not comfortable with that particular lady being in London right now.'

'Why not?'

He gazed at her steadily for a moment before answering, 'Because she was in the camp the night that Richard was murdered.'

Stunned, Chione jumped to her feet. 'What? Do you mean that woman murdered my brother?'

'Sit!' he commanded. 'Hear me out. No, I do not mean any such thing. In fact, I know most definitely that she did *not* kill Richard. But I'm beginning to wonder if she might not know who did.'

She was still on her feet. 'What would a Frenchwoman be doing in camp in any case? And how could you possibly know that she didn't do it? Perhaps she was after the scarab and the Lost Jewel, you can't know.' She paused. 'Unless…'

He stared back at her, silent. Anger and humiliation surged

through her. She was tempted, oh, so tempted to jump over the table and smack the determinedly calm look from his face. But she didn't. 'I see,' she said icily.

'No, you don't. She came to me with some half-cocked story of an offer from Drovetti. And you forget, although she was in the camp at that moment, Richard was not. He had gone to one of the tombs. To meet somebody?' Frustration cracked through his implacable facade at last. 'I don't know, because for the longest time, nobody bloody well told me anything!'

She didn't reply. She couldn't. All she could see in her mind's eye was that woman pressed up against Trey—while Richard faced death alone in a rocky canyon nearby.

'I hadn't even met you then, Chione. I had no idea what you and Richard were involved in, let alone that she might be involved in it, too.'

'And today?' she asked nastily. 'I did not see you protesting when she flirted so baldly.'

'Today I was trying to get information from her. I couldn't let on that I suspected her of anything, or I would have learned nothing.' He paused. 'And I am going to have to try again.'

Chione turned to leave the room.

'Running?' Trey asked unpleasantly. 'You've been running all day, Chione, ever since you saw that clue. Don't you think it's time you stopped and faced whatever it is that has unsettled you so?'

Fighting tears, she kept going.

'Please,' he said tiredly, 'this is far from over, Chione. I have had news from Aswan.'

She paused and he began to talk. She was shocked to hear what Alden and Aswan had been up to. She turned back and glared at him. 'I don't *want* to hear any more. All I want is Mervyn back. I don't want to deal with this any more. Let them have the damned jewel, as long as they leave us alone.'

'They won't. It's gone too far, now. It's all mixed up in one intangible mess.' He came around the table. This time she didn't move. He took her hand. The usual spark of sensation, that indescribable jolt she experienced every time he touched her, threatened to shake her out of her self-imposed numbness. Ruthlessly, she squashed it. She did allow him to lead her across the hall, to the family parlour. A fire crackled in the grate, casting shifting shadows over the room. Trey pulled a chair close to the flames and she settled into it. He brought one over for himself, and positioned it so it faced the fire as well. Together they sat, staring into the flames, the smoke-tinged air settling, like a trance, over them both.

'Eventually, you will have to talk to me,' he said quietly. 'But for now, just listen. Perhaps it will help if you hear what *my* greatest fear is.'

She shook her head, but he paid her no heed.

'I told you that my mother left. She had a horrendous argument with my father, and then she ran away. She left him— us—behind, preferring to live in disgrace with his brother.'

He paused, but she said nothing. She couldn't decide if she was more afraid he would stop, or afraid he would go on.

'What I didn't say, what almost no one knows, is that my father went after them. He got himself raging drunk and chased them. He was gone for two days. When he came back he shut himself up in the library and drank some more. He stayed in there, and stayed drunk, for over a week. I was not allowed to see him, but one night I woke up—and found him staring at me in my bed.'

Chione could see him swallow before he continued.

'"She didn't love me," my father said to me. "Not the way I loved her." He took a swig from the bottle he held in his lap. "She didn't love you either, did she? Not enough. Not enough to stay, not enough to take you with her." Then he was quiet a long time. I think I cried, but he didn't seem to notice. "Be glad," he said eventually. "You'd be dead too, then." He stood, but he didn't leave. He just stood there a long time, looking down at me, but not really seeing me. Finally he gave a massive shudder. "Her eyes are open," he said. "But she can't see me any more." Then he turned and left.'

Trey sighed, but Chione sat frozen in her chair. 'A couple of days later,' he said, 'we received word. The two of them had been in a carriage accident. Tracks showed that another vehicle had forced them off the road and down a steep embankment. My uncle was grievously wounded. My mother was dead. It had taken a while for them to be identified because my uncle had been unconscious for days. The next day my father had an accident of his own. He and his horse went over a cliff, one they must have been by a thousand times. No one questioned it, but we all knew the truth.'

Finally, Trey turned his gaze away from the flames. He stared at her with pain in his gaze, and a hardness that frightened her, but she could not look away. Tears welled in her eyes and she struggled to keep them from overflowing.

'For a long time my greatest fear was that my father had been right. That my mother hadn't loved me, as my father obviously hadn't. What if I was unlovable? What if no one *ever* loved me? Eventually, though, I stopped being afraid. In fact, I began to hope that that was indeed the case. What had love done for my parents? Killed my mother. Made my father weak? Certainly. Turned him into a murderer? Perhaps.'

He looked away again. 'So I scorned the idea of love. Certainly I did not find any reason to doubt my conclusions. Although I lived for the letters from my mother's brother, I couldn't say he loved me. We had never even met. And my other uncle, the one whose custody I was put into? The one who destroyed my parents? I rarely saw him. He sent me a birthday present once, too. Just one. A riding crop, supple and gleaming. Included with it was a note to my tutor, giving him permission to use the thing to beat the arrogance out of me. Which he did. Regularly.'

Chione uttered a soundless protest, but Trey's gaze remained fastened on the fire.

'I was sent away to school before long. If you know anything about Eton, you know that affection and love have no part in the curriculum. I kept my head down, I did well at my studies and I continued the correspondence with my travelling uncle. When I was done I wished to go to him, rather than attend university, but my guardian wouldn't hear of it.'

'So I did what I was told. I waited until I reached my majority. I waited until all the folderol was done and over with and all the privileges of my rank were passed to me. Then I took that riding crop that my uncle had sent to me all those years ago, and I thrashed him with it—to within an inch of his life. I left England and I never came back, until I came to you.'

The tears were streaming down Chione's face now. Trey looked at her and his hard, set expression softened.

'And here, at last, I found evidence that I had been wrong,' he said. 'Here was love and comfort. Here was a family devoted to each other, willing to sacrifice for each other. Here you were, Chione. Everything I never wanted, but had to have. And once again, I was afraid.'

'Stop,' she whispered. She knew what he was doing—telling his secrets so that she would be obligated to share hers. He didn't understand. She could not do it. She'd lived with her secrets for too long. They defined her, had indeed become a part of her. If she gave them up… She shivered, unable to even finish the thought.

'Don't you see?' she cried. 'This is it, what I fear the most. This—intimacy. You sharing your secrets and wanting me to share mine.' She halted on a sob.

'Why, Chione? Why are you afraid?'

There was a huge lump in her throat. It was going to choke her. She'd thought that Trey was safe, but she'd been wrong. She never should have agreed to the betrothal. She had to put a stop to this. Deliberately she hardened her features. She would take a page from Trey's book and strike first. Hurt him before he could hurt her further.

'You're ruining everything, Trey,' she said fiercely. 'Do you think that I didn't know that about you? That I couldn't sense your reluctance to be open? I welcomed it. It freed me. Even when we became betrothed, I didn't worry too much, fool that I was. Don't you see? I don't *want* to be burdened with your secrets. I don't want to burden you with mine. And it's all going to hell now. You're letting in things that will destroy us both.'

She swallowed hard and continued, determined to put an end to this. 'You learned the right lesson as a boy. I've finally learned it now. Emotion destroys. Look at your parents. Look at mine. Love always comes with a price, whether it be heartbreak or mistrust or eventually hatred.' She laughed harshly. 'Even friendships are not immune, and professional relationships suffer too if emotion enters the scene. Look at Mervyn and Batiste.'

She stood, looking down at him with narrowed eyes. 'It's too late now. I was wrong to pull you in.' She took a step away from him, towards the door. 'The betrothal is at an end. It might be better if you leave now.' She walked out, heading for the stairs before he could speak, before he could have a chance to call her back.

Trey sat, stunned. Silently, he watched her go. A black cloud of anger and disbelief filled the room and descended over him. For a moment he wallowed in it. Wasn't this exactly the blow he had been expecting? Hadn't he known it would be a mistake to get involved, to allow himself to hope? And even though he'd expected the hurt—hell, he likely deserved it for going against all the principles of a lifetime—it didn't make the stab to his heart any less devastating. As he stared at the empty doorway where she had disappeared, the temptation to follow her suggestion, to get up and leave, nearly overwhelmed him.

But hiding away from pain was the course that had led him here. He had just watched it lead Chione out that door, too. Trey was canny enough to notice when he was rapped over the head with one of his own tricks. She had lashed out at him to distract him, to protect herself. She was still hiding. From something in her past? Something terrifying that reached right down into the core of her, judging by the change in her demeanour and just how much she was willing to sacrifice rather than expose it.

He puzzled it over, but could not guess what it might be. He thought perhaps that Richard's journals might give him a clue, but they were in Chione's room. He didn't dare consider disturbing her now. He was stumped.

He mentally replayed the conversation. No, she was damned good at hiding what she didn't want the world to see. It made him wonder just how long she had been at it.

Irritatingly, he kept coming back to something seemingly inconsequential. *Even friendships are not immune, and professional relationships suffer too…*she had said. *Look at Mervyn and Batiste.*

For some reason the phrase echoed in his head. Repeatedly. *Look at Mervyn and Batiste.* And then an image of something Chione had showed him in one of Richard's journals popped into his mind's eye. *Drovetti in Thebes today, and in the company of C. G. B. Neither happy to see me. I am getting close.*

C. G. B. What was it that Eli had said? *But Gustavo Batiste? He's a bad character.*

Suddenly all the disparate facts connected. Captain Gustavo Batiste. C. G. B. Trey shot out of his chair, excitement and awe propelling him towards the stairs. He started to climb, had to refrain from shouting Chione's name in his exuberance. He came to an abrupt halt. What if he were wrong? She was in no state to deal with it. It would crush her.

He turned and descended, going to the back of the house and through the green baize door to the servants' quarters. He slipped through the back door, crossed the garden to the mews, and found the groom's quarters at the back of the stables. 'Eli,' he called. 'I hope to God you are not asleep.' He pounded on the door. 'Get your knife, your pistol and your best peg, man. We're going to the docks.'

Chione fled to her bedchamber. She'd hurt Trey; there was no mistaking the flash of devastation her harshly worded rejection had wrought. She was sorry for it, but he had spoken so tenderly and there had been something unquestionably significant in his expression. She had seen it and been at once elated and terrified, and suddenly terribly cognisant of her mistake.

She should never have let it get this far, should never have exposed herself so. She would have been smarter to go it alone, or to marry Orville Stockton, even. She would still be untouched, safe behind the unbroken mask of English reserve that was Miss Latimer. She wouldn't have had to face this fearful choice now, and she wouldn't be facing ceaseless remorse in the years ahead.

She stretched out on the bed, her tears drying. None of that seemed real yet. She felt strangely calm. It was done now. The choice had been made. How was it possible for a person to feel so horrible and yet so relieved all at once? For it was true, the terrible anxiety she had fought all day had drained away. An unnatural, empty lightness came in its wake—blessed numbness that eased the pain of loss and the sting of regret. Gradually, she relaxed and slept.

She awoke in Belzoni's Tomb. It looked much the same as it had this morning, except the flickering gas lights had been replaced with sputtering torches, and in the centre of the chamber sat a luminous, opalescent coffin. The alabaster sarcophagus that Belzoni had described in his book. Chione tried to sit up, but found that she could not move. She looked about and discovered she was surrounded by hundreds of the little *ushabti* figures that Belzoni had shown her.

A faint noise caused her to look to the centre of the room. It came again, from the coffin gleaming in the uncertain light. From its depths rose the gruesome figure of the mummy, its shining death mask still thankfully in place. Chione fought back a moan as the creature reached a sitting position, raised a ghastly arm and gestured to the multitude of tiny figures.

As one they came to life—called by their purpose. Created to be slaves, to do the dead pharaoh's bidding in the afterlife, they answered his summons. Horrified, Chione felt herself responding as well.

'No!' she cried, but her limbs were not her own to command.

'I'm not one of them!' She could not stop. Ever closer her legs carried her, until the withered, bandaged hand reached for her.

She awoke, gasping in terror. Sweat poured from her. She sat up in the bed, struggling for control. A vivid image of Eshe flashed in her mind; her mother forced to bend to a stranger's will. 'I'm not a slave,' Chione sobbed aloud. 'She was more than that. And so am I.'

She dropped her head in her hands and realised that she knew what her greatest fear was. And she knew where the coffer was hidden.

Chapter Eighteen

The morning was just a faint lightening in the eastern sky when Chione dressed and went in search of Trey. His room sat empty, his bed looked untouched. He had gone, then. She'd allowed her fear and feelings of inadequacy to control her, and she'd driven him off.

Still harbouring a faint glimmer of hope, she pushed through the door of the family breakfast room. Trey was not there, but his adopted urchin was going out the door on the other side of the room.

'Bartholomew, wait.'

The boy turned, snatched the cap from his head. 'Yes, miss.'

'Come here for a moment, please.'

She took a seat at the empty table. Bart silently advanced until he stood before her, his gaze fastened on the carpet at her feet.

'Have you seen Lord Treyford this morning?'

He looked up. 'No, miss. Stableman says how he took off in the night. Him and the old groom, the one with the peg?'

'Eli, yes.'

'They got in a hackney and left in the wee hours.'

'I see.' Hope flared briefly. If Trey had taken Eli, then surely he would be back. She focused on the boy. 'How do you like being employed by Lord Treyford?'

Bart shrugged. 'I like it fine. The work's easy. The pay's good.'

'I'm glad. Lord Treyford likes you too. We all do. That is why I am going to ask you to put the silver back in the sideboard where you found it.'

The boy skipped back a step in alarm. 'How did you know?'

'I guessed,' Chione said, reaching gently for his hand. 'But I thought I might be right. I had a feeling, because you see, I used to be just like you.'

'You never!' he scoffed.

'Oh, but I did. It was in a city far from here—but I was most definitely a street rat.' She nodded at his look of shock. 'Yes, it's true. I know what it is to have no home, to sleep in the street, to forage for food, all the while trying day and night not to fall prey to worse dangers.'

'But how?' He waved a hand, speechless, to their comfortable surroundings.

'I was taken in by a kind man. He looked at me and saw more than just an urchin. He gave me a home and a family. For a time I still pocketed stray silver and hoarded food, but then I understood that he was truly offering me a better life. Just as Lord Treyford is willing to offer the same to you.'

He looked down. She doubted whether he believed her.

'It's tempting just to look at him as an easy mark, is it not?' she asked.

He glanced quickly up and then back down.

'You may look at him that way—and perhaps that will be what he becomes. No more, no less. But it will be up to you. I know we would be happy to take you with us when we leave London. Again, this decision will be up to you. You are free to refuse. Just understand that it would be your fear working against you, not lack of opportunity.'

She took his hand again. 'I know what I am talking about. I just let fear ruin the best thing that was ever offered to me. Now I have to try to make it right.' She looked at him, considering. 'Will you help me?'

Bart nodded.

She leaned in close. 'Can you pick a lock?' she whispered.

He looked surprised, but nodded again.

'Good. I have one last job for the two of us. Then, after this morning, I hope neither of us will ever have to steal again.'

It was still very early when the two of them stole out on to the street. Bartholomew led them on a roundabout path that avoided the main thoroughfares and kept to the residential districts. Not many people were out on these streets, just an occasional baker's boy or a maid here and there sweeping the steps to one of the grand houses. Twice they saw a fancy carriage pull up to discharge its late-night revellers. They stopped several times to ensure that they were not being followed.

It wasn't long before they reached Piccadilly and the Egyptian Hall. Carefully they circled around the back. Bartholomew had the back door open in the twinkling of an eye. They entered into a darkened workroom, filled with clutter and furniture left over from previous exhibitions. Chione was glad she had thought to bring along a satchel with a few basic supplies. The early morning light did not reach into the rooms. She pulled out two candles and a flint.

Quietly they eased into the exhibit. In the dim candlelight the Hall had the same eerie, sepulchral feeling as her dream. Chione wished, the thought fleeting and intense, that Trey was here with them. She pushed it away. She had left a note, but with any luck they would be back home with the coffer before Trey returned or anyone knew they had gone.

Silently they made their way through the exhibit, paying particular attention to the models and displays. At last, they found it. She hoped that it was it. A glass display case sat on a dark wooden base in the corner of the Entrance Hall. Inside sat an unassuming collection of objects: a plain bronze strongbox surrounded by the best of Belzoni's collection of *ushabti* figures.

'I believe the case is just a heavy glass box with no bottom,' she whispered to Bart. There was no one to hear, but she couldn't bring herself to speak out loud. 'Do you think you can help me lift it?'

'Can't we just break it?' he asked with a nod to her satchel.

'I would rather not. I think the two of us can handle it.' They set the candles down nearby and set to work. They did struggle with the weight of the case, and with the delicate task of lifting it without disturbing any of the objects it covered, but eventually they got the thing lifted off.

Reverently Chione ran her fingers over the pitted and stained surface of the ancient bronze chest. Could this plain and simple box truly hold the secret to a three-thousand-year-old mystery? There was no obvious lid to the box, seemingly no way to open it. Seamless and mysterious, it offered no answer to her question.

'I'll take one side,' she said low to Bartholomew, 'you take the other. We'll set it on the floor right here in front of the base.'

It was lighter than she expected. They set it down and she moved both of the candles closer.

Nothing. No marks, symbols or messages. Chione looked at Bart and lifted a shoulder. She thought a moment before a notion hit her.

'Help me tilt it up,' she said.

She'd been right. It was there—stamped in the thick metal base of the box. The outline of a scarab, a near replica of the bottom of Mervyn's piece. Her breath caught and her heart raced. After all this time, after everything that had happened to her family and her loved ones, this was it. She had found it.

Carefully they set it flat once more. 'Thank heavens it is not too heavy,' she said to Bartholomew. 'We've got to get this home as quickly as we can.'

They stood and had it lifted between them once more when the voice floated ominously out of the darkness.

'We shall save you the effort, Miss Latimer. Please, set it back down on the floor.'

Chione peered through the darkness towards the arched doorway. From the Room of Beauties a man emerged. His gorgeous white turban and his long, grey-shot beard marked him as a foreigner, but his wardrobe was that of an English gentleman: shining boots, black pantaloons and a form-fitting coat of the finest grey superfine. He even had a watch and fob stretched across his embroidered waistcoat. It was an oddly fascinating mix of cultures, but a cold hostility emanated from him as his dark gaze roamed over her.

'Who are you?' she asked. She and Bartholomew were still frozen in place, the bronze chest suspended between them.

He laughed. 'Ignorant child. I am Hassan.'

Behind him four men stepped out of the shadows. One of them was dressed in ragged Eastern robes; the others also wore English clothes, although of a totally different calibre. They were dressed more like stable hands than aristocrats. As they stepped closer, into the feeble light cast by the candles, Chione could see that while their leader looked sleek and fit, his men were a battered lot, adorned with old scars and fresh bruises. One of them was missing three of the fingers of his right hand.

'The coffer, and what is in it, belongs to us,' Hassan said in a flat voice. 'Put it down.'

She glanced about. She and Bartholomew were trapped in a corner. There was nowhere to go. Slowly she did as he ordered. Bartholomew followed her lead. As the weight of the thing reached a spot just a few inches above the floor she looked across into his frightened eyes and said, low and clear,

'Run. Find Lord Treyford.' With her foot she kicked out at the two sputtering candles.

The darkness fell, sudden and intense. The other end of the coffer clanged loudly as it hit the floor. Sharp words rang out and then the heavy sound of running feet. Chione tried to move quietly away, but she found her arm seized in a cruel grip.

'That was very foolish, Miss Latimer, and to absolutely no avail. My man will find the boy and he will cut his throat.' He spoke harshly again, ordering his men to light the gas lamps. A spark flared and the closest light flickered to life, revealing the icy expression in Hassan's face. Chione had expected to see anger, and its absence was unexpectedly frightening. This man radiated an indifference that rendered her as nothing, and forced her to believe that he was capable of anything.

'It's been you all along,' Chione said with an unnatural calm. 'You raided the house, and attacked us in Exeter. You have followed us, watched us. I don't understand. Who are you?'

He barked an order to his men and watched as they moved to cover the various entrances of the room before he answered. 'I have told you. We are the rightful owners of the Pharaoh's Lost Jewel. For millennia the story has been handed down in our village, kept alive by our tribe—the story of how the Jewel was stolen from one of our own. Many times have my ancestors tried to retrieve it, but I, Hassan, shall be the one to succeed.'

Chione still did not understand. 'Your tribe? Your ancestors?'

'Come, surely your grandfather has told you the tale?'

'The tale—you speak of the story of the architect's daughter?' The concept of so much time staggered her, but slowly the pieces of the puzzle began to connect in her mind.

'Of course,' he answered with a parody of a smile.

'Then, your tribe, you—you are all—the tomb robbers?

The family the story speaks of?' She stared at him aghast. 'It cannot be!'

'It can be. It is. You have been too long in the West. Daughter of the Nile,' he scoffed. 'You have forgotten the timelessness of the East. Does not my family live among the same tombs built back when it all took place? We did not doubt. One day, we knew, we would retrieve what was stolen from us so long ago.'

He was right; it took an effort for her to bend her mind around the concept. 'But to hold a grudge so long?' Just to say it out loud left her unbearably sad. 'It is unbelievable.'

'It is not. The ancient dead have long provided us with a living. But now things are changing, now the Franks interfere.' He gestured at the exhibit around them. 'They steal our treasures. But they shall not have the Lost Jewel. This I have vowed.'

'I don't care what you have vowed,' Chione cried. 'The Jewel never belonged to your ancestor—he was not worthy. His wife was far more clever. If such a thing could belong to anyone, it would belong to the family of the architect.'

Hassan rolled his eyes and gripped her tighter. 'Who can predict a woman's trickery, eh? And you are not so clever as I. For three thousand years we have waited to avenge him.' He motioned for one of his men to retrieve the box. 'Now it is done.' He ran an assessing eye over the bronze vessel. 'A shrewd choice. I had expected something more ornate, more fitting. But the outside matters not, only the treasure inside.'

'I don't understand. You did not know what the coffer was either?'

He laughed. 'No. This is the brilliance of my plan. Over the years the details were lost. For a long time we knew only that the coffer and the Jewel existed. But stories of the Jewel began to circulate outside our village. I listened to the tales, sifted through them. Then I went to the elders. Someone did know where the coffer was, and that was information we could use.'

'Mervyn,' she said flatly.

'Yes. Rumour is a wonderful thing. It flies as fast as a bird. All it took was a whisper here and there into the right ear. We had found the hiding place, I said. It was only a matter of time until the coffer was ours.' He chuckled. 'In just a few weeks Mervyn Latimer was back in Egypt.'

'What have you done with him?' she whispered.

'I? Nothing. Your grandfather has enemies of his own and they got to him before us. I was furious at first, until I saw that the old man was as wily as ever. He'd hidden the coffer away again before he was caught. So I had hope. His enemies came to us, seeking an alliance. I agreed, but they are fools to think we would share the Jewel. I began to plan again.'

He released her and took a step away, running a brazen eye over her form. 'Your family is far more formidable than I first expected. I was shocked to find that you are no exception. When it finally came to you, I had not thought you would be such a creditable adversary.'

She sniffed in disdain.

'It is true. For months I have hunted you and yours. I did not expect you to ever turn the tables so neatly. Nor did I think to lose so many of my men. Have you killed them all?' he asked conversationally.

Chione raised her chin. 'You are the monster here. Not I.'

He sighed. 'I doubt they will fare well in your cold English gaol. But no matter. It is a small price to pay for the Jewel.' For the first time a true emotion showed in his face. An ugly hunger that grew as his gaze lingered on her. He reached for her again and involuntarily she took a step back.

'It is a great pity that you must die, but like your brother before you, you have too much knowledge.'

Tears welled and flowed over. 'You killed Richard,' she whispered.

'A clever lad. Nearly as clever as Hassan. He slipped into my country and found the coffer almost before I knew he was there. A merry dance he has led us all, no?' he asked with a glance about. 'But Hassan is the victor in the end.'

'But Mervyn,' she said desperately. 'Where is he now?'

'He is where he has been.' He shrugged. 'When it is discovered that I have won the prize, his fate will be more uncertain.'

He tilted his head, considering, then like lightning he reached out and grabbed her once more. Chione winced as he tore the pins from her hair. Her long locks tumbled down and he ran a caressing stroke along the length of one ebony strand. His eyes glittered. 'Would you like to see him one last time? A spirit like yours cries out to be broken.' He dragged her roughly against him. 'By all that is holy, I would like to make the both of you beg.'

Panic surged and she struggled, straining to free herself from his iron grip. He let go of her hair and used his free hand to slap her hard across the face. The smack of his hand against her flesh rang out loud in the dimly lit room.

Chione stilled, the stinging of her cheek awakening ugly memories and, unexpectedly, a hidden determination. Hassan's eyes flashed and his cruel mouth curved into a slow and wicked grin. Chione gathered herself and cast her glance about. Die she might, but she swore her death would not come cheap. Her eye fell on the table of *ushabti* figures.

Before either of them could make a move a peculiar grunt echoed from a dark corner of the room. Hassan gripped her tight and turned towards the door to the workroom. The henchman there, the one in the ragged robes, pitched forward and landed in a heap on the floor. He didn't move again.

Silence reigned, broken only by the rustle of the other men shifting where they stood, casting nervous eyes about the room. Hassan jerked his chin at one of them to investigate. Almost fearfully he approached his fallen comrade. He nudged him with his toe, and then turned him limply over. With a cry of alarm he reached down and picked up a small object, brandishing it aloft. 'It is as before,' he cried. 'The mark of the scarab!'

The other lackey started up. 'You see, Hassan! It is as I said. There is a curse on this treasure!'

'Stupid, superstitious fools!' Hassan dug his fingers tighter into Chione's arm and railed at his men. 'There is no curse!'

'Ah, but I'm afraid there is.' Everyone jumped when the new voice stole, calm and unruffled, into the room.

A thrill of hope surged through Chione. She looked up, searching. There, in the corner gallery. 'Mr Alden?' she breathed.

'What did I tell you?' raged Hassan. 'It is naught but an Englishman with a sling.' He peered into the darkened recesses of the gallery above. 'The woman is correct. It is the English scholar.' He gestured at his men. 'Are you women to be afraid of a bookworm such as him?'

'Hassan does not wish you to know,' Alden said evenly, 'but there is indeed a curse.' A flash in the scant light proved to be a gleaming pistol pointed unerringly in Hassan's direction. 'Any man who touches the coffer will pay for his transgression against the old gods. Your master thinks to let you suffer while he enjoys the spoils. I would do you all a favour to put a bullet through his black heart.'

'My men are superstitious, not stupid,' the rogue said with preternatural calm. 'They will kill the girl before they finish you. They will have the coffer and still I will have won.' He gestured to the henchman who still hovered over his fallen companion. 'Kill him.'

'You can try,' Alden challenged. 'Come on, then.' He kept his pistol trained on Hassan and beckoned the other man with a toss of his head.

'Do not waste your effort.' A woman appeared from the shadowed corner of the gallery. She stepped closer to Alden. Her silky tone and curling lips belied the fact that she too held a small gun and it was pointed directly at his head. 'I will deal with this English bookworm.'

Chione gasped. It was Madame Fornier, the woman Trey had suspected might be involved in this mess, the woman who had pressed herself against him in so blatant a manner.

Hassan's reaction was not so restrained. He swore mightily at the woman in Arabic before switching to French. 'What are you doing here? Are you stupid? Did I not tell you and your dolt of a husband to stand watch tonight?'

'Fornier is dead,' she replied in the same language. 'And there is no one left to watch. The prisoner has escaped.'

Hassan let loose with a string of foul invectives. His fingers dug cruelly into the flesh of Chione's arm. She cried out and strained to pull away, but her movements only served to bring the villain back to his senses. He cast a warning glare at the Frenchwoman and snarled at her, this time in English. 'Kill him, then. Quick.'

Alden did not move. His gun was still trained on Hassan. Madame Fornier lowered her gun an inch and protested, 'He is brother to a peer. Unlike the French, the English do not take kindly to those who kill their aristocrats.'

'What do you care for the English? Insolent woman! Do as I say.'

'He will be valuable if kept alive,' the woman argued. 'I dare say his family will pay us well to get him back.'

'And I dare say your precious Captain Batiste has already sailed with the morning tide! We will be lucky to escape ourselves, now that you have blundered so stupidly! Kill him.' He pointed to Alden. 'Or I will leave you to face the English authorities alone.'

Chione saw the woman hesitate, but then she raised her gun with resolution. Behind her something else moved in the shadows. A look of alarm passed over the Frenchwoman's face. In a flash of movement her arm swayed, the gun exploded and both she and Alden went down behind the railing.

'No!' cried Chione.

Like a rat, Hassan knew when an exit became prudent. 'Come,' he said, and his henchmen jumped to do his bidding. 'Bring the coffer and the girl. We go.' He turned her over to one of the two remaining men, whose grip was no gentler. Chione tried to shake him off. He only grinned and pulled her after his master, back towards the Room of Beauties and the front of the Hall.

They had only reached the pillars in the centre of the room when a loud crash sounded somewhere in the back of the building. Hassan quickened his step. 'Come,' he ordered again.

It was too late. 'Hassan!' someone called from behind them.

Chione stopped in her tracks. She stared disbelievingly over her shoulder. The figure stood awash in the flickering light of a gas lamp. He had a face that was lined and dirty, framed with straggling, unkempt hair. His clothes, literally in rags, hung on his thin frame. Chione's vision blurred with tears and it was not until the figure spoke that she knew for sure.

'Hassan, you old devil,' the man said. 'I should have known you'd figure somewhere in this.'

It was too much. 'Mervyn,' Chione choked, caught on a long, shuddering sob. 'Mervyn!'

He smiled at her briefly—one shining moment in which he conveyed love and pride and a subtle warning. Then he returned his focus to his enemy. Chione's eye was caught by movement behind him. 'Trey,' she breathed.

'A-yi,' Hassan sounded truly vexed. 'Like an evil omen you appear at every turn, Latimer. And you…' he gestured to where Trey stood behind the older man '…you are no better.'

'I will accept that as a compliment,' Trey returned.

'You have come too late this time, my old friend,' Hassan ignored Trey to address Mervyn. 'This time I will emerge victorious. I have the coffer and your granddaughter. You shall not block my way.'

'And yet here I am,' Mervyn said quietly.

'Not for very long, I am afraid. You are weak. I see that you did not enjoy the accommodations provided by your old rival.' A spark of amusement appeared in his flat, dark gaze. 'How glad I am to finally see you brought so low! The fact that this victory has been so long in coming only sweetens the taste.' He paused and glanced up into the empty gallery. 'How did you escape, if I may ask?'

Mervyn gestured behind him. 'The gods sent me help. They do not mean for you to have the Jewel. I am afraid it will once again be the bitter taste of defeat for you, my friend.'

The bland and impenetrable facade dropped over Hassan's face once more. 'I tire of this nonsense.' He spoke aside to the henchman holding the coffer. 'Daoud, you will deal with the wretched English lord. Be sure that he pays dearly for his interference.' He reached into his coat and pulled free a short, curved scimitar, its blade catching the dim light. 'The old man I will kill myself.'

The pair of them advanced. Chione twisted hard and jerked her arm free, only to be caught up tight against her captor's chest. He pulled her hair mercilessly until she had no choice but to tilt her head back. Somewhere in front of her the fighting began, but she could see only the high, shadowed ceiling. The cold point of a blade pricked her throat.

'Latimer will win,' she ground out in Arabic. 'Allah has decreed it. He will destroy you.'

'If I kill you now, I can take the box and be gone before anyone wins,' he countered.

'I have a golden amulet,' she whispered desperately. 'I will give it to you if you let me go.'

He hesitated. 'Where is it?' His voice growled low.

'I have it. Under my skirts. Let me loose and I will give it to you.'

For several long seconds he wavered. At last greed won out. Chione had no doubt that he meant to take whatever she had and kill her still. He spun her around and pressed her up against one of the pillars. One hand pressed her shoulder back into the rough surface while his knee braced hard against her hip. The position gave her the opportunity to catch a quick glimpse of the rest of the room.

Trey fought Daoud with grim efficiency, judging by the flash of blades in their corner. Mervyn had a harder time of it. He rocked back and forth, avoiding the savage slash of Hassan's blade time and again. In his hand he held an object— one of the candlesticks she had brought. Not much help against Hassan's deadly blade.

Her captor nudged her, pressing a leg between hers. Chione shook him off, extended her leg and very slowly began to lift her skirts. Glancing up, she saw his leering grin as he focused on the sight. She bent over and reached higher under her skirts, where her hands were hidden from his sight. Working fast, she pulled a knife from her garter—and watched dumbfounded as the man toppled at her feet. She stared down at him in stunned surprise. Blood ran from a gash behind his ear.

Chione looked up and found herself hauled into the arms of Trey. He tucked a blood-tipped *ushabti* figure under his arm, kissed her hard and whispered in her ear, 'I owed you that one.'

Together they turned and Chione saw why he had not used the blade that she had seen him with as he fought Daoud. It glinted now in Mervyn's hand, desperately trying to block the thrusts of Hassan's longer, far more lethal scimitar. She saw that he hadn't been quick enough more than once. A crimson slash showed clear across Mervyn's chest, another had severed the dirty sleeve of his left arm.

'Help him,' she urged Trey.

'I've already been told quite firmly to mind my own business.' Trey's tone conveyed his understanding. He nodded towards the two men, both of whom showed signs of tiring. 'I believe this has been a long time coming.'

Mervyn feinted, then dodged behind a display case. Hassan

took just a moment too long in recovering. The older man came at him from the other side and drove his knife blade hard into Hassan's shoulder.

Red blossomed across his finely tailored coat, but his expression never shifted from its look of implacable determination. 'I shall not lose, old man. It is time the Jewel was returned to its rightful setting.'

'You are correct about that,' Mervyn panted. 'But such a course has nothing to do with you.' He struck hard once, twice, and again until Hassan was forced to retreat from the flurry of blows. But the Egyptian was too crafty to be forced into a corner where his manoeuvrability would be impaired. He struck back, seemingly without consideration for his damaged arm, definitely without any thought of mercy. Mervyn gradually fell back until he was once again braced against a pillar in the centre of the room.

Chione gripped Trey's arm. 'I don't care what he said, he needs help!'

'Wait.' Trey raised a hand. 'Look.'

She did. 'Eli!' she gasped. The groom stood braced in the doorway to the back workroom. A crash sounded and he looked over his shoulder, back into the darkness behind him. A low, silent form erupted past him, easily evading his reaching hand.

'It's the damned dog,' Trey said grimly. He picked his *ushabti* figure up again and took a step nearer the combatants.

Fiercely intent on each other, they had not noticed the new arrivals. Morty noticed them, however, and seemed to have no difficulty identifying the long-lost member of her family. She bristled, her raised hackles and her low, rumbling snarl signalling her deadly intent. She crouched and, moving faster than Chione could follow, launched herself into the battle.

Hassan's instincts were good, even if his blank indifference stood no chance against a four-stone missile armed with large teeth and the snarling promise of death. He turned away from

Mervyn, towards this new and greater threat. One arm poised to protect his face and throat, the other raised to deliver Morty a sweeping blow.

But that moment's distraction was all that Mervyn needed. He blocked Hassan's strike with his own blade and at the same time struck a mighty clout to his temple with the candlestick.

The villain dropped like a stone, Morty following him down. The scimitar skittered across the room and Trey jumped forward to pull off the dog.

All of Chione's attention remained focused on Mervyn. He had fallen to his knees in the centre of the room. His head bowed, he braced a hand on a pillar. His breath came in great, rasping gulps.

Slowly, she approached. His shoulder, when she reached down to touch it, felt pitifully thin. He looked up and her heart thumped wildly to see the look he gave her. Love and acceptance, unconditional and beautiful, undeniably the thing she had missed the most all these months. This feeling inside of her now, it was the greatest gift he had given her, the one thing she had received from no one else in her life—she glanced back over her shoulder—save one.

She started to turn towards Trey, had a vague, silly notion of introducing Mervyn to the man who had rescued him, but a strangled cry sounded in the back of the room. As one they looked to see Eli still framed in the doorway, his hands restraining a desperate, fighting Will. At Mervyn's nod the groom let go. The boy stumbled, sobbing, to his father's arms. Chione's knees gave way and the three of them rocked in an endless, heartfelt and tearful embrace.

Chapter Nineteen

Trey refused to give in to emotion, despite the touching reunion that tugged at even his rusty heartstrings. That way lay danger and his most difficult task still waited. If he meant to get through it with any sort of dignity he must ignore the pain threatening to swamp him. He focused instead on clearing the havoc they had all so thoroughly wreaked.

Alden, thankfully, fared well. It was Aswan who had moved in the shadows and got to the Frenchwoman in time to misdirect her shot. The scholar cheerfully displayed the bullet-razed wound in his arm. 'I think this taste of adventure will hold me for a good long while,' he said with a grin. 'At least my brother never got me shot at.'

'She fights dirty,' was the entirety of the Egyptian servant's report, gesturing to the bound and gagged Madame Fornier.

Hassan sat next to her in the same state. He'd awakened from the blow to his head with his filthy tongue intact and Trey had tired of hearing everyone's ancestors maligned. Morty took the guarding of the prisoners on herself, her lip curled in a permanent snarl until Hassan lashed out at her with his boot. The dog took that as an invitation and helped herself to the shiny leather. Trey figured she'd take it off the villain's foot before too long.

The man Trey had bashed with the *ushabti* figure still lay unconscious. Daoud and the other henchman had disappeared in the confusion.

Trey sent one of the guards that Eli had brought back to Wapping, but Hassan's assessment of Captain Batiste had been correct. His ship had already sailed with the morning tide.

The rest of the men were given the duty of hauling the prisoners off to the magistrate's office. But as they filed past on their way out, Mervyn called for them to halt. He drew close and whispered long and fervently in Hassan's ear. The villain's back stiffened, his eyes went wide. He looked to Mervyn with a question apparent in his eyes. Mervyn nodded solemnly and then he gestured at the guards and they were gone.

Trey watched Will approach his father. The boy leaned against him, his eyes wide with curiosity. 'What did you say to him, Papa?'

Trey leaned in, wishing to hear the answer as well.

'I told him the truth. What he is looking for is not in that vessel.' The old man sighed. 'But an obsession such as Hassan's does not die an easy death, so I hope to point it in a new direction.' He smiled down at his son and ran a hand through his hair. 'The French did indeed abscond with some of the treasure Hassan seeks. Let them deal with him for a while.'

At last all of the details were seen to. Trey even had the display case put back together, minus the coffer, of course. He stood alone a moment, shoulders slumped in weariness and dread. Chione moved beside him and slipped her small, soft hand into his.

'Thank you,' she whispered. She looked at the newly restored display, not at him. He gave her fingers a squeeze.

'All this time,' she said low. 'He's been on Batiste's ship all this time. It was no wonder he disappeared without a trace.' She glanced askance at him. 'How? How did you know?'

'It was something you said last night,' Trey answered.

'When you were telling me so eloquently how emotion destroys whatever it touches. "Professional relationships suffer too," you said. "Look at Mervyn and Batiste." For some reason that kept circling in my brain. And then I remembered Richard's words, in his journal. You showed them to me, do you remember? *C. G. B.* Captain Gustavo Batiste. I didn't know for sure, but it seemed worth a look.'

She ducked her head. 'You didn't tell me.'

'You were upset. I didn't know if I was right, and I wasn't sure you could handle it with equanimity if I was wrong.'

'No, you did the right thing. I was…distraught.' She sighed. 'Thank you,' she said again.

'He'll need looking after,' Trey said gruffly. 'Batiste had him locked in the slave hold.'

'And damned miserable it was, too,' Mervyn said, approaching from behind them, 'but I was allowed on deck when we were at sea. Batiste knew that I had too much to live for, I wasn't going to go over the side.' He looked at the small, roughly shaped figures in the case and then over at the coffer. 'He was after the Jewel, of course. He said he was going to hold me until I talked.'

'Then he didn't know you very well after all, did he?' Chione smiled.

'No, in the end, he didn't. I don't think he could bring himself to kill me, not because I might change my mind and tell him everything, but because I think he enjoyed having me at his mercy even more than he wanted the Jewel.' He sighed, a tired, heart-sore sound. 'He was particularly gleeful when he told me about Richard.' He took her other hand. 'I'm so sorry, Chione.'

She released Trey to embrace the old man fiercely. Trey watched her grandfather hold her close and his own arms ached, because they would never again do the same. She no longer needed him. And she had made her thoughts on their betrothal clear enough.

'I want to go home, Chione,' Mervyn said into her hair. 'I want to sit down with Olivia in my lap and you and Will on either side. I promise, it will be a long, long while before I suffer the urge to get up again.'

'I understand and appreciate your sentiment, sir,' Trey answered before Chione could. 'Things are taken care of here. But I wondered if you wouldn't mind if Chione stayed behind with me, just for a bit.' He paused and glanced at her surprised expression. 'We have some business to finish, and a few things that need to be said in private.'

Mervyn looked from Trey's face, down to Chione's. 'I understand that you have betrothed yourself to this young man,' he said to her.

She flushed and hesitated. 'Yes, sir—but it was just a ruse. Mrs Stockton tried to take the children from me. Trey entered into the betrothal only to protect us.'

The old man regarded Trey soberly. 'It appears I am in your debt in more ways than one, sir. I suppose you are past the point of asking permission, but I thank you for doing so anyway.' He extended his hand and gripped Trey's tight. 'I trust you to bring her home safe.'

Trey nodded. 'Yes, sir.'

Everyone had gone. Trey took Chione's hand and led her to the first chamber. He looked around a moment, and then he moved the bench that Mrs Ferguson had sat knitting upon away from the mummy's case and angled it towards a colourful depiction of Isis embracing the Pharaoh.

'We are an odd pair,' he said, escorting Chione to the bench and waiting for her to settle in. 'We do our best talking when we've something else to look at, had you noticed?'

'No, I hadn't,' she said, intrigued. 'But it has been something of a pattern with us, hasn't it?'

Trey sat down beside her and for several minutes they sat

without speaking. They were close enough on the bench to be lightly touching and he allowed the steady rise and fall of her breathing to calm him. A lock of her hair had fallen across his arm. He stared at it instead of the colourful relief before him and longed to touch it, to lift it to his face and breathe in the sweet scent of her, perhaps for the last time.

At last, she stirred. 'Trey, I—'

'No,' he said, ignoring the sudden press of her against him. 'Please, Chione. This is difficult for me. Let me say what I must before you speak.'

She nodded. 'All right.'

He reached inside of his coat and drew out a small box. 'While we were in Devonshire I sketched out what I wanted and sent it on to London. By the time we arrived, this was ready.' He opened it.

'Ohh…' she breathed, her fingertips travelling to her mouth to hide her exclamation of delight. 'It is beautiful.'

He hoped she thought so. He had been very specific and Rundell, Bridge and Co. had been happy to accommodate the Earl of Treyford. Tucked in its nest of velvet sat a ring of golden filigree. The front piece was in the shape of the Eye of Horus, with a blue lapis as the pupil.

Tentatively, she reached out, shooting him a questioning look. He nodded and she touched it gently. 'It is just exactly the colour of your eyes,' she said.

Trey shifted uncomfortably. 'I hadn't thought of that,' he said. 'But I am glad you like it.' He handed the box to her. 'There is a much more important gift I want to give to you, Chione.'

Still cradling the box, she looked up at him in question.

'Your freedom,' he said.

She drew a long, shuddering breath.

'I want you to know that I understand,' he continued before his courage gave out. 'The heavens know I am no prize for any woman, let alone, as you said, for one who carries heavy burdens of her own.'

Chione started to speak, but Trey raised a hand to stop her. 'Please. I understand that I have dived in and made myself part and parcel of this entire mess,' he said. 'But I am glad I have, because now we can finally put it to rest. The legend won't haunt you any more, Chione. The coffer is found, the Jewel—whatever it might prove to be—is safe and so is Mervyn. You are free—free to live your own life. You can go to America, just as you planned.' He faltered a bit, and paused to breathe deeply. 'Go—find your clean slate. Begin again. Go and be happy.'

He took the ring from the box and slipped it slowly on her finger. 'All I ask is that you wear this and think of me, from time to time.'

She smiled at him with tears in her eyes. 'May I speak now?' she asked with slight exasperation.

'Yes.' He braced himself for what he had no wish to hear.

'Thank you.' She stretched up, ran the fingers of both hands over his temples and curled them in his hair. 'You are the single bravest man I know, Niall Stafford, Earl of Treyford. Do you think that I am going to let you get away so easily?'

Incredibly, her words stung. He was attempting to be noble. For the first time in his adult life he was putting someone else's needs ahead of his own. Did she not take him seriously? Couldn't she see how deeply he felt, how he needed to fulfil her dreams?

She read his reaction. 'No, I am not talking of physical bravery.' She waved a negligent hand. 'Mervyn has us all beat in that category, at any rate. I am speaking of bravery that comes from the soul, emotional generosity—and that is far rarer and infinitely precious.'

One of her hands slid down, gently caressing his face, continuing on across his shoulder, down his arm, to take his hand in hers once more. 'I know, Trey. I know how far you have come. I realise how hard it was for you to share yourself with me, to open your past like a book and let me read the most painful passages of your life.'

She gripped his hand tight. 'Do you think I would reject you because you've entangled yourself in the chaotic mess of my life? Think back, Trey, to the day you first arrived at Oakwood Court. Would that man have taught Will the best canter transitions for his mount or sat in a coach all afternoon and let Olivia put ribbons in his hair? Would he have talked to me of my mother, and his own? Would he have seen my turmoil yesterday and thought to ease it by sharing his? Could he have ever shared his father's secret with me?' She shook her head. 'You've grown, Trey, you've taken a journey that few are ever brave enough to set out on.'

Trey felt peculiarly like crying. Her praise unmanned him. No one had ever said such things to him. 'Only because you showed me the way,' he said gruffly.

'Yes, but you shouldered me out of the way and far surpassed me,' she said, her tone rueful. 'And I could not bring myself to follow.'

'You were frightened.'

She sighed. Her eyes closed and she nodded. 'Richard knew, though, didn't he? My infuriating little brother knew that the hardest thing I could ever do was face the truth about myself.'

Gently he tucked the straying lock of hair behind her ear. 'Then your greatest fear…?'

She shuddered. 'Allowing the secrets of my past back into the light of day. I didn't want to face them again, or ever acknowledge that what happened then had anything to do with the person I am now.'

'It's done now. You don't ever have to worry about it again.'

She ducked her head. 'Yes, I do. I owe it to you.' She

looked up and directly into his eyes. 'I want to tell you everything, for how can we begin our lives together if we are not on the same path?'

He kissed her then, couldn't have stopped himself if he wished. She exhaled, a long, satisfied sigh and then she melted against him. Her lips were warm and eager and tasted of exquisite promise—a pledge of days, months, years of such kisses. The promise of happiness.

She pulled back a little. 'Wait, Trey. I have to tell you.'

He made a sound of protest, but she gave him a pleading look.

'All right, then.' He pulled her comfortably against him and ran his fingers through her glorious hair.

She sighed. For several minutes she just leaned into him. Trey bent and kissed her neck, knowing she was steeling herself for a battle.

'You spoke of the lost little boy you once were,' she began, 'but I can tell you that he would have been no match for the angry little girl I used to be.'

Quietly she told her tale, telling him of Edward Latimer's death, of the harrowing journey cut short by her mother's captors. It was then her voice changed. 'They left us to die, Trey, like dogs in the street,' she said. It made Trey itch to get his hands on the bastards who caused that harsh, unforgiving tone. He listened in wonder and awe as she told of following after the men who had taken her mother, and of eventually finding her enslaved to a Frank.

'My brave, beautiful girl,' he whispered, kissing her temple.

'No. Not brave—furious. A new creature was born on that journey, a being of anger and plain stubborn refusal to be defeated. It is the side of me capable of hate and resentment. I thought she had gone when I found Eshe—but she was still there, lurking.'

Her voice grew quiet again. 'It was a good thing, I would guess, because I needed her again later, when the plague went through. The Frank caught it and my mother as well when she tried to nurse him. Richard and I found ourselves returned to the streets.'

She sat back then and looked at him, her expression hard. 'Do you understand? I was perhaps a little older than Bartholomew. A child alone with a toddler in the Egyptian slums.'

Trey met her gaze directly. To look away now, he suspected, would be the end of any hope for them. 'I don't know how you survived it,' he said simply.

'I did what street rats do, Trey. I stole, I cheated, I lied. I did worse.' She breathed deep. 'And then Mervyn came. He found us. I cried over Richard, kissed him goodbye and handed him over to his grandfather.'

'Why was it goodbye?' Trey asked. 'Didn't you know that Mervyn would take you too?'

'No, I didn't.'

'Why not?'

'Because Richard was Edward Latimer's son, but I was not his true daughter.'

He stared at her blankly. 'I do not understand.'

'I told you that Eshe had run away from her family—she wanted to see more of the world.'

'Yes.'

'She ran away with a Frenchman. A surveyor in Napoleon's grand army of engineers and artists. She lived with him, bore him a child. Me.' She ducked her head. 'But when the French were defeated he went home without us, without a second thought. It wasn't until a year later that Eshe met Edward Latimer. They fell in love, truly in love. She married him and he was the only father I have ever known.'

Trey sat, stunned. 'Then you are… Then Mervyn is not…'

'He is not my grandfather. Not by blood. You can see why I couldn't tell you,' she said, unable to keep all of the anguish from her words.

'I can see why you might think so at first,' he said, indignant, 'but surely later you might have got round to it!'

'I wanted to! I felt terrible, but I couldn't risk it. You railed at me for sacrificing myself for my family. What would you have thought had you known they were truly not my family?'

'You thought I'd be angry?'

She nodded and hid her face on his shoulder. 'I felt so guilty—I know I should never have agreed to the betrothal.' She gave a little sob. 'You deserve so much better in a wife!'

That statement, perhaps, shocked him even more than her revelation. 'What did you say?'

'It's true. You know it is. My mother was a slave, my father some unknown Frenchman. I lied to you. I lied to everyone—through my entire life. I let them all believe that I was someone I am not.'

'Stop it.' Trey's voice crashed through the empty room like thunder. 'You've sorely misjudged me if you think I give a damn about all of that.' He gripped her hard by the shoulders. 'Do you think I care who your father was? My father had noble blood—it didn't keep him from becoming a selfish, murdering bastard. Will you hold what he did against me?'

Anxiety still marred her pretty face, showed in every tense line of her body. 'No, you do not understand. It is not so much who my father was. It is who I am—what I have done. Must I spell it out?'

'I'm afraid you must,' he said gently, 'for I cannot imagine what you could mean.'

'I tried to change, to fit in here in England.' Her eyes rose to his. 'I never did, though.'

He started to speak, but she stopped him with a raised hand.

'No, it is more than my background. It is me—something fundamentally different in me. When I feel…I just cannot…' Her voice fell once more to a whisper. 'That angry, defiant girl—she still lives inside of me, Trey. I've never been able to rid myself of that part of me.'

'Thank God you haven't!' he said fervently.

'What?' She looked utterly shocked.

'You heard me.' He stood and began to pace between the bench and the wall. 'Did you think I didn't know about that bit of wildness inside of you? Good God, you beautiful, hare-brained idiot.' He turned and stared at her. 'Yes, I know that spitfire. I've seen her throw a knife at a bandit in a window, watched her lead her rag-tag family to safety with steely calm. She has saved my life—with a chamber pot, no less!' He came forward again and knelt before her where she still sat. 'She has rescued my barren heart, pressed her body against mine as she came apart. I love her, Chione, because she is a part of you.'

Her hands were shaking. He took them and held them safe in his own. 'You are not just the hissing, spitting Egyptian hellcat from the streets. Nor are you just the well-mannered little English girl. You, my dear, are an endlessly fascinating, sometimes infuriating mix of the two.'

A great, fat tear welled over and tracked down her cheek. She stared at him, her eyes narrowed, her gaze searching, as if looking for the lie in his face.

'I love you, Chione. All of you,' he said simply.

Tears spilled over. Her eyes closed. 'Thank you,' she whispered.

He gently wiped away the tears with his thumb. 'No more thanks, and no more tears. There is only one woman I want you to be right now.'

She made an effort to gather herself. 'Who would that be?' she asked archly.

'Why, the lover of the Niall, of course.'

She laughed helplessly, but it rapidly turned into a sob. Trey gathered her close and let her cry. Gradually it ended, although he still felt her tremble from time to time. Eventually she sat up and wiped her eyes on the ends of her dress. 'You are the only one,' she said. 'The only one who has ever seen all the pieces of me.'

'I'd like to see all the pieces of you. It's been a damned sight too long since I got the chance.'

She laughed. 'Yes, entirely too long.' She tugged at his hand. 'You wanted the lover of the Niall? Let's go, then.'

'Home?' He raised a brow. 'Because I don't think—'

'No,' she interrupted. 'There's a sofa in the back workroom.'

'Lead the way.'

She did, keeping her hand tucked in his like a child. It was no child that hiked her skirts and climbed aboard the sofa, however. She raised herself on her knees and pulled him to her with a finger hooked in his waistcoat.

She breathed in his ear and his skin heated all over. Then her lips slid around to take his own. She kissed him softly at first, then deeper, again and again until her lips were swollen and his cock surged to life, begging for its share of attention.

But something nagged at him. He broke their kiss and pulled back, looking down at the piece of furniture that she kneeled on. It was pink velvet and more than a little ratty. He could see it clearly, he realised, because the early morning light shone through the window. They would not have much time, but there was something that needed to be done.

'Wait here,' he said.

He left the workroom and went through the entire exhibit to the lobby. Ah. The place had been decorated as befitted the occasion. He pulled a large swath of fabric from the wall and returned to Chione.

He closed the door firmly behind him and propped a chair under the knob. He locked the door to the outside. Chione stared at him, puzzled, as he approached and held out a hand to her. 'Hop down from there a moment,' he said.

She complied and he shook out the length of fabric, completely covering the old sofa with cloth of gold trimmed in bright blue.

'There,' he grinned. 'I am going to make love to my Egyptian girl in a more fitting setting.'

She laughed. He swept her off of her feet and laid her gently down upon the shimmering fabric. He gazed down at her, his heart full. 'The most valuable thing I have ever discovered,' he murmured.

She rose to a kneeling position once more. Slowly she reached out to him, untucked the end of his neckcloth and pulled him closer inch by inch. Those brilliant eyes closed as she raised her face to his, even as her fingers worked at the knot. He leaned forward and answered her silent plea with a searing kiss, his own hands busy with his waistcoat buttons.

In mere moments, it seemed, he was bare from the waist up. Lightly Chione touched the long scar where he had once been razed by a knife across his ribs. She bent down and kissed the length of it with nipping, teasing, healing kisses. She did the same for the puckered wound on his left arm and every other mark she found, embracing and accepting each imperfection of his body, just as she had already done for his soul.

His breathing quickened and he fought back a moan. She was running her fingernails over his chest now, scratching lightly through the hair there, trailing teasingly around his nipples just as he knew she liked done to her. His blood surged and his self-control stretched to the thinnest thread.

He made a sound of protest as she drew back, a wicked gleam in her eye. 'You realise, Trey,' she said, her voice thick, 'that we still don't know what was in that coffer?'

'The coffer can go to Hades,' Trey said, turning his head to nuzzle the sweet dampness of her neck. He covered the swell of her breast with his hand and she sighed. He spun her around to get at the buttons of her gown and treat her to the same exquisite torture to which she had just subjected him.

Their coupling this time was like nothing Trey had ever experienced. Never had he given of himself with such openness and never had he been so rewarded. He worshipped Chione's body and savoured her every moan and twitch and whispered plea. When at last neither of them could wait a moment longer, he entered her fully on one slow, heavenly stroke.

She gasped and he felt her muscles tighten. In moments she went over, calling his name and rocking wildly beneath him. It was all the encouragement he needed. He pressed close, rode harder, drove deep and long and endless until he splintered apart and bright, shining joy flowed into him and out of him and he could not tell where Chione's pleasure began and his own ended. He threw his head back and cried out his thanks, for he finally knew that such distinctions didn't matter.

Some time later they still lay in a heap. Trey felt exhausted, sated, and infinitely happy. Until voices sounded in the exhibit outside. He raised his head and listened. After a moment the door knob rattled and they both jumped.

'Chione,' he said, reaching for his shirt. 'I've a sudden burning desire to know what is in that damned coffer. Let's go home.'

Chapter Twenty

As it turned out, it wasn't until the next day that their curiosity was satisfied.

Everyone was gathering in the comfortable family drawing room where Mrs Ferguson had planned a sumptuous celebratory tea. She was wheeling in a heavily laden cart as Chione arrived.

'Bannocks!' Olivia cried happily.

Everyone was there before her. Chione curled comfortably with Trey on a divan and sighed in satisfaction at the sea of faces around her. Mervyn had got his wish—Olivia sat in his lap, feeding him titbits while Will sat at his feet, competing with Bart in a bid to make all the muffins disappear. Jenny Ferguson and John Coachman mooned over each other in the corner and Eli slipped something in his tea when the housekeeper wasn't looking. Jack Alden sat a little apart, talking earnestly with Aswan, who was drinking cup after cup of strong tea.

'If only Lord Renhurst and Drake could be here, we would be complete,' Chione said to Trey over the hubbub of laughter and conversation. He squeezed her hand in response and she laid her head upon his shoulder. Such a small thing, but still it caused the spread of warmth and joy through her insides.

Finally Mervyn called for quiet and Aswan carried in the simple bronze box that had brought them all together. A hush fell over the room and Chione could see anticipation shining in every face.

'So many times,' Mervyn said solemnly, 'I feared this day would not come. Never have I been more aware of how truly blessed I am.' He smiled through the general murmur of agreement.

'But thank the heavens that we are all here, for now the time for secrets is past.' He glanced over to where Chione sat close to Trey and she flushed a little. 'Certainly, they have done us more harm than good. Yet still, I must ask of each of you— please do not talk of what will be revealed here today, at least until preparations have been made for the truth to come out on a larger scale.'

'Aye, we promise,' Eli called. 'Now can we open the coffer?'

'Not yet.' Mervyn laughed. 'First we must tell a story; one that only begins with the ancient Tale of the Tomb Robber and the Architect's Daughter.'

'Not everyone here knows that story, sir,' Trey said.

'Let Will tell it,' urged Chione. 'He knows it well.'

Mervyn smiled down at his son and Will told the tragic tale in his earnest boy's voice. Everyone shook their heads at the sad ending.

'It's so romantic,' Jenny said, wiping away a tear.

'Heathens,' Eli said in disgust.

'As Chione discovered yesterday, that tale has endured—literally lived on—for over three thousand years.'

'Hassan's family, his entire village in Luxor, they are the descendants of the notorious tomb robbers in the story,' Chione explained to the expectant group. 'They believe that the Pharaoh's Lost Jewel is in there.' She indicated the coffer. 'They have kept the tale, along with a thirst for vengeance, alive all this time.' She still could scarcely believe such a thing.

'They've continued the family occupation with some success as well,' Trey said wryly.

'What Hassan did not tell you, Chione, is that the architect's daughter had a family and it still thrives as well.'

Amidst all the exclamations and questions, Chione felt a little breathless. 'Tell us about them, Mervyn.'

'Of course. Chione, what was it that you used to tell Richard? That you worried that the daughter—her name was Nafré, by the way—would ruin her life?'

'I feared that she would let her anger blight her life, yes. I feared that she would never trust again.'

'It was a well-founded fear, for, according to legend, she nearly did let it spoil her life. She nursed her hatred for a long time, especially her resentment towards men. She could not find her way back to contentment. Eventually she left Thebes, abandoned her culture and civilisation in general. She crossed the desert and went to live in a remote spot on the Red Sea. Of course, she could not live entirely on her own, and with her new wealth she did not need to. A little village grew up on that wild and beautiful seashore, far from the caravan routes, visited only by an occasional sailing ship blown off course. She set up a matriarchal system and they flourished under Nafré's guidance, nearly cut off from the outside world.'

Chione's eyes widened. 'You found them,' she said, suddenly sure.

'I did, years ago,' Mervyn confirmed. He closed his eyes. 'I did, and, oh, what a remarkable thing it was. Their small little city is a marvel, a truly unique blend of ancient Egyptian, and later Greek and Roman influences. It is beautiful and pure. They are a simple society, in a lovely setting, always led by a woman—a descendant of Nafré.'

Chione's heart pounded. For the first time in her life she experienced true sympathy with the Latimer family obsession. A part of her longed to go to the spot that Mervyn described, to see for herself these people who had lived isolated for so long.

Next to her Trey sat at attention, staring hard at Mervyn. He started to speak, but the older man stopped him. 'Not yet, Treyford. It is time to open the coffer.'

That broke Chione out of her trance. 'But how?' she asked. 'There are no hinges, there is no seal to break.'

'Bring it closer, please,' Mervyn asked Trey.

Trey carried it over. The two boys made room for it, bouncing in their excitement. Mervyn made a gesture. 'Turn it over.'

Everyone gasped when the scarab imprint was revealed. From his coat Mervyn pulled his own scarab. He placed it gently into the depression in the coffer. It was not an exact match. The legs of Mervyn's scarab were too short, they did not extend as far as the legs stamped into the bronze.

A murmur of disappointment grew in the room, but Mervyn looked unperturbed.

'You have the emerald, I believe?' he asked Trey.

Trey nodded and pulled the jewel from his pocket. He placed it carefully into the indentation in the right wing.

'Push,' said Mervyn.

Trey did so, gently, and an extension sprang from the leg of Mervyn's scarab, filling the empty space and locking it into place.

'But we never found the other jewel,' Chione said, disappointed.

'Aswan,' Mervyn said.

The servant rose and approached. Very slowly he began to unwind his turban. At the end, theatrically, he produced a shining garnet stone—its shape a mirror of the emerald's.

'Aswan is a descendent of Nafré himself, and a very great friend to our family,' Mervyn said over the loud exclamations of wonder and delight. 'Please, Aswan, will you do the honours?'

Aswan settled the jewel into place and pushed. Again the leg extended and locked the scarab into place.

'Now,' said Mervyn, 'turn it back over, and then lift.'

Trey did and the bronze top and walls of the box lifted way, leaving the bottom and the contents revealed.

'Ohhh,' Chione breathed, gazing in wonder at the object on top: an elaborately decorated papyrus scroll. 'May I?'

Watching her closely, Mervyn inclined his head.

Gently she took it up, unrolling it with the utmost care. The detail was amazing. 'It's the legend,' she said in wonder. 'How old this must be!'

Aswan nodded. 'It is nearly as old as the legend itself.'

'It must be priceless,' she said.

'It is, Chione, as are the documents and journals with it,' Mervyn told her. 'It is *their* narrative: the story of each descendant of Nafré. That coffer contains their lives, their deaths, their history as a people. It is put into the keeping of each new matriarch—she who has always been called the Pharaoh's Lost Jewel.'

'Because, young miss,' said Aswan, 'despite the faithlessness of the father, Nafré always knew that her child was the most precious thing that she carried from that tomb.'

'We must return it!' Chione said. She stared up at Trey. 'You will help, won't you?'

There was tenderness in his gaze as he looked back at her. 'I think it has already found its true home, Chione.'

She stared at him, uncomprehending.

'Treyford is right,' Mervyn said gently. 'You are the Lost Jewel, Chione. You are the last descendant of Nafré.'

'Cor!' whispered Bartholomew.

'I should have told you long ago, but I was weak. Marie died, and I could not stand the thought of losing you, as well. I wanted to be sure you would be safe, and I wanted you to be ready to hear the truth, too.'

Chione had gone very still. Her heart thundered and her

mind went dizzily awhirl. One thought emerged from the chaos and she clung to it. 'Eshe!' she said. 'She ran away because her family refused to live in the world. That is what she meant?'

'Yes. Eshe believed her people could not live in isolation any longer. The world is shrinking—she understood that. I had found them. A small party of French explorers found them too.'

'She left with them.'

'She did. She wanted to learn all she could so she could teach her people, Chione. She believed they must be prepared or else their way of life would be destroyed.' A bleak expression sobered his lined face. 'She was right. I have seen it happen in other places. They will fare so much better if they are gently taught, gradually shown how much the world outside has outstripped them.'

'It would seem to be a job for which you are eminently suited,' Trey said, settling back next to her and taking her hand.

She stared at him. What irony, when she had scorned the legend for so long. She thought of what Mervyn had said, and she knew that she hadn't been ready to hear such a thing. Until now. Until Trey had helped her reconcile her past with her present, and paved the way for her future.

'It is like a dream,' she said, staring into the cool blue of his eyes.

'It is not a dream, but your destiny,' Aswan said firmly.

'Think of the stories you could write!' exclaimed Will.

A million questions and concerns flooded Chione's head. She blurted out the one which felt the most urgent. 'You cannot leave again so soon,' she said low to Mervyn. 'Perhaps a map or perhaps we should wait…'

'You don't need me.' Her grandfather laughed and pulled Olivia close. 'And I am going nowhere for a good long while.' He tilted his chin towards the Egyptian man. 'Aswan will show you. It is his home.'

Chione leaned back into the comfort of Trey's embrace. 'It is all too much to take in.' She straightened suddenly and looked to Aswan. 'Wait—is the Jewel allowed to marry?'

'Of course.' He inclined his head.

'How do ye think she'd go about gettin' the next one then, aye?' Mrs Ferguson asked pragmatically.

Chione glanced back at Trey. It was not a decision she could make alone and she knew that the question danced in her face.

He smiled at her with approval and love and she had her answer.

'Mrs Ferguson raises a valid point, Chione. Perhaps you should consider an heir your first duty to your new family.' He paused mischievously. 'On second thought, we'll need two: a girl for you and a boy to take on the earldom. It might be best if we got to work on that right away.'

'I told ye,' grumbled the housekeeper, 'betrothed ain't married!'

* * * * *

CELEBRATE
60 YEARS
OF PURE READING PLEASURE
WITH HARLEQUIN®!

We'll be spotlighting a different series
every month throughout 2009
to celebrate our 60th anniversary.
Look for Silhouette Desire® in January!

Collect all 12 books in the Silhouette Desire®
Man of the Month continuity, starting in
January 2009 with *An Officer and a Millionaire*
by *USA TODAY* bestselling author
Maureen Child.

*Look for one new Man of the Month title
every month in 2009!*

You're invited to join our Tell Harlequin Reader Panel!

By joining our new reader panel you will:

- Receive Harlequin® books—they are FREE and yours to keep with no obligation to purchase anything!
- Participate in fun online surveys
- Exchange opinions and ideas with women just like you
- Have a say in our new book ideas and help us publish the best in women's fiction

In addition, you will have a chance to win great prizes and receive special gifts!
See Web site for details. Some conditions apply.
Space is limited.

To join, visit us at
www.TellHarlequin.com.

REQUEST YOUR FREE BOOKS!

Harlequin® Historical
Historical Romantic Adventure!

2 FREE NOVELS PLUS 2 **FREE GIFTS!**

YES! Please send me 2 FREE Harlequin® Historical novels and my 2 FREE gifts (gifts are worth about $10). After receiving them, if I don't wish to receive any more books, I can return the shipping statement marked "cancel". If I don't cancel, I will receive 6 brand-new novels every month and be billed just $4.94 per book in the U.S. or $5.49 per book in Canada, plus 25¢ shipping and handling per book and applicable taxes, if any*. That's a savings of 20% off the cover price! I understand that accepting the 2 free books and gifts places me under no obligation to buy anything. I can always return a shipment and cancel at any time. Even if I never buy another book, the two free books and gifts are mine to keep forever.

246 HDN ERUM 349 HDN ERUA

Name _____ (PLEASE PRINT)

Address _____ Apt. #

City _____ State/Prov. _____ Zip/Postal Code

Signature (if under 18, a parent or guardian must sign)

Mail to the **Harlequin Reader Service:**
IN U.S.A.: P.O. Box 1867, Buffalo, NY 14240-1867
IN CANADA: P.O. Box 609, Fort Erie, Ontario L2A 5X3

Not valid to current subscribers of Harlequin Historical books.

Want to try two free books from another line?
Call 1-800-873-8635 or visit www.morefreebooks.com.

* Terms and prices subject to change without notice. N.Y. residents add applicable sales tax. Canadian residents will be charged applicable provincial taxes and GST. Offer not valid in Quebec. This offer is limited to one order per household. All orders subject to approval. Credit or debit balances in a customer's account(s) may be offset by any other outstanding balance owed by or to the customer. Please allow 4 to 6 weeks for delivery. Offer available while quantities last.

Your Privacy: Harlequin Books is committed to protecting your privacy. Our Privacy Policy is available online at www.eHarlequin.com or upon request from the Reader Service. From time to time we make our lists of customers available to reputable third parties who may have a product or service of interest to you. If you would prefer we not share your name and address, please check here. ☐

SPECIAL EDITION™

The Bravos meet the Jones Gang
as two of Christine Rimmer's famous
Special Edition families come together
in one very special book.

THE STRANGER
AND TESSA JONES

by

CHRISTINE RIMMER

Snowed in with an amnesiac stranger during a
freak blizzard, Tessa Jones soon finds out her
guest is none other than heartbreaker Ash Bravo.
And that's when things really heat up....

Available January 2009
wherever you buy books.

COMING NEXT MONTH FROM

HARLEQUIN®
HISTORICAL

- **TEXAS RANGER, RUNAWAY HEIRESS**
  by **Carol Finch**
  (Western)
  Texas Ranger Hudson Stone can't disobey orders. He must find
  Gabrielle Price. Hud believes her to be a spoiled, self-centered
  debutante—but discovers she's more than capable of handling
  herself in adversity! Bri enflames his desires—but the wealthy,
  forbidden beauty is strictly off-limits!

- **MARRYING THE CAPTAIN**
  by **Carla Kelly**
  (Regency)
  Oliver Worthy, a captain in the Channel Fleet, is a confirmed
  bachelor—so falling in love with Eleanor Massie is about the
  last thing he intended! Eleanor loves Oliver, too, although her
  humble past troubles her. But in the turbulence of a national
  emergency, Eleanor will fight to keep her captain safe....

- **THE VISCOUNT CLAIMS HIS BRIDE**
  by **Bronwyn Scott**
  (Regency)
  For years, Valerian Inglemoore lived a double life on the war-
  torn Continent. Now he's returned, knowing exactly what he
  wants—Philippa Stratten, the woman he gave up for the sake
  of her family.... But Philippa is not the hurt, naive debutante
  he once knew and is suspicious of his intentions....

- **HIGH SEAS STOWAWAY**
  by **Amanda McCabe**
  (Renaissance)
  Meeting Balthazar Grattiano years after their first fateful
  encounter, Bianca Simonetti finds he is no longer the spoiled,
  angry young nobleman she knew. Now he has sailed the seas,
  battled pirates and is captain of his own ship. Bianca is
  shocked to find her old infatuation has deepened to an
  irresistible sexual attraction....